SHIP MATES

SHIP MATES

Megan Becker

Lattes & Lovebirds Literature

Ship Mates
Copyright © 2024 by Megan Becker

This book is a work of fiction. People, places, events, and names are products of the author's imagination or are used fictitiously. Any resemblance to real-world people, locations, or events is purely coincidental.

All rights reserved. This book or any portion thereof may not be reproduced or used without the express written permission of the author, except for the use of brief quotations in book reviews.

Printed in the United States of America

Front Cover Artwork by Alexandra Aiken

Lattes & Lovebirds Literature

ISBN: 979-8-9898118-0-9

Itinerary

Before Boarding

Day 1: Embarkation

Day 2: At Sea

Day 3: Bermuda

Day 4: At Sea *(Formal Night)*

Day 5: The Bahamas

Day 6: Private Island

Day 7: Miami

Day 8: At Sea *(Formal Night)*

Day 9: At Sea

Day 10: Disembarkation

Post-Cruise Extension

Before Boarding

One Year Prior to Sailing

MEGAN BECKER

Gwendolyn

"GWENDOLYN PIERCE, LOOK what you've done."

When I was five, eight, fourteen, those words from that voice could have me shaking in my proverbial boots. They still could, though I've been careful to not earn my grandmother's wrath in adulthood.

But today. Today the words are different. Dripping with the sweetness I associate with Gram (most of the time), her hands pressed to my cheeks, her eyes afire with excitement and pride.

Books Off Broadway looks amazing. Its vaulted ceilings are draped with paper chains, each link decorated by a local student, and handmade paper snowflakes dangle between the chains. Despite the chilly air outside, it feels like a cozy winter wonderland in here.

Cozy because it's charming, with rich old wood and plush leather armchairs, inviting anyone to sit and browse and stay a while. The personal touches from the local community add to that magic, but I had nothing to do with that.

Books Off Broadway is also currently quite cozy because an extra seventy bodies are jammed inside. It's possible I had something to do with *that*.

Mr. Charles, one of the owners, grabs a microphone and brings the temporary sound system to life with a breathy "Testing, testing, one, two, three" into the mic. "Good evening, everyone. If you can take your seats, please, we'll get started in just a few minutes."

Customers wander to their folding chairs, chatting over hot cocoa that may or may not be (but totally is) spiked with Irish

Cream, carrying copies of my book.

My book. The words never get old. Seeing it in print is a dream come true. Seeing a few dozen women clutching it like a prized possession is incredible. Having seen that six times in the last thirty days is nothing short of miraculous.

As the last few attendees filter into their seats, Mr. Charles steps up to the microphone and introduces himself. My headshot on the easel next to him smiles back at me as I watch him talk, and I can feel my stomach flip just as it's done at the other five events I've spoken at.

"So without further ado, please welcome to our little stage Ms. Gwen Dolan-Pierce!"

I smile at Gram and kiss the top of her head. "That's my cue."

There's the usual applause and I introduce myself, thank Books Off Broadway and Mr. and Mrs. Charles for having me, and give a brief background of both myself and the book. Then the questions start and I forget the world around me and dive instead into the process, the characters, the creative choices along the way.

A woman, maybe Gram's age, raises her hand and asks who inspired me to write. It's a question I've gotten at each interview and speaking engagement so far, and when Gram smiles and winks at me I'm not entirely sure she didn't feed this stranger the question earlier tonight.

I smooth my skirt over my legs and pause, smiling before I give the answer I've perfected. "Are there any teachers in the room?"

A few hands tentatively rise.

"In addition to my grandmother—" I nod Gram's way and catch her wave in return, "—it's because of my teachers that I am where I am right now. It was a teacher who acknowledged my talent when I was young, others who nurtured it in adolescence. They encouraged me to set goals and work toward them. We all owe them our gratitude for what they do, all day, every day. Let's give them a round of applause."

       MEGAN BECKER

The room fills with the sound of golf claps and a few cheers.

A few more questions come my way (my favorite: *Have you planned your dream wedding for your own happily ever after?* my answer: *No, but I'd probably wear black glitter or hot pink or something very unexpected*), and once I'm done speaking, I take a seat at a long table near the register and start signing copies, smiling politely and making small talk as attendees step before me.

The woman who launched me into Ode to Teachers beams at me when it's her turn. "Thank you for saying what you said earlier. About the teachers."

"Absolutely! I really meant it. They're underappreciated, but they do so much."

I credit my teachers with providing some of the most invaluable advice in my life and launching me into my career. But I don't dare say that anywhere near Gram; if she heard that, it'd break her heart.

"Any chance you're single? I think you'd love my grandson," she jokes, in the forward way that grandparents do. I can only imagine her doing this with her grandson next to her and the shade of red his cheeks might turn, or how his jaw might hit the floor.

"Sorry, but I'm spoken for at the moment."

"I believe it. So talented, and pretty to boot. Well," she says, taking back her book, still smiling. "It was great chatting with you. Thanks so much." She carries off her hardcover and disappears into the crowd.

There's another half hour of signing books and shooting the breeze, and as things wind down I refill my cocoa, hunting for Gram. She's hugging the woman, waving goodbye.

"Make a new friend, did ya?" I always tease her at these things, and at the grocery store, or on the sidewalk when she strikes up a conversation with a complete stranger about which custom orthotics they're using to have such a spring in their step. The woman makes friends everywhere she goes.

"I did indeed," she smiles. "New pen pal."

She truly means *pen* pal, because Gram hates email. Finds it too impersonal.

"That sounds nice."

She nods and surveys the store. "Whadaya think the over/under is on clean-up time?"

Gram loves gambling as much as she loathes electronic communication.

We pack up the easel and the display board on it, then help Mr. and Mrs. Charles fold up the chairs they'd brought in for this event. Within twenty minutes, the place is back to normal. *Mental note: I owe Gram ten bucks.*

"Did he call, at least?" Gram asks as we step out into the evening air.

I haven't even bothered to check my phone these last two hours, but I feel confident in my response. "No. He hasn't."

"Sorry, dear. I know you were looking forward to him being here tonight."

I shrug, not wanting to let Gram see me upset. "It's fine. Probably had to work late. I know how that goes."

In reality I'm annoyed and, frankly, pissed off. Tristan's traveling all month for work, and the one time my speaking gig is in the same city he's in, he can't even bother to show up. *Can't* or *doesn't*, it doesn't matter. It sucks either way.

We walk a block back to the hotel, planning our room service order. Gram pushed hard for a New York book signing, and I think a swanky hotel and room service were her motivating factors. I'm just grateful for practice speaking with much smaller crowds in the last few weeks before having to speak to a crowd the size of the one at Books Off Broadway.

"You okay, Sweetheart?" Gram rests a hand on my forearm as I reach for the elevator button.

I shrug. "Fine."

She doesn't believe me, and for a second her lip twitches down and I think she might tell me to "ditch Tristan's ass" (because, yes, she has said exactly those words to me before), but instead she smiles gently, full of pity, and pats my arm. "You were fantastic tonight. Nancy was very impressed." My head tilts and Gram clarifies. "The woman I was talking to at the end."

"Ah, the woman who tried to set me up with her grandson?"

Gram shrugs. "High praise, for a woman to think someone is good enough for her grandchild."

I love reading, but right now I'm not loving what's between the lines.

"Do you mind ordering for me? Chicken tenders and fries, with a Manhattan? It feels appropriate, considering." I gesture toward the city streets around us.

For someone who covered for me when I missed curfew as a teen, Gram seems a bit intolerant of my current need to go meet up with a boyfriend. I smile as innocently as I can when Gram makes a face. Then she nods, and I promise I'll be up soon. There's just one thing I need to do first.

MEGAN BECKER

DAY 1

Embarkation

Gwendolyn

"GWENDOLYN PIERCE, LOOK what you've done."

The suite is huge, expansive and comfortable, and the view is just… *wow*. For now we're soaking up the New York City skyline, but once we set sail it'll be the calming waves of the deep blue sea. We can definitely make this work for us for the next ten days.

"I know I told you not to spend your money on this trip, but this is one time I'm grateful for your rebellious streak."

Gram nudges my side, her bony elbow sharp in my ribs. She presses her fingertips and forehead against the perfectly streak-free glass, leaving smudges behind as she gazes out to the water that laps at the ship a dozen decks below.

It was her idea to book the cruise, to really get away, to help me disconnect and unblock myself, but the interior cabin with two twin beds that she had planned to book would not have been ideal. We'd considered separate rooms, but when I saw the suite, I knew I had to book it. We'll get great sunrise and sunset views from the chaises on our private balcony and lots of extra space when we're just relaxing in the room. I've also volunteered to sleep on the living room's sofa bed for some extra separation, because Gram's snoring would intimidate a lumberjack.

"Consider it a thank-you gift for all you've ever done for me."

"You mean a deposit on a thank-you gift for all I've ever done for you?" And that right there—that smart-ass, sharp-as-a-tack humor—is Gram, all wrapped up in a punchy one-liner that she says with a wink and a smirk that we've always been able to share.

Gram's always had a soft spot for me, I guess. As her only granddaughter, and her only grandchild to be raised nearby, she would spoil me with books and cookies throughout my childhood. When it became clear that my parents were not the spoiling type, she'd spoil me even more: a spa day when I turned eighteen, a beach weekend when I turned twenty-one, and a door that was always open when I needed someone to talk to or a fresh-baked cookie. And sure, I'd gotten my fair share of stern warnings about boys and underage drinking when I was in high school and my own parents couldn't be bothered to see me as a teenage girl in need of guidance, but overall, things have always been great with Gram.

"Are you going to explore the ship a bit?"

She's already easing herself into an armchair near the door, already sliding out of her tie-dye slip-ons, reaching for her swollen ankle. "No, dear, I think I'll stay here a bit. Maybe sneak in a nap before dinner."

"Sure." I unpack a bit while she sits there, relaxing after a busy morning on our feet, waiting in lines, navigating to our suite. When she's not looking, I sneak my laptop into my beach tote and slide the straps over my shoulder. I wrap my free arm around Gram and kiss her temple, promising to be back in time to escort her to dinner.

I saw a *lot* of children—like, a number I'm uncomfortable with, considering it's the middle of the school year—when we were boarding, so I head straight to the adults-only section on the top deck, appropriately yet ironically named The Retreat, all the way at the front of the ship.

It's chilly outside, but the November air is calm for New York and will only improve as we sail south in just a few hours. Tomorrow will be primo balcony time, but right now I'm heading inside to claim a chair in The Retreat's indoor pool area, desperate to get a head start on the heat and humidity promised to us by the Caribbean islands we're heading to.

     MEGAN BECKER

Naturally, every chaise along the windows is taken, claimed by blue and white striped pool towels and temporarily discarded flip-flops. Most chairs, actually, seem to be reserved for one of the many adults in the various pools and hot tubs housed here. I take a lap, and on the far side I finally find a solitary, available chair.

It feels so nice to sit, and I take a moment to rest my eyes before pulling out my laptop and opening the document I've stared blankly at for days. Everyone's expecting another hit, another runaway success. But right now I just want to hit someone and run away.

Specifically, I want to hit the person next to me who is dripping chlorinated water all over my tote, my dress, and my laptop.

"Do you *mind*?" I ask, swiping the droplets off my keyboard.

More drops fall.

"*Excuse me*!" I twist and look up, coming face to—well, not face, that's for sure—with a pair of flamingo-covered swim trunks. I catch my shriek on its way out, so it exits my mouth as some choked *gargh* sound, high-pitched and rumbly all at once.

The waist twists, and this man has the gall to look at me with big brown eyes and an infuriating smile. "Oh, sorry," he says, lowering himself to his chair, saving me from having to look at the lines and curves his wet trunks stuck to just a moment ago.

My cheeks burn, but surely it's rage from the fresh patches of water landing again on my chair as he shakes a towel through his hair, and not lingering embarrassment from my first glance at him.

"Dude, honestly." I snap the laptop closed and make a show of smoothing the now-damp shoulder of my dress.

"Dude, sorry," he mocks, his grin glitching. "You know you're at a pool, right? And there's typically lots of water?"

"Yes, and if I wanted to be wet I'd be *in* the water. This seat wasn't marked as being in the splash zone."

He grunts and rolls his eyes, then kicks his feet up onto his chaise and throws his hands behind his head, elbows out, taking up space in the way that men do but women shouldn't even consider unless we want a handful of less-than-complimentary labels assigned to us. And he does it all with a maddening smirk on his face.

"Do you always bring high-value electronics to the danger zone? Do you at least unplug your laptop before you bathe with it?"

"I came in here to escape from all the children on this boat, thank you very much, but I see they allowed at least one in the adults-only area."

His expression shifts, and his lips curl into an actual smile.

"Of *course* she hates kids," he tells the air around us.

"I didn't say that."

He ignores me, and I don't know why, but I become immediately defensive.

"I just have work to do, and I was hoping it would be a little calmer here. Not that I need to explain myself to you."

He twists, adjusting his chair to a near-horizontal position, and looks at me. His yellow T-shirt has dark patches from his dripping hair, but I hardly notice anything beyond the way the shirt pulls against his chest and inches up his arm to reveal a firm, curvy bicep.

Oh, Gwen, you always did find the jerks the most attractive.

"You do realize this is a cruise ship, right? Not an office? There are going to be people, and children, and water, and it won't be calm, and you're not supposed to work."

I feign awe. *Clutch-my-pearls* hand to the heart and everything. "I didn't realize I was next to the cruise ship MVP." He shoots a puzzled look my way, and I clarify. "Most Vehement Pain."

He rolls his eyes. "Okay, OCD. Obnoxious, Cranky Dictionary."

I give up on doing anything productive here and decide I'd rather take my chances with the real children beyond the confines of this space and not this quasi-attractive manchild next to me. I shove my laptop into my tote and swing my feet off the chaise.

"Leaving so soon? But we were just getting to know each

other," he taunts, because he knows he's won. Satisfaction sparkles in his eyes.

Just like I'm blocked on my next book, I can think of no clever comeback for this stranger I'd like to strangle. Instead, I take satisfaction in ramming my tote into his *taking-up-space* elbow, hearing the sharp breath he draws, thinking there's a chance he could fall overboard before we have an opportunity to run into each other again on this ship, and storming off.

THE CONCEPT OF vacationing in November—really, traveling in the months between Labor Day and Memorial day to anywhere but a dated convention center in the tri-state area—is foreign to me. Packing swimsuits and flip-flops in the fall? Normally I'd say it's either an HR issue waiting to happen, or a luxury for the non-public servants. Yet here I sit, swim-suited up, flip-flops tucked under my chair, already a swim and a soak into a November vacation. Already relaxed, in body, at least, if not in mind.

Because that did not go well. At all.

It would be just my luck that a random stranger would be awkwardly flirting with me from across the hot tub, complete with aggressive eyebrow waggling and attempts at physical contact by way of awkward leg-stretching and toe-to-toe caresses. So I felt lucky when another woman—here in The Retreat solo, by the look of it—took the seat next to mine. I figured I could pretend to know her to fend off the lady with the eyebrows. I felt less than lucky when I realized the woman in the chair next to mine was one of the most maddening humans I've ever met.

I'm not sure why she brought her laptop to a pool area, I'm not sure why she seems to hate children, and I'm not sure why she seems to hate me. Okay, that last one, maybe I can understand. I did call her a cranky dictionary, after all. Most of all, I'm not sure why I'm so intrigued by—and attracted to?—all of these things.

It's nice here. Quiet, but in a loud way. The bubbling of the hot tub jets reverberates throughout the room, so this place is like a giant white noise machine. I can enjoy this type of quiet; there's enough distraction that I'm not stuck with my thoughts. And thank God, because my thoughts have been terrible company for months.

The last time I was truly relaxed was… when I was seven, maybe? When life was simple. Not that it's exceptionally hard now, it's just… complicated. Confusing. Stressful. So when I was invited to come along on this trip, I couldn't turn it down. Ten days? In *November? Not* having to listen to people toss around buzzwords like *pedagogy* and *rigor* while tossing back Long Island Iced Teas? It sounded like a dream. Plus, what's better than a week away with one of your favorite people? Very few things.

So here I am, ready for a fresh start. Ready to be surrounded by strangers and ready for the chance to be whoever I want to be, which is the *me* I was before everything went to shit. I'm ready to be unknown and unjudged and untethered to the perception and the mistakes I left back home.

Part of that is confidence. I've been working hard to not shy away, to own my presence and feel like I belong. There's no better place to do that than here, where no one knows me as anything but who I show them that I am.

Granted, I'm maybe not off to the best start. The one person I've actually spoken to does not seem to be a fan of my new persona. But, Miss Mystery Workaholic doesn't get to bring me down. Not today. Not this week.

There's not a chance in hell I'll let someone who brings their laptop to the pool—and then complains when it gets three drops on it—affect me on this trip.

Gwendolyn

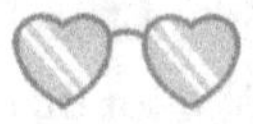

I PEOPLE-WATCH a lot, and the sailaway provides ample opportunity to see throngs of people being who they are.

It's windy, and there's one guy whose Yankees hat keeps flying off his head. He chases it down, plops it right back on his mop of red curls, poses for a photo, and runs along the promenade deck to chase it when it inevitably flies off again. Dumbass.

Some people never learn, I think, and that jerk from earlier flashes into my mind. But I *did* learn, and I'm not repeating my mistakes.

Instead, I'm watching the social media superstars in front of me, their duck lips and peace signs in every selfie. There's an older couple, wrinkled and beaming, posing with the Statue of Liberty behind them as we make our way toward the Verrazzano-Narrows Bridge. Then everyone looks up, making sure we'll fit, like there's still a question about whether this behemoth vessel can fit under the bridge it sailed under to get to the terminal where we embarked in the first place.

Spoiler alert: it fits.

I weave through the crowd, eager to get back to the room, to Gram. She wanted to enjoy the sailaway from our balcony because she's "done this enough times," and she just wants "to relax and enjoy the views." And it's so unlike her, this not wanting to be surrounded by excitement, that I worry for a moment. But she cruises frequently, at least three times a year, and I've never joined her until now (not that she hasn't asked, but because I was full of excuses that I have been too blocked to fabricate recently). Maybe

     MEGAN BECKER

this is her favorite part, this peaceful pulling away from land, this separation from the real world as we prepare to spend a week and a half floating in God's swimming pool.

Sure enough, Gram's there, her arms propped on the balcony railing and a smile tugging at the corners of her lips.

"Hey, you."

"Hey, yourself," she says, shifting to let me squeeze in next to her. Not that any squeezing is needed, because our balcony is huge.

"Are you soon ready for dinner? Or did you want to skip the dining room tonight and just hit up the buffet later?"

She shoots me a look that says she thinks I'm crazy. "Gwen, we do not 'skip' the dining room on this ship. You can't even get lobster tails and filet mignon at the buffet, but in the dining room, you can have as many as you want."

"Sold!" I laugh. I hook a thumb toward the suite's interior. "I'm going to get changed."

Gwendolyn

"WELL, LOOK WHO it is." The words are punctuated with performative surprise as we approach our table in the dining room. The familiar-looking woman already seated there rises and greets us.

"Nancy. Fancy meeting you here!" Gram doesn't fake it any better than her friend just did.

I greet Nancy, who wraps her arms around me like we're old friends, despite meeting once, about a year ago. "You look beautiful, dear," she says, her eyes skimming my navy sheath dress, her brow furrowing slightly. "Didn't you tell her, Maggie, that she doesn't need to dress up on the first night?"

Gram and Nancy are both wearing tropical-print tunics over Bermuda shorts, and a quick glance around the dining room shows most people are casually dressed.

"She stopped taking my fashion advice long ago."

"Yes, when I was twelve, and you took me on a shopping spree that made my Lisa Frank notebook look bland," I say, smoothing my napkin over my lap, and Gram laughs.

Nancy shifts in her seat across from Gram, craning her neck toward the entrance. On her side of the table there are two glasses full of water, two full of wine. She's waiting on someone, and I know from Gram's pen-pal stories that she's not seeing anyone. So that leaves one guess, and I'm *pissed*.

"Are you two trying to—"

Gram and Nancy exchange a guilty but unapologetic look. "Set you up, dear? Yes." Gram's so forward, so matter-of-fact, like she's shocked I hadn't guessed it already.

"You'll love him, Gwendolyn. He's such a nice young man."

"You have to say that. You're his grandmother."

Gram snorts in the seat next to me. "We're also honest to a fault, because we're old women who don't care what other people think. Trust me—" she smirks in a way that tells me she's not afraid to be honest about me, too, "if he were a little shit, she'd tell you."

Nancy laughs again. "He's wonderful. After all, he gave up a week of his life to join his grandmother on a cruise, so he can't be *that* bad."

I think about the lesson learned last year—that the handsome bad boy will break your heart—and I consider that maybe it would be nice to meet a "nice young man" for a change. Then my brain is full of that infuriating face from this afternoon, with his brown puppy dog eyes, messy hair, shirt stretched across broad shoulders…

I try to shake the memory loose, but it's no use. When I open my eyes I still see him, dry this time and in a T-shirt and jeans, with that stupid smile plastered across his lips. I groan, and those lips huff deep laughter into the air. Gram backhands my shoulder, and Nancy looks concerned.

"What's gotten into you?" Gram asks me before apologizing to the man lowering himself into the seat across from mine. "She's not normally like this."

"You sure about that?" he winks in reply, and Gram is smitten.

"I like him." She could at least whisper. Her approval clearly pleases him, and he gloats as he sips his wine.

Nancy clears her throat. "Gwendolyn, this is my grandson, Sawyer Dawson."

The way he leans back, stretching an arm to rest a hand on the back of Nancy's chair, taking up space again, still smirking—this guy is the worst.

"We've met," we say together.

"How fortuitous," Nancy smiles. *Read the room, Nancy.*

The waiter comes and I order a glass of wine. Something stronger would be nice, but I don't want him to have the satisfaction of thinking he's getting to me. I plan to show him that he's *not* getting to me—even if he really, really is—by rocking this dinner and then never seeing him again.

This all would have been so much easier if he'd just fallen overboard between his pool time and dinner.

Gram and Nancy have so much catching up to do that they fill the time until dinner arrives at our table, but once the crab cakes are served, they are radio silence. That opens the door for Sawyer to open his mouth.

"So, Nan. Did you really think I needed a week of rest and relaxation, or did you just invite me along so Gwendolyn here wouldn't be third-wheeling at dinner?"

Nancy swallows down her rice pilaf. "Maggie and I both thought you two could use a little break. I think you'll have a wonderful time getting to know each other, instead of hanging out with us boring old ladies."

I glance at Gram, who's oddly quiet, and I wonder if she's really planned to ditch me this whole trip in some misguided attempt to help me find a man.

"It's very considerate," I say, "but I'm content spending time alone, if I'm not with Gram."

Nancy chances a look across the table, her expression crestfallen. Gram nudges my foot under the table, and her lips are pinched, eyebrows knitted in a scowl when I meet her eyes.

We're saved by the waiter again, and he fills Gram and Nancy's mugs with decaf, which they both drink black. I'm so glad they met last year—notwithstanding the headache in human form seated at our table—because they're clearly cut from the same cloth. It's good for Gram to have a friend to talk to, write to, and vacation with,

    MEGAN BECKER

even if that last part was a surprise to me.

"So what's on the agenda for the evening?" Gram asks. She and Nancy turn their attention our way, like we've suddenly become the social planners for this whole operation.

Sawyer finishes his dessert and stretches back again, and I wish I could say why it bothers me so much when he makes himself bigger. But all I can think to say is "karaoke," which I instantly regret.

Sawyer pounces on that word and rattles off a list of songs he thinks I should sing, each one about some pissed-off, jilted ex. *Kerosene. Goodbye, Earl. Before He Cheats. Anything by Taylor Swift.* Each title digs deeper than the last, though he can't possibly understand why, and his smirk shows he thinks his little game is hilarious.

My heart hammers in my throat. I turn to Gram and Nancy and excuse myself, dodging waiters and cruisers on my walk out of the restaurant and to the elevator bank. I hate that I press the button eight times, because I know it won't call the elevator any faster, and because I'm sure it makes me look a certain kind of desperate in front of Sawyer, who's striding toward me through the crowd waiting to be seated.

"Hey." His smile has faded, and his thick dark brows draw together. "You took off pretty fast there."

I bite my lip and turn so I'm parallel with the elevator doors. When I punch the button again with my thumb, he presses a hand to my shoulder and turns me, making me face him. He ducks his head to bring his eyes level to mine.

"You okay?"

If he were anyone else, I'd believe that what I'm reading in his eyes is worry, but I just spent three minutes listening to Sawyer laugh about the idea of me singing vindictive and petty songs, and now it actually makes me feel *extremely* vindictive and petty, even though I wouldn't normally describe myself that way. Plus his hand is still on my shoulder and it warms me through my dress, and he's taking up space again—*my* space—the way he bridges this gap between our bodies.

I peel his fingers off my shoulder, and that smirk plays again on his lips at the methodical removal of his appendages.

"Our grandmothers were extremely misguided, trying to trick us into some fling."

He laughs, head thrown back, Adam's apple bobbing. "It's cute, that you think that's what this is." When I glare at him, he quiets and rolls his eyes, speaking through his smile. "They're trying to make us fall madly in love with each other."

My body shudders.

"Don't look so disgusted. You could do worse."

"The whole idea of it grosses me out, and the fact that you just said I could do worse makes my skin crawl like I've got head lice."

"That's very dramatic, and a little hurtful."

I square my shoulders and cross my arms, waiting for the elevator. I'd take the stairs, but it's ten decks up, and I'm in heels. Plus, no way am I going to let him think he's won twice in one day. Imagine the gloating.

"I just don't understand why they think they have any right—"

"They're our grandmothers. This is what they do. They meddle and try to make sure we're happy."

I glower and hope he interprets me correctly: *Does it look like I'm happy right now?*

Instead, Sawyer shrugs. "It would be nice, you know. To get along for them. It's only ten days."

Finally an elevator arrives. A crowd pours out and I dart to the back corner, holding onto the railing. "Twelve, please," I tell Sawyer, as a family and two other couples pile into the elevator with us.

Sawyer slides in next to me and pulls one of my hands from the grab-bar, inserting his massive body between me and the glass wall. He puts a hand on my hip and nudges me away from the side, and

     MEGAN BECKER

I hate that he's turned an elevator ride—my escape route—into something close and physical and almost intimate.

We stop on three different decks on the way up, and the car empties along the way. When it's just us, I move to the opposite corner and grip the bar again.

"Why do you keep doing that?"

"Doing what?" he asks, perfectly calm, leaning back against the glass wall with his ankles crossed and his arms folded against his turquoise T-shirt.

"Getting in my space like that. *Encroaching.* It's rude to touch people and move them without their consent."

His forehead creases with worry. "I was only trying to help," he says, as the doors open again on deck eleven.

"Help with what? Getting shrimp cocktail fingers on my favorite dress?"

He backs out of the elevator, the worry lines replaced again by that ridiculous smirk. "Trying to keep you and your short dress out of view from all the people below you as you ride the glass elevator."

I jump away from the wall and smooth my dress behind me, twisting to make sure I've put enough space between me and the glass that no one can see up my dress anymore. By the time I turn back to Sawyer, the doors have closed, and he's gone.

Gwendolyn

"YOU REALLY SHOULD join us for the comedy show."

Gram made it to the suite about ten minutes after I did, wondering why I took off so quickly. I've already changed into leggings and an oversized sweater, with my hair pulled into a messy top knot and tortoise-shell glasses replacing my contacts, my laptop open and my legs stretched out on the couch.

"I'm good here, thanks. But you and Nancy should go have fun."

"Well, I'm sure Sawyer will be there, too."

"Like I said. I wish you and Nancy the best."

She huffs. "Gwendolyn. You were not raised to act this way toward a perfectly kind young man."

Because I don't want to burst her bubble about her BFF's obnoxious grandson, I bite my tongue about the pool encounter and that smug elevator experience. I lower the laptop lid and stretch my arms high overhead—a *power pose* I learned about at work—and simply say, "I was just surprised. I didn't like being blindsided."

Gram nods. "Fair. But he was just as surprised as you were, and he still seemed to have a good time."

Yeah, a good time making fun of me. "I thought this trip was for you and me, so we could connect and relax and I could write. But now the focus seems to have shifted, so I go home with a boyfriend instead of a finished draft."

"But what a souvenir," she smiles, nudging my shoulder. All I hear is, *'You could do worse.'* "Just try to have an open mind, okay

Gwen?"

I force a smile, because there's no fighting Gram on this. There's just faking it, playing nice when I have to and making up an excuse why it doesn't work out when the cruise is over. "Sure. Fine. But I'm in the zone, so I think I'll still skip the comedian tonight."

"Sure, dear. Whatever you need. It starts at nine in the forward theater, if you change your mind." She kisses the top of my head and takes off for Nancy's cabin and the game of dominoes they've also invited me to, like that would sell me on joining in their evening adventures. Gram sure knows how to pre-game.

I write for a bit, but so many thoughts are swimming around my head that I still can't make progress. Plus, I'm hungry again, and I've heard great things about cruise ship pizza.

The main deck is easily walkable; most guests are in the bars that line the walkway, or at the comedy show or the family movie night upstairs at the outdoor pool. I wait in line for a personal Hawaiian pizza and stroll with my box past one bar where, sure enough, it's eighties karaoke night. The thought of Nancy and Gram duetting to Cindy Lauper fills my mind, and I can't help but laugh.

I've brought my laptop, too, and I work my way to the back of the ship where I'd seen a high-top table earlier, just outside a bistro, and I open the computer and the pizza box next to each other. For an hour I'm in the zone—the zone I lied to Gram about being in earlier—and only notice *him* when he starts speaking.

"Do you ever stop working?"

I wish I wasn't mid-bite of pizza, with a room-temp cheese blob dangling from my lips, but you don't always get what you want. With my mouth full, my eyes have to do all the talking; I hope their dramatic roll says *"Keep on walking."*

If it does, he ignores it (I'm *shocked!*), and he leans across the table, twisting his head to see what I'm working on.

I lower the laptop screen and finish chewing, careful not to choke on congealed cheese, but if it doesn't kill me, the embarrassment might. "What I do or don't do really doesn't concern you."

He plops onto a stool next to mine. "Why do you hate me?"

It's a trick question because if I give him a reason, I sound unreasonable, and if I say I *don't* hate him, he might interpret that to mean I could possibly, one day, like him.

"Who said I hated you?"

He spins on his stool until he's facing the wall, his back propped against the table, and he shoves his hands in the pocket of his black hoodie. "You've acted disgusted with me since we met."

"I'm not acting."

"You're insufferable, you know that?"

I *do* know that, because I've been told. I'm too high-maintenance, too needy. But Sawyer doesn't deserve to know that bit about me. "Now who's the dictionary?"

He shifts in his seat, and I see his smile from my periphery. "Touché." After a few half-swivels from him while I clean up my pizza trash, he asks, "So, what do you do, anyway?"

"Data analytics for a tech firm." I risk just enough of a glance back to see his eyes widen, and he stops twisting in his seat.

"Seriously?" But he reads me right away when our gazes meet, and he picks up on the smile I can't fully stop from forming. "Oh. Funny."

"You don't think women can work in STEM?"

He shrugs. "I know they can. I just didn't think *you* were one of them."

My jaw drops, but I recover quickly. I narrow my eyes at him, choosing to ignore his implication that I'm not smart enough to work in that field. "What about you?" I ask instead.

He twists on his stool again. "I'm a teacher."

It all makes sense: *'Thank you for saying what you said earlier. About the teachers,'* and *'I think you'd love my grandson.'* Nancy's a tricky one, for sure, and wildly off-base with her assumption.

"What do you teach?"

He shrugs. "High school math."

"I bet your students are missing you, with you playing hooky."

He crumples at that, shoulders sagging and curling in on himself. Even if I didn't like him taking up space earlier, there's something about him making himself smaller that feels wrong. "I bet," he says, and it's so pitiful I have to change the subject.

"Did your grandmother really not tell you anything about me?"

"She really didn't," he answers. "She wanted us to get to know each other."

"When did you find out about their little plan?"

He shrugs. "Right before dinner, I guess. She told me to be on my best behavior because the future Mrs. Sawyer Dawson might be there across from me."

I cringe, and he laughs.

"If it makes you feel better, I told her no way, no how, was I going to entertain this idea of letting her hook me up with a random stranger on this ship."

"Good."

"Because I'd already met a feisty stranger in the adults-only part of the ship, and I wanted to spend a little more time with *her.* Assuming I could find her again, of course."

I freeze, nervously glance his way, and say, "Liar."

And *shit,* the way his skin pulls and folds itself around his lips and eyes when he smiles.

"Why don't you let me buy you a drink, so we can actually get to know each other?" He's already rising, like it's a done deal that I'll say yes and drop everything I was doing to go with him to one of the bars.

"That won't be necessary," I tell him, tugging my sweater sleeves past my hands, curling my fingertips inside its cozy cocoon. I feel his eyes on me and the sweater, a silent judgment about who I am, dressed like this.

I grab my laptop. "I'm going to head back to my room so I'm there when Gram comes back from the comedy show. Good to see you, I guess."

He takes two steps toward me. "That dress earlier—the one you wore to dinner—it was nice. It really suited you."

"Thanks." I love that dress. It's polished and chic and *smart*.

He smirks again. "Sure. I thought it was really safe. Very stiff."

This man is the absolute worst, and I don't hold back. "What is your problem?"

He shrugs, playing dumb. "I don't know what you mean."

I roll my eyes in return. "You've been a jerk since the minute I met you today. Between the pool and dinner and now this…"

"I offered to buy you a drink and get to know you, since we're going to be forced to spend a lot of time together over the next ten days."

"I am not obligated to get a drink with you or anyone else."

He retreats at the words' punch. "I didn't say you were. I'm just saying, I'm *trying*, Gwendolyn. To play nice. For *them*."

A family meanders by, the children searching a planter along their way; what they're looking for, I'm not sure. Sawyer watches them pass, and suddenly his whole expression shifts.

"They should be in school, right?"

"I'm sorry?" he asks, snapping his eyes back to mine.

"Shouldn't they be in school, and not on a cruise? Seems like a lot of missed days."

He shrugs. "It could be fall break for them, plus an educational trip for a week. It's not outside the realm of possibility."

"Is that how you could swing this trip? Fall break plus vacation?"

He hunches again but recovers quickly. He forces a smile and says, "Now *that* would have been a great question to ask over a drink," before turning away and strolling toward the elevators.

     MEGAN BECKER

DAY 2
At Sea

Gwendolyn

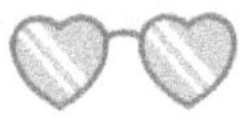

GRAM IS A creature of habit, so I'm up and dressed well before eight o'clock for breakfast.

I pack my tote with a book, our lanyards, sea-sickness medicine, bottled water, pens, and my laptop. Gram raises an eyebrow at the last item, then asks, "How did it go last night?"

I'd pretended to be asleep when she came back from the comedy show (and, as I could tell from the smoke that clung to her clothes when she'd kissed the top of my head, the casino), so I didn't tell her about bumping into Sawyer.

"It was fine. I got a few hundred words out."

"What's this one about?"

I shrug, and she laughs.

"I thought you just said you wrote a few hundred words."

"I didn't say they were *helpful*." And they weren't, because they were all alternate endings for my own love story with Tristan.

She pats my shoulder on her way to the door. "Things will look up, I'm sure of it. Between the sun and the sand and Sawyer, you'll find something to write about."

SAWYER

A GOOD RUN should help clear my head. It does at home, anyway, and there's something kind of nice about running with nothing in front of you but the treadmill screen and infinite ocean.

When she first suggested I take up running, I thought it was a little too on the nose. But she clarified: I'm not running *away*, I'm running *toward* something. Still, I'm running, putting distance between myself and all the things I want to get far, far away from. This trip accomplishes the same goal: there's no cell service, no WiFi, no communication with anyone back home. No social media stalking of Gwendolyn Pierce, which is frustrating, because I know I know her, but I don't know how.

The treadmill belt squeaks a steady rhythm, punctuated by each footfall, and I hear every thud, even with my headphones on, over the pulse that pounds in my ears under the electric guitar and scream-singing of the band that occupies most of my training playlist. I'm not sure why the fitness center seems to be the least air-conditioned part of the whole ship, but sweat is dripping from my hair, nose, and arms by the time I start my cooldown.

Afterward, the shower feels incredible, despite having to duck down to wash my hair. I let the water run down my back and watch it circle down the drain, imagining my problems are carried away in that swirling vortex.

But it's not that easy, and being still for too long makes me itchy. My legs are starting to tighten after this morning's run. I need potassium, hydration, and a walk.

The breakfast buffet is still crowded, but I'm not looking for a table. Instead, I swipe a banana and a carton of chocolate milk, then fill a cup with water and down almost everything before I even leave the room. A few laps around the sports deck should help to loosen my muscles.

From up here, the view is incredible. The breeze off the unending sea is comfortable, and the water rises and falls around us in a gentle greeting. The sun climbs, and wisps of white clouds dot the sky. And then a familiar figure pops into view.

Gwendolyn

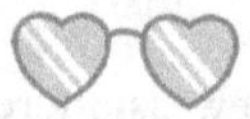

SAWYER'S A NO-SHOW at breakfast, but Nancy's quick to point out that it's because he's at the gym this morning. "He's training for a marathon," she says, with such reverence you'd think he's the only person ever to do so. Fine by me—I get to fill up on pineapple and French toast without being harassed.

After breakfast we head to the sports deck, but we part ways there. I'm ready to relax, and they're itching for a game of shuffleboard. I grab a chaise that overlooks the ocean and settle in to write. To *actually* write this time, not just to create a happily-ever-after for myself on paper.

My fingers rest on the laptop keys and I tap away at the home row, but I never press hard enough to put words on the screen.

I'm still stuck.

The ocean is a nice distraction, and I watch the waves glitter in the sunlight. Maybe there's a story there, in the glittering surface of the sea, aboard the ships that pass through it. I could break from my usual style and write a pirate love story, maybe a mermaid love affair, or a combination of the two.

It all feels too overdone, but at least they're ideas. Instead of diving into a story that has no subject, I dive into brainstorming more possibilities. Anything. *Everything.* I type the most random words I can think of: *Radio. Lamp. Silver. Werewolf. Slippers. Umbrella. Knife. Rum. Condo. Ballerina. Orange. Blanket. Yeti.*

An idea starts to form. Not with *all* the words, of course, but a few of them. This could be something, and I'm a full page into

MEGAN BECKER

summaries and plot lines when I feel it: that creepy kind of sensation, when you can tell someone's watching you.

I half-close the laptop lid and twist to my right to grab my water bottle from my tote—my excuse to look around. The next chair over is empty, but beyond that there's a woman in all black sitting upright in her chaise, reading a book with a cover I know by heart.

"Wow."

I jump a bit at the voice behind me. I don't even have to look to know whose it is.

Why couldn't Gram and Nancy have planned a trip to New York City, or Disney World, or Las Vegas, or somewhere open and roam-able, where I wouldn't have to risk bumping into Sawyer every five minutes?

Actually, scratch Vegas. Too many chapels.

"What a coincidence," he says.

I drop the bottle back in the bag and settle back into my seat. "Yes, what a coincidence, that on our ship—currently in the middle of the ocean with no escape route—we have bumped into each other again."

"Not that," he laughs, and when he says nothing else, I'm forced to look at him. He simply jerks his head toward the woman with the book and lowers his voice. "Gwen Dolan-Pierce. I *knew* that name sounded familiar."

"Look at that. Now you know something about me, and you didn't even have to buy me that drink." I slide the laptop into my tote and stand. He trails me as I weave through the people now swarming the deck.

"Is that what you've been working on? Another book?"

"Yes."

"What's it about?"

"It's a romance novel. That's what I write."

He pauses, and it's so abrupt that I stop too and turn his way. He's making a face.

"Now what?"

He must realize he's making the face, because he shifts and stammers. "I just—I—you don't seem like you…"

I could save him, because I know exactly where this is going, but I refuse. "I don't seem like I *what*, Sawyer?"

He swallows, and there's something fascinating about watching a man like him be speechless. Those broad shoulders don't know whether they should slump in defeat or puff up with false pride; he toes the deck boards and crosses his arms. Finally, he clears his throat and meets my gaze. "What made you want to get into writing?"

Solid deflection. "Do you mean, what made me want to get into writing romance novels? Because what could I possibly know about love?"

"No," he says. *Yes*, he means.

I roll my eyes. "What time is it?"

"I don't know. Around eleven, I guess?"

"Good enough." I grab his hand and pull him toward the forward staircase. "Come on, you owe me a drink."

The Billiard Bar is hosting Oldies Music Trivia downstairs, but upstairs it's relatively empty, and we nestle into two cozy velvet armchairs next to a railing that overlooks the game below. Gram and Nancy have wandered to the lower level of the bar, and based on Nancy's excited sipping of her Bloody Mary, I can tell she thinks they're the team to beat.

Sawyer surprises me when he orders what I'm having—a cosmo with a splash of pineapple juice. Really, he's full of surprises,

     MEGAN BECKER

because he's almost *nice*, asking me about my background in writing.

"I knew your name was familiar to me, and I just couldn't place it until I saw that book."

"You definitely cracked that code. Are you secretly an FBI analyst or something?"

Despite my sassy, smart-ass tone, he smiles warmly. "No. I've just spent too much time at Nan's house. She's had that book out on her coffee table for a while."

"Planting seeds, I guess. You know I met her last year, right?"

"I'd imagine it was when she met Maggie?"

"Right. At a book signing I did in New York. She actually told me about you then."

A rush of pink shoots up his neck and into his cheeks, and he tries to hide it by taking another sip of his drink. "She did?"

"Mhmm," I nod. "She asked me if I was single and said I'd love you." Now it's my turn to blush, but I don't know which part of what I just said causes it. I hope he doesn't ask me about either.

"What made her so sure of that?" He asks what feels like the most dangerous question possible. Asking me why his grandma is sure I'll love him? That's a door I prefer to leave closed, deadbolted, and barricaded.

I try to turn the focus away from the *L*-word and turn it back to what Nancy brought up at that event. It should be a safer conversation. "The only thing that stands out is, she thanked me for thanking teachers during the Q-and-A portion of the talk. Do you think that's what it could be? The teaching thing?"

He scowls at his drink and turns his glass on its cocktail napkin. "Could be."

I ask if he enjoys teaching; he grunts what I interpret is a *'yes.'* But when I ask a few more questions—these questions I'm supposed to be asking over getting-to-know-you drinks—he shuts down.

"I've got a headache," he says. "I think I'm going back to my room for a bit."

He had seen the world: every ocean, clusters of islands, jungles and mountains and shores. Yet none of these things, not the crystalline waters of the Caribbean nor the views of rolling meadows nor the colorful pageantry of the tropical birds and flowers could compare to her beauty.

When the water shimmered white, he knew she was close.

"Shall we cast the anchor?" his first mate had asked, catching him gazing overboard. But he didn't know how many there were below, didn't want to risk hurting them.

"No," he said, his callused hands braced against the railing, his eyes fixed on the water. She would appear at any moment, her body glimmering as it met the sun. And he would feel himself fall in love all over again, as he did every time he saw her.

"Captain," the first mate said, "we have a place below, if you want to keep her close."

Oh, how it tempted him. She had vowed, in a secret lagoon on the Isle of Amori, to follow him anywhere. "You won't," he'd replied. "The journeys are long and the ship is too fast. You'll tire of it." And she had sworn she would never break her vow.

But he was fearful of what he couldn't see. What mermen swam in her pack? When he couldn't see her, who was she with? She said she loved him, but she never promised it was only him.

Okay, this pirate-mermaid-love story is maybe also turning into another writing-as-therapy session. Everything comes back to Tristan. To how things ended. Maybe I don't know how to write

   MEGAN BECKER

happily-ever-afters anymore.

I'm relieved when my alarm goes off and it's time to meet Gram for dinner.

Gwendolyn

SAWYER SKIPS DINNER, but Gram, Nancy, and I have a wonderful time. These women were destined to be friends, and now they're cramming seventy years of missed memories into ten days. Sure enough, they won their trivia game earlier, and they're planning an outing to karaoke later.

"Come with us, Gwen. Show those other kids how it's done." Gram turns her attention to Nancy and adds, "She's always been a wonderful singer."

"I'm *okay*," I clarify, rolling my eyes at Gram. I promise to go along. No guarantees on picking up a mic.

"Sawyer's a good singer, too, though he'll never let you know it. That boy's so shy."

This is literally the *worst* time in my life to have a mouthful of wine, because somehow I choke it down, nearly spit it out, and feel it burn in my nose all at the same time. It's like slow motion, the way Gram and Nancy turn their heads toward me at this awful sound I make.

"Something wrong, dear?" Nancy asks.

I set down the wine glass and wave a hand to signal I'm fine. "I just never would have guessed I'd hear him described as 'shy.'"

Nancy nods, like Shy Sawyer is the most obvious thing she's ever discussed. "He hates being the center of attention. In the fourth grade, he decided to do a comedy routine for the school talent show. He passed out on stage, and they had to bring out the smelling salts."

I blush, because I'm embarrassed for the kid who was trying

something new and different when he failed so spectacularly in front of a crowd, and because I'm embarrassed for the man who's skipping dinner and whose grandmother is telling stories he'd probably rather she didn't tell.

And I blush, thinking about how I'm thinking about him, caring about his feelings, wondering how he is now and if his headache's gone away.

When dinner wraps up, we make plans to meet for karaoke.

"I promised I'd bring him a pizza after dinner," Nancy says when Gram asks if she wants to play Bingo.

"I can take something back for him."

Nancy looks at Gram, then at me, then back. I, too, am stunned I've volunteered for this mission. She smiles. "That would be very nice. Thank you, Gwendolyn."

I show up at his cabin twenty minutes later with a piping hot personal pizza, pineapple-free because I saw the way he wrinkled his face at mine last night.

He and Nancy have adjoining cabins, one deck below ours. They've got to have amazing sunset views from their balconies right about now.

"Oh. Hi," he says, holding open the door. He's got a book in his hand and a comfortably rumpled gray T-shirt on. His hair looks messy, wind-blown. I can't tell if he fell asleep while reading or if he'd taken the book out on his balcony.

"Hi."

"Hi," he repeats. He's kind of cute, when he's not being an asshole.

"I brought you—"

"My pizza?" He takes the box and cranes a neck down the hallway. "Where's Nan?"

"Oh, she and Gram went to play Bingo."

"I see." He shifts in the doorway like he's doing a cha-cha-cha: a step backward, a step forward, a thought about moving to the right, inviting me in.

"Are you feeling better?" I ask, taking my own step back, deeper into the hallway, to signal my desire to *not* be invited in.

Sawyer readjusts his pizza box and book and runs a newly freed-up hand through his hair. "A little. Thanks for asking."

"Sure. Anyway." I check my watch, though I don't pay attention to the numbers. "Well, I don't want to keep you from your pizza, so…"

"Thanks, Gwendolyn. For the delivery."

"Sure." I force a smile. "And hey, if you're feeling better later, we're going to check out karaoke. You should come along." It's a peace offering: inviting him to join us, knowing he probably won't. A very safe peace offering.

"Uh, yeah. Maybe, I guess," he says, which catches both of us off guard.

It's the weirdest goodbye from there, with barely a wave, a noncommittal "see ya," and me, power-walking away from his door.

     MEGAN BECKER

SAWYER

WELL, *THAT WAS* weird. Was Gwendolyn just being nice to me? First by bringing me a pizza, then by inviting me to karaoke later tonight?

There's been some weird role reversal since our first meeting yesterday, and now she's the fun one while I feel like the downer. I know she's just trying to get to know me, and she has no way of knowing that her questions feel invasive. But regardless of her intent, I'm not ready to answer most of them. Getting some separation seemed to be the best option this afternoon, and avoiding dinner meant avoiding additional uncomfortable conversation.

Seemed is the key word here, because instead of being around other people and the distractions offered by the rest of the ship, I've been stuck in my room alone with my thoughts for hours. Maybe it's that *alone* piece that had me considering inviting Gwendolyn in, or maybe it's insanity. Regardless, I didn't. Or maybe I did, sort of, with whatever weirdness happened around the doorway, and she took off. And that would be par for the course, I guess—being rejected.

It's a nice enough night and the walls on the balcony keep the wind from feeling overpowering, so I'm able to comfortably enjoy the sunset and my pizza outside.

There's something freeing about being out here, almost like a windows-down drive along back roads: wind in your hair, Bon Jovi blaring through the speakers, the openness ahead of you. Finally, for the first time in months, I have nothing ahead of me, but in the best way possible.

Out here, I finally feel relaxed. I feel like I can *feel*, like I don't have to drown out my stress with the sound of footfalls on a treadmill or pavement. My concerns are lifted and carried off by each rolling wave. I don't have to think; I can just be. It's nice to not have to be in charge of something, to just let life happen for a few days. To let someone else steer the ship, quite literally.

Another helpful realization is that no one here knows me. I'm not the sum of my mistakes from back home; I'm just Sawyer. I'm the random guy on a cruise with his grandma. Perfectly normal. At least, as normal as any other guy on a cruise with his grandma.

I finish the pizza and enjoy a few more moments of the remnants of the sunset, but then the sky darkens and that openness I'd loved a few minutes ago turns into a black void. The nothingness feels oppressive. Luckily, I don't have to dwell in it. I grab a long-sleeved shirt and head out in search of the one place that will make me feel less bad about myself: the karaoke bar.

   MEGAN BECKER

Gwendolyn

"THANKS AGAIN FOR taking him some dinner," Nancy says when she and Gram get to the table I've been holding for half an hour.

"Of course. How was Bingo?"

They look guiltily at each other, and Gram breaks her silence first. "We may have skipped Bingo."

Normally I wouldn't think much of Gram's plans changing, but the sideways glances and the squirrely looks raise some red flags.

"Spill it, ladies. What were you up to?"

Nancy laughs and thrusts a foot my way, and her skin has the unmistakable sheen of a recent pedicure. "We treated ourselves to the spa," she says, wagging her turquoise-trimmed toes at me.

"Don't be mad," Gram adds, like I'd hold it against her that they pampered themselves for an hour.

"I think it's great. Just make sure I get a heads up if there's a group outing for massages."

Karaoke starts a few minutes later, and it's exactly what we all expect: people who've spent far too much time at the bars already, ballads and drinking songs, and everything is off-key.

Gram nudges me and gives me a twinkling look—a 'go show 'em' look—and I know she wants me to sing, more for herself than for me. This is one of those times, just like at Books Off Broadway last year, when she wants me to put myself out there so she can brag and boast. Not that my singing is anything for her to brag and boast about, but if it means we don't have to hear an old Meatloaf song from the handsy couple in the corner, I'll happily sign up.

When it's my turn, I grab the mic and ignore the lyrics screen, because I know "Castle on the Hill" by heart. It's the best kind of karaoke song—one that was played almost hourly on the radio at the height of its popularity, a former top 10 that hasn't gotten much attention in the past few years. The music starts, and the toe-tapping kicks in automatically in the crowd, along with the smiles of recognition. We *all* loved this song, and we're happy to hear it again.

The third verse slows and the music quiets, and as I sing the lyrics, I scan the crowd. Gram's beaming—the bragging and boasting are surely coming—and Nancy seems impressed, and the man sitting front-and-center is amenable to my performance.

Then my stomach twists, because there at the bar's entrance, propped against the doorway with his arms folded across his chest, is Sawyer Dawson. Thank goodness I'm not singing an angry breakup song—I'd hate to prove him right.

I finish the final chorus and give an over-the-top bow to the audience before returning to my seat with Gram and Nancy. Sawyer arrives at our table just after I do, just in time for Gram's first round of gushing, and just in time for a bachelorette group on stage to warble out the first few lyrics of "Lady Marmalade."

"Should we go?" Nancy asks, cringing at the act on stage. The girls giggle their way through their performance, entertaining each other more than they entertain the audience.

"Aw, but Sawyer just got here! I'd hate for him to miss this," I say in mock protest, and he snaps his gaze to me. His horrified look convinces me that I can't subject him to such torture. "Okay, fine. We can go."

We sneak out of the bar during the applause for the bachelorette party and wander the deck. Gram and Nancy set the pace along the way, and Sawyer and I follow a few steps behind.

"So, you're feeling better?"

He shrugs. "A little bit. Dinner helped. Thanks again."

"Sure. Glad you're out and about."

He nods and shoves his hands into his pockets. "You were, uh, really good up there. Do you sing a lot?"

I'm confused by this version of him, which is so unlike the obnoxious guy at the pool yesterday and so much like the Shy Sawyer Nancy described at dinner that I'm half tempted to carry a bucket of water with me to throw on his face in case he passes out.

"I used to," I answer. "I guess I still do, in my car, around the house, in the shower."

He clears his throat. "Well, it's good. You're good."

I feel heat flood my cheeks, knowing he was thinking about me in the shower. "Thanks."

We follow our grandmas into an elevator, out onto the pool deck on fourteen, and to the ice cream machine for some soft serve.

It's still chilly enough that the outdoor decks are near-deserted. Gram plops herself into a plush chaise and props her feet in front of her. I can tell her ankles are bothering her already. The rest of us lower onto the coordinating sectional across the coffee table from her and start planning out our day tomorrow between licks of ice cream and crunches of cone.

"We can get off the ship at nine o'clock," Gram says. "So if we plan for breakfast at seven-thirty, maybe?"

"That sounds fine," Nancy replies, biting off a piece of her cone, but I catch Sawyer slump in my periphery.

"Actually—" I'm sure it comes out *ack-muh-ley* because my mouth is full of soft serve and I'm desperate to keep it from touching my teeth. "Mind if I skip breakfast and am just ready to get off the ship at nine? Seven-thirty's a bit early for me." Then, so I don't sound like I'm lazy, I add, "At least for vacation."

Gram gives me her stern voice, the one I've heard since I was little, more parent than grandparent. "You'll need breakfast. You've got a busy day tomorrow."

Sawyer chimes in from the opposite end of the sectional. "Maybe we could just grab something at the coffee shop. I bet they have a decent selection."

Gram shifts her gaze to him, then back to me, like she's wondering if it's okay with me that Sawyer just inserted himself into my plan. *She* is certainly fine with it, of course.

He must realize what he's said, because he adds, "If you want company, of course."

"Sure," I say, and we exchange a smile. I wonder if he can read in mine that I volunteered to sacrifice pancakes just to get him off the hook for an early breakfast. All because I saw him slump, make himself smaller, and I didn't like it.

When Gram and Nancy agree that they need seconds of ice cream and a "good sit," Sawyer invites me to walk with him. It's late, and I'm shocked Gram's not getting her rest in now, since she planned an early start to her day tomorrow.

We loop around the pool deck, past the spa and the fitness center.

"So, a marathon, huh?" I ask him, and his brow furrows in a blink-and-you'll-miss-it flash. Then a half-smile turns up the corners of his lips.

"Yeah. Race is in February."

"How long have you been training?"

He shrugs. "About two months so far. I'm about halfway through my training plan."

Writing requires a similar dedication: working toward the craft regularly, taking much-needed rest days, and spending hours on weekends ignoring everything else in your life.

"Won't it be cold?"

He turns his head my way, not missing a beat as we approach the forward stairs. "The race?"

"Yeah. February. That's got to be freezing for twenty-six miles."

     MEGAN BECKER

He mutters something; I can't make it out. "What was that?"

"Point two," he says. "Twenty-six point two miles. The *point two* is the hardest part." He smirks like it's a joke, but I'm not privy to its meaning.

"Ah, sorry, Mr. Math Man. Won't it be cold for twenty-six *point two* miles?"

"It should be in the fifties or sixties at least. Pretty perfect weather for running."

"Sure. Keep dreaming, buddy. I know we've had a few warmer days in the winter before, but that seems like a pretty high hope for February."

He stops and turns fully toward me. Wind sneaks between the plexiglass barriers around the front of the ship in half-inch-wide wind tunnels, snagging his shirt, rippling it across his chest. He's layered a zip-up hoodie over the gray T-shirt I saw him in earlier, and it pulls and plays in the ocean breeze.

"Gwendolyn." His eyes narrow, and he purses his lips. "I can't tell if you're joking or not."

I swallow, confusion settling in. "No?"

He rolls his eyes, but in a nice way, and laughs it off. "It might be cold back home, but my marathon's in California."

"Oh. I just assumed." I shake my head. "So are you going out just for a weekend? To run and come back?"

He shakes his head, continuing our walk, opening a door to head back inside. "I'm planning to explore a bit. Do some hiking, visit a vineyard my friend told me about."

"Wow—your school must have a great vacation policy."

We'd found ourselves, moments ago, at the top of the forward stairs, and now he bounds down them two at a time. He pauses for a moment on Deck Eleven, his deck, like he can't decide if he's just going to call it a night or keep going until he runs out of stairs.

His Adam's apple bobs, and his eyes meet mine, and I feel like he's looking for an answer to a question he can't bring himself to ask.

"I think I'm going to get to bed." I hear myself say it, saving him twice tonight.

He clears his throat. "Probably a good idea. I'm gonna—" He hooks a thumb in the direction of his room and clears his throat again.

"I'll walk you," I say, because I can't keep my mouth shut. Except I do, the whole way back to his room, and he does, too.

"Thanks, Gwendolyn," he says at his door.

"I didn't do anything."

He holds his cruise card up to the lock and props the door open with his foot when the light goes green. "You did." The saddest smile forms on his lips, and my mouth goes dry. "Anyway, I should—" he jerks his head toward the room.

"Yeah, me too. Big day tomorrow, apparently. Goodnight, Sawyer."

I trek toward the back of the ship—*aft*—and up a set of stairs to my room, where I climb into bed, wondering who the hell Sawyer Dawson is.

DAY 3

Bermuda

Gwendolyn

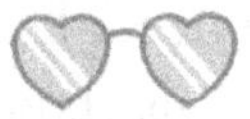

"I THOUGHT SEVEN-THIRTY was too early for you," Gram says, eyeing my tote, my sundress, and my lightly made-up face. It's not a statement: it's a trap, like she's trying to figure out why I'm ditching her for a breakfast I said was "too early" when I'm awake, dressed, and packing my beach bag for the day.

I shrug. "I guess I went to bed earlier last night than I'd expected to."

"The way you and Sawyer went off together—I was surprised to see you here when I got back."

"Yeah, well. We just did a lap around the ship. I think he was tired."

There's a knock on the door, and Gram passes me the sunscreen from the shoe organizer hanging over the closet door. "I'm sure that's Nancy. Since you're up, would you like to join us?"

"No, it's okay. I'm supposed to be going to the café with—"

"Sawyer!" Gram swings the door open, and Nancy and Sawyer filter in. "We were just talking about you," Gram says.

"Is that so?" Nancy smiles, turning and winking at Sawyer, not discreetly.

"Just about breakfast," I clarify, lest Sawyer (or Nancy) get any ideas.

Sawyer avoids his grandmother's gaze. "I figured I'd come up and see if you were ready. We never planned a time or meeting place last night."

"Last call for the buffet," Gram announces. "Have you two

changed your mind?"

"No," Sawyer and I reply together. He flashes me a smile before turning back to Gram. "Thanks, though. Have a great breakfast."

Our grandmas leave, and it's just us. Sawyer ambles around the room while I finish packing for our beach day.

"Do you mind passing me that book on the coffee table?" I ask, adding my tie-dye beach towel to the tote.

Sawyer shuffles around me and passes the book my way, then surveys the rest of the suite and the giant picture window that frames a stunning Bermuda as we approach. "You've got quite the room here," he says, and I can't tell if there's judgment in his voice.

"We thought it would be nicer than two separate rooms." *My* voice is judgment free, but my words might seem like a dig, if someone wanted to take them that way. "For us, I mean," I add.

"Mm." Sawyer clasps his hands behind his back, and it makes his shoulders seem broader. If he were in all black, he'd look like a Secret Service agent, standing there massive and stiff. But he's in tan shorts and an open button-down over a white T-shirt, so he just looks pensive as he gazes out at the sea.

"You ready to head to the café?"

He turns and nods. "Sure."

Once we get our order—a vanilla iced coffee and a muffin for me, black coffee and an egg sandwich for him—Sawyer checks his watch and suggests a walk. Which is how we find ourselves on Deck Fourteen, the sun warm on our skin and bright in our eyes.

A jogger passes us on her lap around the track that's painted on the deck. It seems dangerous to run—the deck is so slippery from its early-morning cleaning that I've slipped a few times already, thankfully without making too much of a spectacle of myself.

"Do you ever just sit around and watch people?" He glances over and down at me while he takes a sip of his coffee. "Not in, like, a creepy way. Just observing."

"Are you kidding? It's a huge part of my job."

     MEGAN BECKER

He looks over my head, his eyes sweeping the perimeter of the deck. "Here," he says, grabbing my arm, pulling me off the track and past a row of chaises to the railing. His hands are warm and gently firm, and I'm annoyed that I'm not annoyed that he just manhandled me. Again.

"What are we doing?"

He shrugs, and it looks like some pink is creeping into his tanned skin. "I thought it would be fun. To people watch." He rests his coffee on the floor and picks at his sandwich.

I prop my forearms on the railing and scan the deck, seeking out a good subject. "Over there," I say, gesturing my head to the left. "That couple."

Sawyer glances up and looks in the same direction. "Matching jackets?"

I shake my head. "Not that one. She's in the pink bikini, he's in the—"

"Speedo? Ugh. Gross."

"What do you think their story is?"

Sawyer turns his body toward me so he can more naturally watch the couple in question. "Story? I'm not sure."

"Oh, come on." I angle toward him, looking up into his big brown eyes. "When you people watch, don't you wonder about their stories? Or make them up, at least?"

He shakes his head and a half-smile forms, and for the first time in twenty-four hours I feel like Day One Sawyer is peeking through. "I'm a logic and facts kind of guy. I just observe. I'll leave the story-telling to the professionals." He nods toward the couple. "What's their story, Gwendolyn?"

When I look back, the Speedo man is bent over, applying a generous amount of goopy white sunblock to the woman's shoulders. The woman sweeps her hair to the side, twisting it, fiddling. "They do this often... at least a half-dozen cruises a year. Mostly for the duty-free shopping, I'd imagine. They don't need to *explore* the world, just see it from their lounge chairs. They'll spend the day in the sun, looking out at Bermuda, but they're not getting off the ship. They don't do excursions. They apply sunscreen once in the morning and never again and marvel at how their skin is always perfectly tanned."

I turn to Sawyer when I finish my analysis, and I blush, because instead of looking at the couple I just spent a minute describing, he's looking at me. "What?"

"That was very…" he pauses, his eyes shifting between the couple and me. He lands on, "specific." I shrug under the weight of his gaze on me. A breeze sends strands of his hair across his eyes, and his shirt flutters.

"Like I said. All in a day's work." I look away from his chocolate eyes and find a new subject. "There, on the other side of the pool. Jean shorts. Chevy T-shirt. Trucker hat. Your turn."

He shakes his head. "I really don't think—"

We volley, back and forth, the smirking and the blushing. I plaster a grin on my face and watch color creep into his. "What's the matter? You scared?"

"Of what?"

"Losing. To me."

He chuffs. "It's not a contest."

"Sure it's not," I laugh. This time when I make eye contact, I wait for him to break it. It takes a few moments, but he finally looks away and spins a stranger's story. I realize I've been holding my breath.

"Okay," he says. "This guy, he's a dad. His job is to claim the poolside seats while his wife gets the kids ready. He'll have a cheap domestic beer can in hand well before lunch, and he'll be in the pool playing with his kids, who are five and two. I bet if he'd turn around, you'd see tattoos on his calf muscles. Probably the kids' names. And he's totally going to enter the belly flop competition at the end of the week."

     MEGAN BECKER

I start a quiet slow clap, nodding approval. Sawyer shakes his head, like he's coming back from a trance, and fixes his eyes on mine.

"Bravo," I say, still clapping. "That was a top-notch story."

He shrugs and takes the final swig of his coffee. "You gave an excellent demonstration." He gives me a half-smile, and I almost think he might be nice, and that his demeanor during our first encounter was a fluke.

"So, what are your plans today? Living dangerously? Laptop at the swim-up bar?"

Like I said, I *almost* think he might be nice. But I can't keep from smiling this time.

"Very funny." I elbow him. "Gram booked some kind of excursion for us today. Not sure what, though. She said it was a surprise."

"Nan's been doing that a lot, too. Planning parts of this trip in secret, I mean."

At first, when Gram wanted to take the lead on the planning, I thought it was great. But ever since her first surprise—that she was trying to set me up with a total stranger—I've been wary of her intentions and her plans.

"I guess we should get back to them." He nods in agreement, and we head back toward the elevators, returning to our separate rooms to prepare for whatever our grandmothers have in store for us.

Gwendolyn

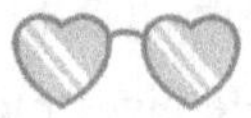

"YOU HAVE *GOT* to be kidding me."

After breakfast, Gram let me know that I needed to change. Instead of lounging on the beach (I was hopeful our excursion was a taxi to the pink sand beaches), she booked us for some kayaking in a harbor at the far end of the island.

Except, when we got off the ship, she said her leg had been cramping all morning, and she didn't want to risk it cramping in the kayak, so she was going to "find Nancy and sit this one out." So I'd be commandeering a two-person kayak on my own.

Except, I won't be, because freaking Sawyer Dawson is waiting on the beach when I step off the second water taxi to the harbor. And he's Nan-less.

"We've been played," he says, a grin crossing his face. Admiration, no doubt, for these sneaky senior citizens.

Sawyer insists I take the front seat, and while I don't love that he'll be behind me unsupervised, I do appreciate that he won't be obstructing my view. He offers a steadying hand as I lower myself into the flat-bottom kayak.

"I'm fine," I assure him, just before the neighboring boat bumps ours, shoving the front end crooked and making everything wobble. Instinctively, I reach out and grab his arm as I try to maintain my balance and not fall on my ass into the water.

"Clearly you're a professional," he laughs.

I roll my eyes and get situated in my seat, trying not to think about the way his skin felt, warm and smooth under my hand.

Once everyone is settled in their kayaks, one of our guides paddles out in front of us and explains what we'll be doing: short trips to various parts of the harbor, then some time to explore on our own. But first, a few minutes to practice our teamwork and paddle around this cove.

"So it'll probably work best if you just paddle, however you can, and I'll make sure I counter your strokes to keep us moving in a straight line." Sawyer's already alternating as he paddles, left, right, left, and when I twist and glare at him he's watching where my paddle dips into the water, focusing so intently that it's like keeping us going in a straight line is a mathematical formula that requires Einstein-level genius and concentration.

"Tell me, do you feel everyone's skills are inferior to yours, or do you reserve this level of condescension just for me?"

His jaw drops, and I read panic in his eyes. "You just—I didn't take you for—"

I skim my hand over the water and flick droplets off my fingertips at his face. "Relax. I get that you don't think the writer can do outdoorsy things. But it's just kayaking. It's a pretty chill activity—lots of people do it."

"Noted. Sorry."

"It's fine. But don't think you're going to sit there and judge my skills the whole time. I'm an excellent stroker."

Fuck. Me. I feel my cheeks burn red, and his mouth gapes and closes, then gapes and closes again, like he's trying to figure out the wittiest possible response without crossing a line. I whip back around so I don't have to see the smile on his lips or the mischievous glint in his eyes.

We've traveled literally four feet, probably all of which are due to the water's gentle movement, because we've spent the whole time bickering instead of actually practicing. The guides, John and Denny, call us back together, and we form a haphazard convoy with one guide leading us and one in the rear. This is *leisurely*, they remind us. We're not going for Olympic gold.

Sawyer doesn't seem to get the memo, because he paddles deftly, advancing us past three of the seven other boats. I sabotage his efforts by dragging my paddle in the water, and I nearly lose it twice. It also causes us to turn sideways.

"I thought you were excellent at *stroking*," he huffs behind me. There's a hint of amusement in his tone, but it's definitely not reflected on the face of the woman in the kayak next to ours, with her pre-teen son sitting in front of her.

"I'm so sorry about him," I say, jerking my head toward Sawyer. The mom rolls her eyes and steers away from us, and I feel our boat shaking with Sawyer's laughter. I flick him with water again, and he retaliates in grand fashion by scooping water into the slight curve of his paddle and pouring it onto my leg.

"*Jerk*," I mumble, editing myself, avoiding the name I want to call him because I don't want this woman to be even angrier with me for cussing in front of her child.

I wonder: If I chanced a look back, would he wink at me? Would that playfulness from our first meeting be spread across his face? I'd love to know, but I can't look back, because I don't want him to see what's written on my own face. Best to stare straight ahead, paddle left-right-left, and pretend that I'm not at all enjoying his ridiculous antics.

The next hour is mild—touring the harbor, learning about sea turtles and the island—and then we round a bend into a cove larger than the one where we started. The land around us here is different. Earthier, with more mud than sand, more trees than houses on the banks. The water is brown and deeper-looking, full of sediment and mystery, unlike the clear shallows where we started. We stay close to the shoreline.

"Do you think there are snakes out here?" When the question escapes Sawyer's lips, it's barely a whisper. I turn, as much as I can, to look at him, and his face is Casper-white. I think he's just revealed his biggest fear, the way he stares at the land.

"No," I answer. "I'm pretty sure there are not."

He swallows, and his Adam's apple bobs. "But you can't be sure."

"We're on an island, barely twenty square miles, hundreds of miles from any other land mass. How would snakes have gotten here?"

His eyes move to mine, and they're so full of worry I want to put my arms around him and tell him it'll be alright, like Gram did for me when I was seven and had night terrors during a sleepover at her house. Instead I just smile, and I watch his tension dissolve.

"That's a good point," he offers.

"I know."

"You're smart."

"I'm aware of that."

"For a *romance writer*," he says. But his lips curl upward, and this teasing, playful version of him is back.

I want to splash him, want to dip my paddle into the harbor and pull it back hard, letting water rush off the blade and onto his leg. If I pull back far enough, draw my shoulder blades close together, let the paddle drip closer to his waist than his knee, I could make him look like he peed himself, and wouldn't that be hilarious?

Just as I'm about to do it—my grip is tight and I'm biting my lip so premature laughter doesn't betray my intentions—movement in the water startles me. I bobble the paddle but recover, though now the whole kayak has shifted, and I brace my feet against the foot pegs to steady myself.

"You okay up there, Madam Expert?" Sawyer asks. There's so much mockery in his voice that I really regret not having been able to carry out my plan.

"I'm fine. I just… I thought I saw something." I peer over the edge, looking for whatever it was that caught my attention just a moment ago.

"It's not a sea snake, is it? Because *those* could be here, right?"

"No, I don't think so. It was… *whoa*." I tuck the paddle next to my leg. The plastic side of the boat is warm under my hands, and I crane my neck, still steadied by my feet, to look at what's just below the water's surface a few feet ahead.

"Take us straight forward. Slowly. *Gently.*"

Sawyer obeys with a short paddle on each side of the kayak, guiding us away from the shore.

"*There!*" I point, and he drags the blade through the water to slow us down.

"What are you looking at?"

The boat tilts, just slightly, as he shifts his weight and follows my gaze to the right.

"Are those—"

"Turtles!" I whisper-yell. "Sea turtles. Aren't they amazing?"

I'm not sure how long we sit here like this, but it's long enough that John, one of our guides, must be concerned.

"Everything alright?" he asks, pulling up alongside us. His voice interrupts the gentle lapping of water against our kayak and startles me.

"Oh! Yes, everything's great. We found some turtles."

"They're smaller than I expected them to be," Sawyer says, and leave it to him to be picky about the size of the sea turtles we've happened upon.

"But they're not snakes, so that's a plus." I shoot a wink in his direction, and I can't for the life of me figure out why. He grins in return, squinting into the sun.

John looks confused, like *of course* turtles are not snakes. He eyes Sawyer and replies, "Most turtles here are juveniles, which is why they might be smaller than you'd imagine. Once they grow, they could be seven hundred pounds." He rests his elbows on his knees and watches them like they're his favorite film.

Similarly, I can't peel my eyes from the cluster of turtles around the boat. They move so effortlessly through the water, floating and gliding with the help of their flippers. Despite them being just under the water's surface, they're nearly camouflaged; ripples on the water reflect the sun's light in the same pattern as their shells.

"We need to rejoin the group now. Time to learn about pirates!" John says. He's maybe forty, tan and lean from the kayaking and mountain bike excursions he leads on a near-daily basis on the island. He's friendly, but not overly so. He's got a lot of knowledge but very little patience, so we don't argue when it's time to follow him back to the rest of the group.

Denny, on the other hand, is a native of Bermuda but a nineties California surfer-boy type. He can't be more than twenty-two, and I wonder how he came to absorb so many traits from four seasons of *Saved by the Bell* in his young life.

I could sense John's interest in the sea turtles we encountered and the information he shared throughout our excursion so far. Denny has the same enthusiasm for the pirate stories he tells us about the island: apparently early settlers would intentionally cause trade ships to wreck in the reefs along the western side of the island, then take what they wanted from the stranded vessels.

I love a good story. Even more, I love a good story-*teller*, and Denny's delivery is equal parts suspense and laughter, married together for an engaging experience.

"You might have some competition on the bestseller list," Sawyer says as we turn ourselves around and begin the journey back to the beach, with John as our guide. "That Denny… he was pretty good."

"I might. Not sure we write the same genres, though."

"Yeah, but if we had a people-watching story contest—"

"I'm sure he'd win."

"Glad we agree."

I can practically feel Sawyer's smile at my back and droplets of water from his paddle as he alternates left-right-left, balancing my right-left-right.

There's commotion behind us, and I follow John's gaze as he turns to see what's happening toward the rear of our group. Some of the other excursioners are laughing, flailing their paddles in the water. Denny muscles toward, then past us at an impressive pace.

"First 'yak back to shore gets free Rum Runners!" he shouts.

John rolls his eyes and stops his kayak, ready to bring up the rear now that Denny has taken the lead.

The only way I can describe what happens next is to say we are *launched* forward. Sawyer is taking this seriously, leaning so far forward with each stroke he's practically in front of me. I paddle too, but the way the laughter takes over makes it hard to dig as deep as I should.

"You might have some competition, too," I tell him. Denny's got some distance on us, but Sawyer's closing the gap, and no one else is even close. I chance a look back, and two lines crease his forehead between his brows.

"What do you mean?"

"In the brute-strength, Mr. Muscles competition."

He misses a stroke on the right before his lips curve up and he raises his eyebrows in a *hubba-hubba* way at me. "You like my muscles?"

"I didn't say that. I simply noticed that you have them. Or—I noticed that you seem to *think* you have them, and that you need to prove they're bigger than anyone else's."

He takes another long stroke on each side of the kayak, flexing and showing off as he does. "If your books are as dirty as your day-to-day innuendos are, I may need to grab a copy or two. And a cold shower."

Heat rushes to my face, and I'm thankful that the sun has been beating on me all day so I have an excuse for the redness there. Without thinking, I scoop the water into my paddle and flick it behind me, drenching his leg. I repeat on the other side. Back and forth, a few times.

Sawyer returns the favor by taking a sip of his water and pouring the rest of the bottle down my back. And damn him for taking his water intake seriously and having a quality, insulated bottle, because there are still pieces of ice left over from when he filled it this morning, and now they're down my spine and under my shorts. One may have found its way into my bikini bottoms.

I arch my shoulders back, willing the sun to find my skin in any separation I can create between my body and the mandated life vest strapped around me. "You ass." I might be laughing as hard as I can tell he is.

"Your face was so red that I thought I should help you cool down."

The competition is lost. We're almost there, but we've been passed by everyone but John and an elderly couple who take turns paddling while the other looks through a pair of binoculars.

I roll my eyes at him. "You just lost us free rum, you know."

"If only there was some hot-shot, fancy-pants celebrity who could afford to buy a couple drinks for us. Especially because she's the one who tanked our chances of winning." For good measure, he turns his paddle sideways in the water and gives me one more quick flick. "We even? Truce?"

"Fine. Truce. If you buy the drinks."

"Gwendolyn Pierce, are you asking me out?"

"Never."

"Bummer. Nan and Maggie will be so disappointed."

When we reach the sand, Sawyer hops out first, then offers a hand to help me out of the kayak. We have an hour until the water taxi takes us back to the ship, and Sawyer returns our gear while I get ready for relaxation.

Without the bulky life vest, I can see that the backs of my arms and shoulders are burning. I grab my sunblock from my tote bag and strain to apply an even coating.

"Do you want help with that?"

I turn toward the voice, just as Denny's eyes make their way up to mine. My skin prickles under his leer, and I glance at his outstretched hand and swallow. "I, um, I think—"

"Hey, baby, need a hand?" Sawyer slides in behind me and seamlessly transitions into rubbing the lotion across my shoulder blades, like Denny doesn't even exist.

I shrug at Denny as Sawyer's hands crest my shoulders, his fingers curling up and over, his thumbs massaging circles at the base of my neck. He looks up, so close his breath is warm, dangerously close to my ear, and acknowledges Denny's presence.

"Oh, hey man. Great job out there today. Really enjoyed the ghost stories."

Denny cocks his head and squints back. "Ghost stories?"

"I think he means *pirate* stories," I interject.

"Yes. Pirate stories." Sawyer deposits a performative kiss on my temple. "Can you blame me for not paying attention when this gorgeous woman was my view?"

I can't tell if the goosebumps on my skin are from the words he said or the warm-honey way he said them.

It could be the kiss, I guess. Yes. Definitely the kiss. But these are the *I-just-got-jump-scared-by-the-clown-in-the-haunted-house* kind of goosebumps, not the *I-like-how-that-felt* kind. Right. Definitely.

"Alright, well. You guys enjoy the beach then, I guess." Denny takes the incredibly unsubtle hint and saunters off toward the equipment hut to join a brooding John.

"I guess I really might have some competition after all. If, you know—" Sawyer clears his throat, and he rubs in the last of the sunscreen more aggressively than when he had an audience. "If I were actually… which I'm not, of course."

"Of course. No." Denny looks my way again, all sad puppy eyes and surfer boy muscles, and I can only imagine that the words spewing from John's moving lips are a scolding for fraternizing with the clientele.

Sawyer regains his voice. "You should take your shirt off."

"*Excuse me?*"

"Relax, Miss Mind-in-the-Gutter." He dangles the bottle of sunblock in front of me. "I need to get the rest of your back."

"I'm fine like this, thanks."

"You're just going into the water fully clothed?"

I nod, like it's a perfectly normal thing to do.

"Did you bring something to change into?"

"No," I answer, biting the inside of my cheek. I'd thought I'd be spending the day tanning on a beach, and while I put on more practical clothing in my quick-change before leaving the ship, I didn't think to change the bikini underneath. No chance I'm baring more skin with Denny's eyes and Sawyer's hands nearby.

"So, just to make sure I'm following here. You're going to sit in there—" he points to the water as it swells onto the beach, "in that." He gestures toward my tank top and shorts.

"Mhmm."

He rolls his eyes and drops the sunscreen back into my bag. Then he looks past me, peels his shirt off, and tosses it into the sand with a smile. Sunlight plays with the beads of sweat along his collarbone, and he's totally showing off.

"What was that about?" I ask. He steps toward me, his expression growing serious and his hands finding my hips. "What are you doing?"

He leans down and presses his forehead to mine.

I'm glad he's got such a firm grasp on my hips, because otherwise I might disintegrate. I'm hot all over, and my insides are goo, just melty and gross, and for what? Because he's touching me? No, not touching… *holding* me. And his eyes are deep like melted chocolate, warm and enticing.

His stupid, ridiculous mouth is inches away from mine, and I wonder what would happen if I angled my chin higher…

"I win." There's still a hint of coffee on his breath.

"What?"

"I said, *I win.*"

I pull my fingertips from his hair—not sure how they got there in the first place—and take a step back.

He reads my confusion and half smiles. "The competition. With Meathead McMuscle. I don't think he'll be bothering you anymore." He releases my hips but takes my hands instead and leads me toward the water's edge.

We sit side by side in the shallows of the crystalline harbor, our outstretched legs only half covered by the lapping water. Maybe he wants to tan the six-pack I totally did *not* take notice of, or maybe he wants to save my shirt from getting soaked through, but whatever his reasoning, it's nice, just sitting together and talking.

     MEGAN BECKER

I CAN FEEL the creep's eyes on us even now, as the water laps over our legs in gentle undulations. There's no real way to escape him, since we're stranded on this beach with him until we're stranded on a boat with him until we're back at the port.

She looked so uncomfortable when Denny approached her, and I panicked, I guess, and threw myself in to fend him off. The *"baby"* probably could have been enough. The kiss may have been overkill, and there probably wasn't really a need to put my hands on her hips.

But now that I have… Well, I have.

Her hand skims the water's surface in slow, graceful strokes, and her head is low, eyes glued to the ripples she makes, as we trade travel recommendations. So far, I know she loves New York and Washington, D.C. She's also a fan of amusement parks and 'any place with museums.'

"I'd figured you for a secluded-cabin-in-the-woods type."

She meets my eyes, grimacing. "Like some middle-of-nowhere place with no cell service so I can't call for help when the ax-murderer in the woods comes to get me? What on earth makes you think that?"

"Who said anything about an ax-murderer? I was thinking more along the lines of cozy cottage, surrounded by a peaceful stream and colorful wildflowers, with a wraparound porch—"

"With a swing?" Her eyes are big and bright, and she's pulled her legs to her chest, resting her head on her knees.

"Of course there's a swing. There's also a big stone fireplace, so if you go in the winter you can cozy up and watch a movie after a long day of writing, and your boyfriend could bring you hot chocolate, or something."

Where a smile had started to form, now there's a scowl. "Despite what our grandmothers seem to think, I don't need a man involved to enjoy a vacation."

Talking to her is like playing a game of Battleship, and that was a direct hit. "Right. You were well on your way to handling the stranger-and-the-sunscreen problem solo."

Right on cue, we're summoned to collect our things and board the water taxis back to the main port. She wraps her towel around her waist and wrestles her tote bag onto her shoulder, then trudges along the sandy path to the boat.

It's clear she doesn't want to talk, but I promised her a drink, and I extend it to her as a peace offering shortly after we board.

"I was going to ask him to make it extra strong for you, but he nearly filled it to the brim with rum anyway. Must be the standard recipe?"

She doesn't want to laugh. It's so obvious, which is why it's so rewarding when she rolls her eyes, smiles, and takes the drink. She slides her tote bag onto the floor, clearing the seat next to her for me.

Five minutes later, I catch Denny's eyes on her again.

"Damn. This guy just won't quit."

She whips around to face me. "What do you mean?"

I bring my cup to my lips so he doesn't see me mouth his name, then I throw back the last half of my drink. "Don't freak out, Gwendolyn, okay? Just play along." I stretch an arm around her shoulders and pull our bodies closer together. The outside of her thigh is pressed against mine, and her eyes dart to my still-shirtless chest, which has really encroached on her personal space.

She shifts and clasps her hands tighter around her cup. I'm

     MEGAN BECKER

saving her from this dude, but she seems so damn nervous for some reason, the closer that I get.

This could be fun.

The condensation on the outside of my cup is still cold, and when I trace it along Gwendolyn's arm I'm rewarded with an outbreak of goosebumps from her sunburnt shoulder to her wrist.

I lean in to whisper in her ear, to tell her that it's working and that Denny looks like a kid who just got an F on a project he worked really hard on. Maybe she thinks I'm going to kiss her again, just like I did on the beach. Whatever it is, she turns inward in defense, raising her shoulder and pinching it to her chin, and her lips just miss mine.

I can't help but laugh. She does that to me. *Has* done it, a few times. She brings the sound out of me in the most carefree way, and for a second I forget. I forget that I'm miserable, that my life is falling apart, why I have the time off to be on this trip anyway.

"Relax," I tell her through the laughter. The breeze sends her hair across her face, and she looks for a moment like the girl from *The Ring*. It makes me want to laugh even harder, but I keep it in my chest this time. My fingers tuck the strands back behind her ears. "I wasn't trying to do anything."

The boat hits a wave and everyone lurches in their seats, and she and I are now closer together, with my hand in her hair at the base of her neck.

There's a cracking sound from the plastic cup in her hands, and her leg goes rigid, and she holds my gaze before her eyes move to my lips.

And then her mouth crashes into mine.

DAY 4

At Sea: Formal Night

FUCK.

I'm an author, for crying out loud, and yet I can think of no other word to better describe how I'm feeling right now. Possible contenders include:

- embarrassed
- regretful
- mortified
- ready to throw myself off this ship

but we'll stick with the four letters that really sum it up.

I didn't mean to kiss him yesterday. I didn't even *want* to kiss him yesterday. But it almost felt like I was *supposed* to kiss him, if that makes any sort of sense. He'd done this really nice, protective thing, keeping Denny away from me—a few times—and his laugh was so warm, and then his hand was on me, and I just did it.

I wonder if I could get an endorsement deal with Nike.

The clock reads 5:00 a.m., and I'm starving. I told Gram last night that I'd found a problem in my story I needed to work on, which is totally true, if "my story" equals my life, and kissing Sawyer Dawson is a problem. Which… of course it is.

The only way I could be sure to avoid him was to not leave my room at all, so when Gram went to dinner, I ordered a mango-salsa pork chop from room service, which I ate half of, because I found myself more inspired to write than I've been in the last year. Sorry, pirates and mermaids: you've been replaced.

My stomach growls again, and I don't think my smuggled

supply of KitKat bars is going to help with this level of hunger. I roll out of the sofa bed and slide my feet into flip-flops, brush my teeth, throw on a sweatshirt, and quietly close the door behind me so I don't wake Gram.

I try the buffet, but it's closed until seven. Instead, I change course and head toward the café, grateful that they're open so early, and order a large latte and chocolate chip scone. A sign near the exit catches my eye, and I follow the arrows upstairs toward the ship's library.

I'm happily surprised to see two walls lined with shelves, their glass doors displaying everything from board games and children's books to hardcover biographies and dog-eared romance paperbacks.

The other pleasant surprise is the row of plush armchairs in the next room over, each framed by a window that provides a gorgeous ocean view to anyone who looks up from their book long enough to enjoy it.

I open a cabinet; my fingers trace the spines of the old romances and land on one that's weathered to softness. It's an old bodice-buster: *Touch of the Fieldhand's Hand.*

The light of sunrise is a whisper among the clouds, and I sink into a velvet chair to read as I wait for the sun to come up.

It's gloriously empty here. Quiet. A break from the bustle of the ship and the fast pace of home. But the quiet is also an invitation and an opportunity to think.

About the whirlwind of the past year.

About Tristan.

About what could have been, and what is.

The book takes me back, too. Visiting Gram's house growing up, I'd see stacks of these period romance pieces, with the long-haired male models on the cover, doe-eyed damsels in distress melting into them. "They're a nice break from reality. A guilty pleasure. Mindless reading," Gram had said, trying to get Mom to pack one for a family vacation. "But that's the problem: they're mindless," Mom had replied, leaving the paperbacks behind on Gram's kitchen table.

I check the sunrise's progress after each page. Out here, on the sea, it comes little by little and then all at once, and if I blink I might miss it all.

After four pages, I'm distracted by the view out the window: the vast expanse of navy, peaks of white in the moving waters. At the water's edge, there's a medley of color so vibrant it's like a toddler opened a pack of neon Crayolas and started scribbling on the sky. Orange, yellow, turquoise, purple, hot pink—they're all streaked above the horizon, punctuating clouds and chasing away the hazy blue remnants of night above me.

"Beautiful, huh?"

His voice snaps me from my trance. He's in a chair facing mine, across a narrow aisle, a book in his lap. He gazes out the window— no, not gazes. It's not wistful; it's intentional. And his eyes flick to mine and a smile tugs at the corner of his mouth.

"I didn't hear you come in."

He swallows, and his smile grows. "That's because I was here first, Gwen."

Gwen. It rolls off his tongue so naturally, this name so few people use for me in my personal life. Despite it being part of my pen name, so many people use the full name that it always sounds like Gwendolyn. Away from writing, I am almost exclusively Gwendolyn—to my teachers, my family (except Gram), and most of the people I've counted as friends. Even Tristan called me Gwendolyn, at least in daily life. *Gwen* was the breathy moan that escaped his lips exactly twice, both times when we were tangled up together.

Maybe that's why it sounds so intimate to hear it fall from Sawyer's lips. His stupid, full, coffee- and rum-flavored lips. The lips I kissed yesterday and definitely have *not* thought about since then.

"Gwen?"

Crap—all this *not* thinking about his lips has drawn my eyes right to them. I meet his gaze and read concern in his eyes, amusement on his mouth.

"You okay over there?"

"Yeah. Fine."

"Nice spot to watch the sunrise, isn't it?"

I give the window another look, the brightest colors fading to orange and yellow as the sun climbs into view.

"Yeah, it is." And then, because he feels too close and I have to remind him I don't like him, I add, "It's also a nice spot to read. In the quiet."

"Point taken," he says.

I shift in my seat and raise my book again, the steady hum of the ship's engine drowning out the voices in my head that tell me I should talk to Sawyer. Almost. After a few pages, I dare to glance at him again.

He's sunken into his seat, left ankle over right knee, the book open in his lap. His eyes are on the page on his left, but his index finger is already poised to turn to the next page, like he's hungry for it, starved for more of the story, needing to devour every page.

"It's hard to focus when you're staring like that," he smirks.

"I'm not staring. I'm just amazed that you actually know how to read. Or that you're really good at faking it."

"I don't believe in faking things, Gwen."

My jaw drops and I try to close my mouth before I drool. It's a real possibility when I think about him and *not faking* things. It shouldn't be a problem. I shouldn't think about him like that, but it's been so long since I've had a kiss like the one I had yesterday, and now I wonder what *not faking* with him would be like.

He snorts out a sigh and examines the book. "Someone told me this book was half decent, so here I am."

   MEGAN BECKER

"Oh." I take the deepest breath I can, which is not very deep, because my chest won't allow much oxygen in while it's simultaneously tightening around my thumping heart.

"Well, I will leave you to your mediocre book then." I close my paperback and take off, but not before I hear him say my name again, and not before I see that the book in his lap is mine.

I DON'T BELIEVE in faking things. What the hell was that?

Flirty. Gross. Unlike me. Bad enough to scare her away.

The list could go on, but does it need to? She's gone, and I seem like a creep. Even when I called after her, she took off. No opportunity to explain.

When it comes to explanations, I'm waiting for one, too. Her kiss came out of nowhere yesterday. It would be easy to imagine it was just part of the ruse for Denny's benefit, which was what I thought at first, but she took off as soon as the boat docked, then disappeared for the night. That reeks of something more than a fake kiss meant to repel someone else.

I try to read more, but if Gwen's presence this morning was distracting, her absence is brain-numbing. I can't focus. Can't think about anything other than what she might have been thinking when she kissed me. Can't think about anything other than that kiss. If I'm being honest, I can't think about anything other than her.

A change of scenery doesn't even help. Alone in my room, all I can do is think about her. On the pool deck, in The Retreat, at the bar… all I do is scan the crowd and try to find her.

Nan recommends a few rounds of trivia, and we do well as a team. We always have, and we've always been close, which is why it wasn't too unusual for her to invite me along on this trip. She likes her independence but has a hard time traveling alone anymore. Having help with bags and transportation makes things easier for her, and she knew I needed to get away.

"Are you enjoying yourself, Sawyer?" She drops her new highlighter—our prize for winning TV Theme Songs trivia—into her purse.

"Yes, of course," I answer. "You?"

She looks at me, her lips quirking into a smile. "It's simply terrible, vacationing with my favorite grandson."

I roll my eyes in response. "I bet you say that to all your grandsons."

"Maybe," she winks, and her face goes earnest. "I hope you and Gwendolyn are enjoying getting to know one another."

"She's nice." I say it too quickly, and it's too vague, and it's not really representative of the person I'm supposed to be describing. And Nan knows it.

"Sawyer."

"She doesn't make it easy, getting to know her."

"Hm. Can you imagine? Trying to get to know someone who's a little closed off?"

It's different. I'm different. I have reasons for not sharing everything about myself and my past; Gwen's just being difficult. But Nan would have no patience for that answer, so I tell her I'll keep trying.

"Great," she smiles. "Now, make sure you're ready for dinner in two hours. I'm heading off to the casino."

"Going to win some money for your favorite grandson?"

She pats my cheek and winks. "You would be my favorite even if you weren't my only, dear."

SAWYER

FORMAL NIGHT SEEMS to bring people to the main restaurant in droves, wearing everything from dress shorts and polos to tuxes and bowties, sundresses and sandals to evening gowns and heels. One couple passes our table, and I'm sure they've taken a wrong turn on their way to a James Bond cosplay convention.

Nan and Maggie have interpreted the theme more comfortably, and they both wear sparkling tops and wide black dress pants that look like skirts from a distance. And Gwen… Gwen is breathtaking. That first night, there was so much structure to what she wore, but tonight the stiff lines of that dress are replaced by fabric that drapes over her curves, like melted silver that was poured over her skin, pulling in just the right places, showing off a gorgeous figure underneath. It hugs her body like a lover might. Not that I'm thinking about Gwen and her lovers.

Normally I'd stand when a woman arrives at the table, but now I pull my napkin into my lap and take a drink of cold water, considering the idea of dumping it onto myself for a makeshift cold shower.

Gwen lowers herself into her seat and avoids eye contact as she straightens the silverware.

"Don't you look lovely," Nan tells her, and Gwen smiles shyly and thanks her. Nan nudges me and clears her throat, and I take a hint.

"You look really nice," I add, and suddenly bashful Gwen is masked by something else. She shoots daggers my way.

Maggie looks between us and tries to keep the conversation flowing. "Did you have a nice day today, Sawyer?"

I take another sip of water and feel Gwen still staring at me. "It wasn't quite as eventful as yesterday, but it's been good."

"I'm sure the kayaking was a wonderful experience."

This time when I answer Maggie, I meet Gwen's eyes. "Right. The kayaking." I know both grandmas are confused about what else I could mean, but I ignore the silent request for explanation and flash my brows at Gwen. If she's going to make it difficult to get to know her, I'm going to be equally as frustrating.

Her foot grazes my shin and I brace for the impact of a swift kick, just as our server brings us each a glass of wine. Gwen bites her lip before raising the glass. "A toast," she says, "to the unexpected."

Nan and Maggie exchange a look and shrug; Gwen arches a brow at me, clinking her glass against mine before taking a sip. Then it all makes sense, this coyness from her, because her foot follows the line of my shin in gentle strokes as a devilish grin spreads across her lips. I swallow my wine, ignoring the desire to melt into her touch.

"Gwendolyn," Nan says, "Sawyer tells me you two found the library this morning."

"Sure did. It's a great place to catch a sunrise. Actually, I found an old romance novel like the kind Gram used to read all the time."

"Used to?" Maggie chuckles. I love that there is not an ounce of shame in this woman when it comes to smutty books.

"And," Gwen adds, "it looked like Sawyer was really enjoying his book."

I shrug my answer. "It's alright, I guess." I swear a kick should be connecting with my leg at any moment, but Gwen's retaliation is even more diabolical than physical pain. She sinks lower into her chair and wraps her foot behind my calf, then readjusts and slides it between my legs, past my knees. And *shit*. It's all I can do to silence the moan that longs to escape my mouth. Gwen drinks her wine and moves her foot higher. I clear my throat and straighten the napkin on my lap, which makes her laugh and nearly spit her wine back into the glass.

Maggie looks at her like she's lost it. "Gwen, my goodness. Are you okay?"

If Gwen wants to play dirty, I can do that too. I drop my hand to her foot, skimming my fingers around her ankle. Her expression betrays her, and her cool demeanor breaks for just a moment. I'm more than a little smug when I ask, "Yeah, Gwen. You okay?"

"I'm fine." She pulls her foot back just as our food is delivered, and spends most of the rest of the meal with her eyes down, avoiding my gaze.

After dinner, Maggie and Nan take off to change. "You can find us on the pool deck if you need us," Nan tells me, nudging me with her elbow. "Hopefully, you won't."

Gwendolyn

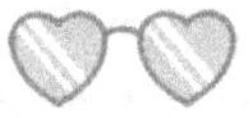

"WHAT THE HELL *was* that in there?" he asks when Gram and Nancy are out of earshot. "Are you starting to like me?"

"Oh, please. You started it."

He laughs that infuriating laugh of his. "I started it? Are we playing that game? Because some might say that you started it—yesterday—when you kissed me. In fact maybe we should take a survey—" Sawyer takes a long stride toward our grandmothers, and I reach for his arm.

"No!" I say, far too loudly, and he turns back to me with a knowing grin. "No. We don't need to survey anyone. They don't need to know about my momentary insanity."

He slows again and we walk side by side. I hate that I notice when he shoves his hands into his pockets. I hate that he does it when he feels embarrassed or unsure. I hate that I make him feel that way, but I kind of love it, too.

When I packed my dresses for the two formal nights, I must have been drunk, or thinking I was on a honeymoon cruise instead of on vacation with my grandmother. Maybe I'd secretly hoped that pictures would make their way back to Tristan and he'd be so devastated by my sex appeal that he'd come crawling back, and I could humiliate him the way he humiliated me. Instead, I'm humiliating myself, standing here in this ridiculous dress next to Sawyer, who looks equally uncomfortable.

"About yesterday." He takes a hand from his pocket and massages the back of his neck.

"Yesterday was nothing, Sawyer. Denny was watching, and I did something to let him know I wasn't interested."

"Right. Yeah. But—"

"That's it. Honestly." Full disclosure: it might not be *it*, but no way am I telling Sawyer that. "Can we please stop talking about it?" He nods, and we walk in silence farther down the deck.

"So, Gwen," he says, and I miss the rest.

Just like after I kissed him yesterday, I feel naked and embarrassed. Then he calls me *Gwen* again, and I feel even more exposed. My name on his lips might as well be his hand on my thigh.

"Gwen?" He touches my shoulder, and there's heat between us. I know he feels it by how quickly he pulls away. "Where do you want to go?"

"The library."

Sawyer arches a brow at me. "You're all dressed up, and you want to go to the library?"

I nod. "There's a café on the first floor. Books on the second. A great view. What could be better?" *Comedy show. Yodeling competition. Falling overboard.* All actually sound more appealing than going to the library right now, with its dim lights and romantic atmosphere. "Are you coming?" If I were an editor, I'd scribble a huge *wc* by that line. Poor word choice, Gwen.

"Do you want me to?" He winces as the words come out, like he immediately regrets accidentally continuing my accidental innuendo.

I have no idea what this man wants. Does he want me to invite him, and if I do, what is he expecting will happen? Or does he want me to let him off the hook and tell him I'd rather go solo?

"How about this," I say. "I am going to the library. You are a grown adult who is free to go wherever he wants."

     MEGAN BECKER

SAWYER

THERE IS A zero percent chance I'm letting this woman out of my sight. Especially in that dress. I could blame it on the Denny incident, say that I'm worried someone else might get too handsy with her and make her uncomfortable. But I've been focused the last few months on being honest with myself and managing my feelings and my truth better, so let's say what it really is: I don't want to let her out of my sight because she looks incredible, and I am attracted to her.

Her lips, painted a deep purple-red, part when she turns and sees me trailing three steps behind her. If she plans to say something she reconsiders, closes her mouth, and turns away from me. It's only after we have our coffees and are climbing the stairs to the library that she engages with me again.

"This might have been a mistake," she whispers, taking in the full room. Most chairs are surprisingly occupied, and it's quiet; everyone actually seems to be reading. She looks up at me, biting her bottom lip, and it would be totally wrong to kiss her right here in the middle of the room, but it's all I want to do. "Wanna get out of here?"

"Yes," I whisper past the lump that's formed in my throat. I would love to get lost in a real library with her, like exhibitionist undergrads sneaking to a hidden corner of the campus library where no one ever goes and the overhead light flickers, and I suspect she'd be just as sexy in an oversized college sweatshirt as she is right now, and I'd pin her against rows of books and have her there, half-dressed and hushed.

But we're not college kids, and we're not in private, and *oh God* I need to stop thinking about that scenario immediately, or I'm going to poke someone in the eye as I walk past them.

I follow her back down the stairs and match her pace as she wanders.

"Did you need to change your shoes or anything?" I ask, though I'm hoping she doesn't change a thing, because she looks great… but also, I could do without seeing all that flesh when I'm trying to keep my flesh under control.

She shakes her head as she sips her iced coffee. "Nope. I'm good."

We pass through the concourse, crowded and congested with deal-seekers shopping the two-for-one T-shirt sales and browsing discounted watches.

"Here," she says, once we've woven our way through a cluster of people fawning over $9.99 jewelry. Gwen darts up the stairs and collapses onto a bench that overlooks the mayhem below. "Let's people watch."

"Here?"

"Um…" she gestures dramatically at the scene below. A drop of coffee spills out from her straw and lands on her wrist. "Yeah, here. Do you not see the characters before us?"

We spend the next twenty minutes crafting backgrounds and telling stories about the unlucky, unsuspecting crowd below.

"How did you get so good at this?" I ask her, because just like yesterday morning, her stories are detailed and feasible.

She shrugs. "I've had a lot of time to study people, I guess." It seems like there's a story there, but she bites her lip like she's holding it in. "Anyway, I don't think it's fair that Gertrude—" (our name for a tall, middle-aged woman with fire-red, Texas-sized hair that we keep circling back to) "—gets to monopolize the jewelry station like that. Bianca clearly wants a turn." She nods her head toward a lithe blonde who keeps craning her neck to see what is being offered at a fifty-percent discount.

"Well, Gertrude isn't worried about anyone but herself these days," I add. "Ever since she found out Rex was cheating on her, she's focused on número uno down there and doesn't give a shit about Bianca's or anyone else's feelings."

I turn to Gwen, expecting her to wear a smile that matches my own, but her expression has shifted. Her eyes narrow and her jaw sets, and she smoothes her dress over her lap.

"Alright, enough of that. I could use a drink. You?" She's on her feet before I can object, and I'm following her to the elevators. She pushes the button four times, then leans an arm against the wall to brace herself while she massages her foot. Luckily these elevators are not glass, because when the door opens she presses the button for the pool deck, moves immediately to the back corner, and crosses her arms.

"Did I say something?"

She avoids my gaze and stares at the changing number over the doors. "No. I was just tired of the game."

It feels hollow, and as much fun as I had teasing her at dinner, I get the sense that now isn't a good time to push back.

We find two chairs together at the pool bar and lose track of both time and the number of drinks that get passed our way. Gwen finishes a pineapple martini and waves for another within five minutes of our arrival. A fan recognizes her and buys her a glass of wine. A woman in the shortest dress I've ever seen, white and strapless, wearing a pink sash that says *Bachelorette*, stumbles over in too-high heels and smudged eye makeup and offers to buy me a shot if I will just kiss her cheek for a scavenger hunt she and her friends are doing. I look to Gwen for approval (or at least for confirmation that she won't murder or lecture me later), and there's a twinkle in her eye before she cheerily announces, "Only if you buy me one, too!"

I read concern on Maggie's face as she and Nan towel off after their time in the pool. I nod confirmation that I'll take care of Gwen and make sure she makes it back to the room safely.

"Who knew Sawyer Dawson was such a player, kissing all the women on this ship." Gwen hiccups a laugh, twirling the shot glass on the counter.

"Well, to be fair…"

Her eyes shift between mine. "What?"

"I mean, if we're being accurate, *you* kissed *me*."

She drops her gaze to my mouth, then raises it to my eyes. "Maybe." She bites her lip and leans in, dangerously close, and her breath is warm and fruity on my face. "But you kissed me back." I only realize my face is moving toward hers when she cackles and pulls back. "You didn't even deny it! And I think you want to do it again."

"Not even close."

"Really? So if I did this—" she traces the hairline around my ear, "or this—" she slides off her stool and positions herself between my legs, her hand on my thigh, "you wouldn't want to kiss me? Even a little?"

I do. God, I do. "Even if I wanted to kiss you back, Gwen, it would require you to kiss me first. Are you going to kiss me? Do you *want* to kiss me again?" The strap of her dress has found its way over the smooth edge of her shoulder, making her neckline plunge further than it should. I hook a finger into the silver fabric and replace it. All I want is to kiss her. Whether returning a kiss or initiating it, I want to. And I want her to be stone-cold sober so she can tell me to touch her, to let my fingers linger at her collarbone, to kiss her. But she's not, and she can't, so I won't.

Her eyes dart to the place my finger briefly touched, and before I know it she's back on her stool. "No. I don't want to kiss you again. I don't even think I like you all that much." *Hiccup.* "You're kind of annoying."

     MEGAN BECKER

She orders another drink and seems to decide that this is all the discussion we need on the topic. Her demeanor changes and there's no attempt at being the sultry version of herself she just showed me.

Quiet Gwen from the first few days of this trip is gone, and in her place is this version of her I only glimpsed the tiniest bit of at karaoke: she's loud and laughing and unapologetic. She sings along to most of the songs that come on the speakers behind the bar, and she has a story for each one about some random life moment connected to it. And she tells each story with this energy I haven't seen from her before.

I know she's drunk, but I feel that maybe she's also *her*. Uninhibited. Messy (there's a stain on her dress from a grenadine-soaked cherry she dropped on herself). Honest (she told me twice that she thought I was an ass that first day but now she's not so sure). Funny (she makes the two guys in Eagles jerseys and cargo shorts next to her crack up when she leans over to tell them her favorite knock-knock joke). And fucking beautiful (see: all of the aforementioned traits).

I get an alert through the ship's in-app messaging system while Gwen's telling me about the time she thought she was going to get arrested because she ate a grape at the grocery store before paying. Maggie's making sure we're still okay; she's going to bed and was just a little worried. I message her back that things are fine, and I'll bring Gwen back soon.

The phone display shows that it's well after midnight and Gwen doesn't want to go, but once I remind her she can carry her piña colada with her, she's fine. I help her off her stool, and she eases down on her heels with the steadiness of a fresh-from-the-birth-canal deer. She knows she *can* walk, but she questions the *how* part.

Her first few steps are… successful. She makes progress, gets a few feet closer to the elevators than she was before. I offer to carry her glass—which she agrees to as long as I promise to let her have a sip whenever she wants one—and follow behind her as we make our way along the freshly cleaned floor. We're halfway there when her foot slips on a wet patch and she reaches out for something to steady her. What she finds is my free hand, and she stares at it for a moment, turning it over in front of her like she's never seen a hand before. Then she weaves our fingers together, beams her sparkling eyes right into mine, and gives a wicked smile.

"Take me to my room, Sawyer."

     MEGAN BECKER

DAY 5
The Bahamas

Gwendolyn

MY HEAD IS killing me.

It makes it hard to get my bearings when I can hardly open my eyes because the sunlight is streaming in, and *ow.*

What I remember from last night is 1) lots of drinking, 2) feeling inspired to write, 3) having a decent time with Sawyer, and 4) literally nothing else. The hard corner poking into my side confirms that I fell asleep writing, and thank goodness my laptop didn't tumble off the sofa bed in the middle of the night and break. The empty cocktail glasses on the nightstand come into focus, which further explains the headache, because I lost track of how many drinks I had before I got back to my room.

I sink deeper into the bed and try to pull the comforter over my head, but there's resistance. Suddenly there's an arm next to me, and *oh my God did I murder someone in my drunken stupor?*

Peering out, I'm relieved to not see a corpse, but consider it might be better than the alternative, which is Sawyer Dawson half covered and half clothed. In my bed. Next to me. Also half-ish clothed, because my pajama shorts barely cover anything.

Sawyer stirs, then startles awake when I shove him.

"What are you doing here?" I hiss. Anything louder would not be in my hangover's best interest.

"Good morning to you, too," he mumbles, stretching an arm over his head. From what I can tell he's wearing a white T-shirt and boxer briefs that leave very little to the imagination, and when paired with my overactive imagination, well…

Heat rushes to my face and I duck under the covers as much as I can. "Good morning. But also, *what are you doing here?*"

His expression is worried but amused. Like he's concerned about me but also knows I'm okay, so he's not *too* concerned. "You really don't remember?" I shake my head (in hindsight, a mistake). "Not surprising. Okay so last night, you were found by a group of fishermen, just floating in the ocean. There's a chip that was extracted from your back—"

"Okay, funny guy. I know I'm not Jason Bourne, so how about you explain why you're here and why I feel like I've been hit by a bus."

The concern vanishes and the amusement on his face takes center stage. "I'm here because you begged me to stay."

"Bull."

"It's true. You wouldn't even let me leave to get pajamas. Hence..." he looks down at his body, and I try so hard not to follow his gaze.

Flashes of last night come back to me. *Drinking. Laughing. Sawyer's hand in mine. Leading him here.* "A gentleman would have slept in his suit. Or on the floor."

"All of a sudden I'm a gentleman?" he mocks. "Also, you wouldn't let me, Gwen. You said you wanted me here. And I can't sleep in my suit, because we still have another formal night, and you said it was no big deal anyway."

I hear the words, but I've stopped processing anything after 'Gwen.' It was one thing before, out in the busy ship, surrounded by people, but it's entirely different here, in my bed.

"Don't worry," he continues, "nothing happened." He flips the comforter aside to show that I am under the sheet and he's on top of it. Okay, this guy has some gentlemanly qualities.

"Why did you let me drink so much?" I groan, giving up on the other fight.

His response, a scratchy, early morning laugh, is possibly one of the sexiest sounds I've ever heard. Then he speaks, and it gets even sexier: "You don't strike me as a woman who needs or wants permission, Gwen. You just *do*. It's one of the things I like about you."

Something happens. *Down there*. Muscles move and roll like they're telling me to have him right here, right now, because I've never had a man talk to me like that before. I haven't even *written* a man like that before. We've already kissed, anyway, so it would be so easy (morning breath be damned) to do it again, tangle my fingers in his hair, let him show me what else he likes about me.

"Also," he says, and I notice that his cheeks are red, like he didn't mean to say that last part out loud. "You said you wanted to write the Heming-way, and who am I to question your creative process."

There's a shuffling sound, movement, and I hear my name. It's Gram, awake and either ready for breakfast or checking to make sure I didn't fall overboard.

"*Shit!*" I pull the covers over Sawyer's head and plop a pillow over him for good measure, then I flop to my other side and prop myself up on my elbow, making myself as big as possible, trying to hide this mountain of a man beside me. "Don't say anything!" I warn him through clenched teeth.

"I'm surprised you're up," Gram says as she closes her bedroom door behind her. She glances my way but largely avoids my gaze. "I was just heading to breakfast. Did you want anything?"

I shake my head, instantly regretting it again. My brain and my eyes are running at different speeds, and it takes a moment for my vision to clear. "I'm good." I'm so *not* good right now.

"Okay, dear," Gram says. She grips the door handle and turns back one more time, smiling, eyes twinkling. "Thanks for getting her back safely, Sawyer."

I DROP OFF coffee and the largest muffin I can find for Gwen, walk-of-shame-ing it the whole way in last night's suit, the shirt and jacket open over my T-shirt. I could have changed first, probably should have changed first, based on the knowing looks I get from a handful of people I pass along the way, but my singular focus was to get a hangover cure to Gwen as quickly as possible, and that did not allow for a detour to my room.

Nan and I somehow find ourselves approaching our rooms from opposite ends of the hall at the same time. She sees me from a distance, and I can sense her reaction before I can see it clearly. Her smile widens as we near one another, and I know her well enough to know she's dying to make some smart comment.

"Nothing happened," I tell her.

"Not yet," she says, and she disappears into her room with a wink.

Our excursion today is for all four of us, and fortunately it's booked for a later time slot. We figure Gwen should have a chance to recover a bit before we need to disembark. Unfortunately, that's not the case, because we're being ferried from our port to a separate part of the island for the event and boats only leave within the first ninety minutes of docking.

When she sees the ferry, her face goes gray-green. "I am going to puke over the side of this boat."

"Sounds like maybe I should look for a new seat buddy."

She doesn't turn toward me as she continues, probably trying to move her head as little as possible. "It's going to be humiliating."

The line stretches behind us, and I estimate that the boat can hold about a hundred people on the lower level, nearly as many upstairs. "How about this: I'll make sure we get a seat by the side, near the back, and I'll hold your hair back if you need me to."

"So chivalrous, Sawyer Dawson. You might be a gentleman after all."

The boat ride is, thankfully, uneventful, and we have two hours to explore and enjoy the beach before our scheduled rendezvous with dolphins. Nan and Maggie decide to check out the gift shops and then wade in the water, but Gwen drops herself into a lounger under an oversized umbrella and declares that this will be where we can find her for the next 120 minutes.

Maggie looks at me and I dip my head to say *I've got this. Go, have fun.* Then I lower myself into the chair next to Gwen's.

"I feel like I have my own security guard." She drapes an arm across her eyes.

"It's easier to pretend to be one for you now than to hire one for myself later if something bad happens to you on this trip."

She lifts her arm and opens one eyelid to stare at me.

"Your grandmother. I'm pretty sure she'd kick my ass."

"Don't be silly," she says, still watching me. "She'd hire someone else to do it." Her lips curve into a smile before she settles back into her avoid-the-sun-at-all-costs position. "How'd you know about the hair, anyway?"

For the life of me, I can't figure out what she's talking about. "What hair?"

"Holding my hair back. If I threw up."

I shrug, though she can't see it. "The joys of being raised in a house full of women, I guess."

"Did you have a lot of sisters?"

"No." I slide out of my flip-flops, then readjust my own chaise to a 45-degree angle and nestle in with my hands behind my head. "Actually, growing up it was just me, my mom, and Nan."

"Really?"

"Yeah. Mom was an only child. My grandpa died before I was born, and my dad took off when I was three. Mom never really pursued a romantic relationship then, because she was so focused on me. So it just made sense for the three of us to live together. When Mom got sick, Nan always helped with her hair, rubbing her back, and I learned pretty quickly that that was an important technique in caring for someone."

She turns fully to me now, her eyes meeting mine. "Your mom was sick?" There's concern there, and it's sweet, but misplaced.

"Oh, like, normal sick. Like when I brought the flu home from school or something and she inevitably picked it up."

"Oh. Good." She leans back into her chair and lets a moment pass. "That whole boat ride, I was wondering how you knew. I was scared you were going to say you'd had long hair, like a man bun or something. Please tell me you never had a man bun."

"I never had a man bun, Gwen." I pause for effect and revel in her reaction when I add, "Except that one year in college."

One wink at her and her jaw drops, like she can't tell if I'm joking or not. (I'm not, but I was double-majoring and taking on a lot of extracurriculars and just didn't make time for a haircut.) Finally, Gwen rolls her eyes, smirking. "You're such a pain in the ass, Sawyer Dawson."

     MEGAN BECKER

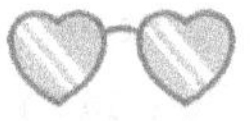

Gwendolyn

IT'S TRUE, HE *is* a pain in the ass, but he's also thoughtful. Some might say sweet. Growing up with his mom and grandma explains his awareness of things like my dress in the glass elevator that first night and his caring for me last night. I could have done without the nightcap back in my room, but I appreciate his respect for an independent woman, letting me make my own choices.

Nancy and Gram find us at lunchtime, their arms full of snacks from the gift shop. After our smorgasbord of Reese's Pieces and pretzel nuggets, it's time to head to our excursion.

We file in, part of a group of about a dozen, onto a wooden platform that floats in the bay just behind the gift shop. Gram and Nancy are the first to enter, with Sawyer and me right behind them. Winston, the trainer, explains what we'll see and do today, and after reminding the parents in the group to keep their kids' hands and bodies out of the water, he calls up our dolphin.

Her name is Freddie, because the way her silver body glides through the water reminds Winston of mercury. I can see it: her missile-like body darts under the far end of our platform straight through the center opening, right up to Winston for a high five and a fish. Gram is loving it; even with Nancy and Sawyer between us, I hear her distinctive laughter and *oohs* and *aahs*.

Winston teaches us about dolphins and their unique characteristics, like echolocation and how their pregnancies last for up to sixteen months—and yes, there is a collective shudder from the women in the group at that fact. Sawyer groans, then leans toward me and says, "They'd better get great Mother's Day gifts."

Winston sets up a few tricks with Freddie. We see her jump, fetch a football, spin in circles, and splash an unsuspecting tourist who's been so preoccupied with taking the perfect photo that she fails to see what's right in front of her until she's drenched. Freddie laughs, her strong tail propelling her upright and backward across the water.

Then we're pulled in groups of four onto the front platform for a flipper shake, kiss, and photo op, starting with the family across from us. It's fun to see the kids in each of the first groups either beam or blanch when Freddie approaches, and Sawyer and I both let out an *awww* when a little girl no older than five tells Freddie she loves her.

When it's our turn, Gram gets the first kiss. She crinkles her nose against the fishy smell but leans in, lips puckered and ready. Nancy whispers something I can't hear in her ear and Gram laughs, and Sawyer whispers under his breath to me that it's a good thing the children have all left the area. Then he turns toward Nancy, and his broad back blocks my view. I lean in, trying to see around him, just as a wave rolls in against the platform. Everything shifts and I'm off-balance, flailing to avoid falling into the water.

Some fearful noise (I choose to erase it from my memory) gurgles from my throat, and Sawyer whips around, throwing an arm out to steady me. He succeeds, but it would have been ideal if his hand had landed somewhere other than my boob.

"You okay?" he asks, scanning my face with concern etched on his own.

"Yeah, fine." I can't decide whether it's more awkward to draw attention to his hand or to just let it stay there until he moves it naturally on his own, but Winston saves the day. And by 'saves the day' I mean 'mortifies us both.'

"Sir." He clears his throat. "This is a family-friendly activity."

Sawyer's eyes flit to Winston, then follow the trainer's gaze,

     MEGAN BECKER

then double in size. "OH! Sorry," he mumbles, jerking his hand back. He turns again toward Nancy, who's been shaking a dolphin's flipper for what feels like an eternity, and I watch color flood his neck and ears.

We both take our turns without incident, and Freddie even gifts me a smooth stone from the bottom of the bay before we pile in for our photo. Sawyer kneels behind me at the photographer's command, and Gram and Nancy fill in behind us. When Freddie makes her appearance in the photo, it's with a kiss on Gram's cheek.

We wave goodbye to Freddie and climb up the ladder and off the platform. Sawyer and I offer assistance to our grandmothers, though Gram smirks when she lets Sawyer take her by the arm and cracks a joke about him getting handsy with multiple women in one day.

I lag a few steps behind Gram and Nancy, who take off giddily for the lockers, and cross my arms over my chest. "Thank you, for earlier," I say. It's an invitation, a peace offering, and Sawyer falls into step beside me.

He runs a hand through his hair, then shoves both into the pockets of his swim shorts. "Of course. And sorry, again, about…"

I force out a laugh when his voice trails off. "Sure you are."

"Hey. Gwen." He stops, so I stop, and if he was avoiding my gaze before he makes up for it now, staring straight into my eyes. "I'm not like that. I would never—"

"I know."

Our gazes are locked another long moment, until he nods and shifts. "Good," he says, resuming our walk back.

We get to relax another thirty minutes before it's time to be ferried back to the ship, and Sawyer spends the whole ride with his hands wrapped in the swirling terry of the beach towel in his lap, his eyes fixed firmly on the water ahead.

THE COLD SHOWER is exactly what I've needed since the "incident" with Gwen. I didn't mean to grab her there—I just wanted to keep her from falling into the water. But since I *did* grab her there, since I know how she feels in my hand… Yes, the cold shower is perfect.

I meant what I told her, which is that I'm *not* that kind of guy, and I feel guilty for even thinking about it now. It just felt right, our bodies being connected like that. And last night? Best sleep I've had in months. It was nice, being close to someone. To *her.* And to be fair, I'm not just thinking about her body, but about her smile, her laughter, her brain, and her maddening wit, and I'm so fucking hard, despite the cold shower, despite knowing how very much I should not be thinking of her right now, like this.

Logic kicks in, and I reason that it's just been a while. Chelsea and I broke up months ago, and I haven't been with anyone since then. Maybe that makes Gwen my rebound, which is why I feel this longing for her—to finally be able to move on.

I do everything I can—think about sports, what I want for dinner tonight, the fishy smell of that dolphin—but I'm in physical pain. I rest my forehead against the shower wall, increase the water temperature, and curse myself for thinking of nothing but Gwen when I wrap my hand around my erection and give myself a much-needed release.

 MEGAN BECKER

After sequestering myself in my stateroom for three hours, I venture out for pizza and a sea breeze. I bite into scorching hot pepperoni as I wander the outer decks, enjoying the slow ship speed and ocean air. If the afternoon's shower was any indication, I need more cooling down on this trip.

A movie's just started by the outdoor pool, but hardly anyone has gathered to watch it. It's dark and chilly, and there's a good number of indoor activities that might be more appealing than some decade-old family-friendly adventure flick.

I make a quick stop at the poolside bar and put in an order for a piña colada—the colder the drink, the better.

"The hermit reemerges, boring pizza in hand, searching for a libation to drown his shame from an unfortunate incident earlier that day."

I don't know how I missed her, but there's Gwen, perched on a stool at the far end of the bar. She's got a journal, a pen, and three empty glasses in front of her, and she looks comfortable in a pair of faded black leggings and an oversized sweater, her hair braided over one shoulder.

Half a smile forms on my lips, and I shake my head. "You don't stop, do you?"

She shrugs and smirks. "Sorry. Writer."

The bartender sets my drink on a napkin and Gwen eyes it suspiciously.

"Plot twist," she says. Her words slur a little, and her eyes shine. "That was an unexpected drink choice, Dawson."

I set down the box of pizza and her eyes move to it. She looks greedy for it, so I nudge it her way. She grabs a slice and takes a ravenous bite.

"Didn't you like dinner tonight?"

"I didn't go. I've been writing for hours." She finishes chewing and takes a swig of her beer, her face twisting at the drink. "What about you? Why'd you skip?"

My mouth opens, but no words come out.

"Afraid they were serving chicken breast?" She launches into uproarious laughter and slaps her leg. "Too soon?"

I shake my head, unable to keep the smile from forming on my lips. God, I love the way she does that. The way she finds the humor, makes the punchline, and lets me off the hook while roasting me all at once.

"I didn't take you for a shy one, Sawyer," she says, once she's calmed down. "That very first day, I thought you were such a douche. You're a very interesting character."

Desperate to change the subject from this afternoon's Grabgate incident and eager to hear more from her mind, I settle into the conversation. "Tell me more about myself, Gwen. I want the people-watching treatment."

She thinks for a moment while chewing the last bite of her slice of pizza. "Grumpy goofball likes things just so. He's shy, but his size doesn't allow him to hide. He's loyal. Fun. Kind. A little handsy sometimes."

Gwen takes another sip of her beer and cringes again, so I wave for the bartender and motion toward my drink. He nods his understanding and slides her a piña colada just a few moments later.

"How am I doing so far?" she asks. She's nibbling at the cherry from her drink, and so help me, if she ties that stem into a knot with her tongue.

I shrug. "Kinda basic, don't you think?"

She takes the bait and drops the (thankfully) untied stem onto her napkin. "Okay, fine." She looks me up and down and narrows her eyes at my shorts and hoodie. "You're effortless. You don't take

    MEGAN BECKER

yourself all that seriously. You have women lined up to hook up with you, but here you are, on a cruise with your grandma, because she wants you to settle down instead of sleeping your way through the single moms at your school. Am I close?"

"Not really."

"None of it? Not the line of women so long it could wrap around a city block?"

"Especially not that part."

Maybe it's the drinks catching up to her, but when she scans me again it's slower, her eyes lingering on all the places they probably shouldn't. "Interesting," she drawls, her eyes nowhere near meeting mine.

"Don't get me wrong," I start, and that gets her attention. "It's not that women haven't expressed interest." They just haven't expressed interest recently. Not since Chelsea. Not since everything happened. Regardless, I add, "I'm not typically a hook-up kind of guy. Maybe that's why Nan planned this trip, so I could—"

"Don't you even imply what I think you're about to imply," she says, and she's suddenly sharp again. "I'm not easy, Sawyer."

"Oh, I'm well aware, Gwen. You're one of the most difficult women I've ever met."

Her brows pinch, but she catches her reaction before revealing too much emotion. I settle my tab and try to pay for Gwen's drinks, too, but of course she's upgraded to the beverage package.

"I'm an independent woman, Sawyer." She slides off her stool as I stand.

"I'm aware, Gwendolyn." I thank the bartender and start to walk away, but she hollers after me.

"Where are you going?"

I motion for the empty loungers by the pool. "I was going to watch this cinematic masterpiece. Is that okay with you, Gwendolyn Shakes-Pierce?"

She scowls, and she won't admit it, but I think she's jealous I came up with that one before she did. She looks back at her papers, then up to the movie screen.

"Did you want to join me?"

Her eyes retrace their path. "No. I have work to do." She turns and plops back down in her stool, and I find a lounge chair where I can see her just as well as I can see the movie.

      MEGAN BECKER

Gwendolyn

CASSANDRA COULD FEEL it in her bones, this aching, yearning need to touch the water. To feel its power, and maybe to steal some for herself. She loved it and feared it, respected it and revered it. She wasn't sure how often other people sat around thinking about which element was the best, but she knew without a doubt that it was water.

It powered cities and leveled them. It was vital for survival and could easily kill. It could heal and it could destroy. It could carve its way through rocks, and it could be still, serene. And, Cassandra knew, it could hold memories.

Theo busied himself with the blanket, the basket, his cell phone. Even when they were traveling, even when they were about to sit down for a picnic on the beach, even when he was presumably minutes away from pulling out the velvet box she'd glimpsed as they packed, work found him.

Or maybe he found work. Maybe he chose it in all these moments: Christmas Eve at her parents' house, a dinner date with friends, intermission of her favorite show. Now, a few minutes before proposing.

Cassandra dipped her toes in the water. She wondered: if she walked straight forward into the crashing waves, beyond them where the water was deeper, over her head, would he even notice?

Austin. Austin would notice.

SAWYER

"I CHANGED MY mind."

She drops into the chaise next to mine half an hour later, and of course I saw it coming, because she's far more interesting than this movie could ever hope to be, and she's kept my attention accordingly.

"I see that."

"What's happening?" she asks, jerking her head toward the screen.

I can't tell her, because I don't remember from the last time I watched it, and I haven't actually been paying attention. "Not sure," I admit. She cocks her head, and I add, "Fell asleep."

"Sure," she says, a knowing smirk spreading across her lips. "Sure." She tucks her journal under her chair and sips at the piña colada she's brought up with her. "It's cold."

The temperature has steadily dropped throughout the evening, and I've been grateful for the blankets the ship provides specifically for their movie nights. But with a low turnout and the movie more than half over, the attendant is gone and the extra blankets are locked behind a roll-up door. I offer Gwen mine.

"No." She shakes her head. "That'd be rude, to take it from you."

I snort. "You're worried about being rude now? After your very telling little psychoanalysis over there?"

She laughs and shakes her head, and the moment is broken by her shiver.

"Just take it. It's fine." I've wrapped myself in pretty tight, because I'm not too afraid to admit that my legs are absolutely freezing, and I start to wriggle myself free.

Gwen eyes me and puts a hand to my forearm. Then metal screeches against the deck as she slides her chair closer to mine, curls up half on her chair and half on mine, and cocoons us both inside the blanket.

"This okay?" she asks, her chin quivering.

With her nestled at my side, there's not much space, and I end up with an arm draped around her. "Yeah. This okay?" I ask in return.

"Yeah."

Twenty minutes later, she shifts. "You're hot, Sawyer."

"Oh. Sorry. This thing really traps the body heat—" I scoot farther away to give her space, but her arm darts across my stomach, her fingers finding bare skin where my hoodie and shorts have separated in the movement.

"No, I mean…" She sighs. "Earlier. I'm surprised, I guess, that you aren't playing the field a little. 'Cause you could, if you wanted to."

"I don't."

"Okay."

For the rest of the movie, her fingers linger on my waist. They absently draw circles and lines, her skin against mine, and it's like a compulsion for her to touch me. Which, of course, means I don't watch the movie at all, because my eyes are torn between staring at the top of her head while I wonder what it would be like if I took her back to my room and really felt her skin against mine, and staring at the insides of my eyelids while I try to force myself to think of very unsexy things.

The movie ends, but we stay there through the credits, then the blackness that follows. Gwen stretches like she'd been sleeping, like she's trying to create an excuse for us lying there together so long.

When we finally stand, I wrap the blanket around her shoulders and tug my sweatshirt down.

"Walk me back?" she asks. I nod and grab her journal for her, then stay a step behind her the whole way down the staircase and the narrow hall to her suite. She swipes her card at her door and steps inside. When she turns and looks at me, I can practically hear her internal dialogue.

I make the decision I know she's struggling with easier on her. "I'll see you in the morning."

She looks conflicted and reaches out as I turn away, wrapping her fingers around my wrist. If I thought my body was hot earlier, I feel absolutely molten now. It would be so easy to go in, lay her down, show her how hot I think she is, too. But I don't do hookups, and I don't think she does, either, though I don't know for sure. And the not knowing tells me exactly what I need to know, which is that Gwen and I cannot happen. Not now, when we're still strangers.

I cup a hand around her jaw, and she watches my eyes as I lean in. God, the confidence of this woman. It's clear from the way she angles her face toward mine that she thinks I'm going for her mouth, and she wants to see the kiss unfold.

There's an ache in my chest, knowing I'm disappointing her, but my lips never make it to hers. I kiss her temple instead, as I'd planned. "Goodnight, Gwen."

My thumb strokes her cheek, and I have to consciously take my hand off her face and remind my body how to walk away from her door.

My sweatshirt's off before I ever reach my room. I fling my shoes across the cabin and head straight to my balcony. I'm on fire for this woman, ignited by her charm, and I hope that the brisk breeze will help extinguish the flames and not fan them.

 MEGAN BECKER

DAY 6
Private Island

Gwendolyn

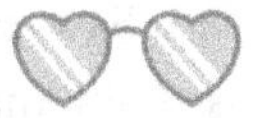

WORKING OUT IS, admittedly, not my favorite thing. Working out on vacation downright *sucks*.

My ass is so sore from the seat of this bike, but I pedal on. I know a good cardio workout is great to clear your head and get your endorphins going, but right now I'm so freaking envious of the people doing Upward-Facing Dog on cushy yoga mats outside under the sunrise instead of bruising their tailbones on a bike in the darkest corner of the fitness center.

I give up after an hour, ready for a shower and a day on the beach. It's boring up here anyway, and I'd feel happier if I'd just gotten the extra hour of sleep. Not sure why I thought coming up here would benefit me.

Gram's waiting on our balcony when I come back to the room, sipping her coffee and watching our approach to the cruise line's private island. Another ship has already docked, but we've booked a cabana for ourselves today, so we don't feel rushed to try to beat others to a cluster of chairs. Today is all about relaxation, and Gram is starting early.

"Skipping breakfast?" I ask, lowering myself into the far chair and propping my feet on the railing.

"Not hungry."

"Uh-oh. That's problematic, because I hear they bring platters to these cabanas, and I can't afford to eat both of our shares."

That lifts the corners of her lips, just a little, and she takes another sip of coffee. Her hand shakes under the weight of the mug.

There are very few times when I consider that Gram is an old woman, but her demeanor this morning is a reminder that she's not as young as she used to be. Even if she and Nancy forget that sometimes.

"You spending the day with Sawyer?" she asks.

I shrug in return. "I guess? I assumed all four of us would be in the cabana."

She changes course. "I can never tell if you two actually like each other or resent us for planning this whole thing."

"Can neither be true?" She turns her head toward me, and I explain. "I could never resent you, and I think what you did was very sweet." A little unconventional, but sweet. "I just don't think he and I would ever work together."

Gram rolls her eyes and sets her coffee on the table next to her so she can turn her body my way. "Gwendolyn. He is everything you have been looking for, and then some."

I open my mouth, ready to object, but Gram narrows her eyes at me, knowing exactly what's coming.

"Gwennie, you have closed yourself off for the past year, ever since that… that jackass broke your heart. Don't take that out on a nice guy like Sawyer. He's different. It's obvious. Stop being so stubborn and give him a chance."

"We don't even know each other, Gram."

"So get to know each other, Gwen. Let him in."

"We have half a week left," I protest, shaking my head.

Gram tuts at me and rolls her eyes. "You act like you'll never see him again when the cruise ends. You live two hours away from each other. You have phones. You have cars. You'll figure it out."

An announcement echoes through the ship that we'll be able to disembark within an hour. Gram pushes herself up with help from the arms of her chair. "I just want what's best for you," she says, shuffling toward the door.

"And you really think that's Sawyer?"

     MEGAN BECKER

She shrugs. "You'll never know if you don't give him a chance."

Gwendolyn

LET HIM IN.

Gram's words (and her sudden frustration) stick with me throughout the morning, through a quick shower, getting dressed, and lugging my beach tote, with Gram's smaller tote nested inside, down the stairs to Nancy's room so we could all walk together to disembark.

What I didn't tell Gram is that I've tried—twice now, apparently—to *let him in.* Like last night, when I invited him into my room, but he kissed my head instead and walked away. I could tell Gram he's just not interested in me, but I don't want her and Nancy to harass him, so I'll let it go and deal. I can't force him to like me, and I don't think I can get much more obvious than telling him he's hot and holding the door to my room open at midnight.

Speaking of hot. Sawyer steps into the hallway in a breezy, half-buttoned white linen shirt and navy swim shorts with little sunglasses and pineapples printed in neon colors all over them. The shirt pulls and twists as he reaches for my bag; the stark white looks great against his tan.

"Morning," he says, and he slides the bag onto his shoulder and shoves his hands into his pockets.

"I can carry that," I tell him. Nothing says *Come on in! I'm a great person! You'll like me!* like not appreciating the help he offered without being asked. He looks over and down at me, a subtle shift in his gaze, and I feel the tips of my ears burn. "Thank you. It was heavy."

"Anytime."

We're swept up in the wave of guests rushing down the stairs.

Gram and Nancy are waiting for an elevator with what seems like a million other people and wave us onward, so we decide to take the stairs down to Deck Two. We wait for them outside so we can all head to the cabana together, and Sawyer is absolutely silent.

"Listen," I start, clearing my throat. "I'm sorry if I made things weird last night."

He readjusts his sunglasses on the bridge of his nose and crosses one ankle over the other. "It's fine."

"It doesn't seem like it is."

He shifts again, his eyes trained on the exit ramp. "I'm just confused, Gwendolyn. I don't know what we're doing here."

Those two extra syllables on my name make him feel so far away. "I thought we were getting to know each other."

The huff he lets out tells me how he thinks that's going.

"Okay," I admit. "Maybe I've been a little confusing. But what if today we actually try to get to know each other better? I'll be nice, but not inappropriately nice."

The side of his mouth that I can see quirks up. "Why the sudden push to have a normal interaction?"

Gram and Nancy emerge on the pier, and I gesture my head in their direction. "I'd like to not be murdered by my grandmother on this vacation." His smile fades and he uncrosses his ankles, looking straight ahead. "Plus," I add, trying to be cautious with my words, "I think we could actually be friends. Or something."

"Or something," he repeats.

FOR ALL MY trying not to think about her after thinking about her in a way I shouldn't have been thinking about her, I can't help but think about her. She's taken up residence in my brain, and I was taking solace in the fact that we know nothing about each other so nothing will happen, but now she wants to get to know each other, and I'm screwed.

Also, *damn*, she looks incredible in a black strapless bikini, with a floppy hat and movie-star sunglasses and a sheer black cover-up cascading down her legs and billowing in the breeze. She might be some hot-shot author who loves touring the big cities, but this woman is in her element on this island.

She rests her forearms against the cabana's railing and inhales, and I can see her shoulders fall, relaxed.

Nan and Maggie have set up shop on the shaded lower level, but Gwen headed upstairs right away for sun. I followed her for access to the slide into the ocean.

"It suits you," I say, unbuttoning my shirt and folding it into my backpack.

"What does?" She basks in the rays' warmth, her face fixed skyward.

"The sun. The sea. You seem… I dunno. At peace. It's good."

She turns, leaning back against the railing. Her eyes are hidden by her ridiculously large sunglasses, but they don't hide the way her jaw moves and her throat tenses with a swallow. "Thanks," is all she says, her voice restrained.

I wonder whether the tension stems from the physicality of last night or from what comes next: tearing herself out of her comfort zone and telling me more about herself. I don't know which type of closeness unnerves her more.

"Mind if I—" I nod toward the railing. She shifts sideways, then turns back to the water.

"Free country," she says, taking an extra step away from me when I reach her. She settles in after a moment of quiet, relaxing again, taking it all in.

"It's really beautiful up here."

"Sure is," she answers. Then, "The water looks so warm."

"Only one way to find out." I lower myself onto the slide and let it carry me into the Caribbean. It *is* warm, and it feels great to be like a kid again, so I climb up the ladder into the cabana, then up the steps, then into the slide and do it all over again.

The next time I reach the top, Gwen's throwing her cover-up and hat onto the wrap-around couch, and she races me toward the slide's entrance. "Don't think you get all the fun," she taunts. She grabs the bars at the top of the slide; I grab her waist. She curls in on herself, shrill laughter escaping her wide smile. It's incredible, this easiness between us right now, and I hope she can view getting to know each other in the same way, instead of it just being something her grandma wants us to do.

"Oh my God, Sawyer!" she shrieks, squirming in my arms, and if it's the only way I ever hear her scream my name I'll still die happy, because there's joy in it. Boundless, limitless, free joy.

I set her on a padded chair a few feet away and send myself careening down the slide again, beaming when she collides into me at the bottom.

"Nothing has ever let me get to know a person better than having their elbow break my ribs."

She flicks water at my face and smirks. "Well, maybe next time don't cut the line, and I won't have to hurt you."

"You kids okay down there?" Nan asks. She sits up to peer at us over an old issue of *People* and I send a nod her way.

"Fine, Nan. We're good." I look at Gwen's face for approval, and it's amazing how she looks so pretty with her makeup on, but so stunning here, with none of it. Her smile turns more content than playful, and the blue in her eyes matches the water that dances around us.

We're *so* good.

There are two floating mats hanging on the wall of the first floor, so Gwen and I drape ourselves over those in the water and venture further down the shoreline, out of earshot of our grandmothers and other guests in their own cabanas. It's time to learn more about each other, and part of me hopes Gwen will fess up to being a hoarder, or someone who bites their toenails, just so saying goodbye in four days doesn't suck so bad.

"Tell me everything, Sawyer Dawson. Who are you?" She's piled her hair atop her head, and it curls where it escapes her messy bun. She stares me down through her dark glasses.

"Well, I'm six-three, a Pisces, and I'm on a cruise with my grandmother."

"Ha, ha. I'm serious."

"So am I. If you're looking for something specific, just ask. What would you like to know, Gwen?"

She thinks for a moment, then asks, "How's your marathon training going?"

"It's fine," I shrug. "Hard to keep up with it on the ship, but it's just a week, and I'm getting some cardio in, at least." Never mind that my heart rate was more elevated just sitting with her last night and thinking about her afterward than it has been on any of my workouts on this trip.

"Have you always been a runner?" She nods when I shake my head. "You don't really have a runner's body."

I feign offense. "Ouch."

"No… it's just that, you're really tall. And muscular. Like…" she motions to her chest and shoulders. "Anyway. I was just surprised when I heard you were training. But it's cool. What made you decide to do it?"

She has no way of knowing how dangerous a question that is, and I can share as much or as little as I want here. "I needed a hobby." There. It's safe, not too revealing.

She tugs up on her swimsuit top and readjusts her arms on her mat. "And you picked running? Training for a whole marathon?"

"I had some… free time," I admit, opening the door to more. Maybe I shouldn't have, because maybe she'll be turned off by everything I have to say and I'll ruin anything we could have before we get a chance to have it.

But all she says is "Oh," and then "My therapist told me I should take up a hobby, too. Do you think lounging in the ocean counts?" And I'm so relieved that I don't even respond. "Sawyer?"

"Hm?"

"Nothing. Sorry. You were talking about having free time."

"Right. So, extra time, needed an outlet, needed discipline."

She shakes her head. "I don't know how you do it. I know teachers are always so busy."

My chest tightens, and I take three quick, deep breaths to ease away the tension there. "I, uh… I haven't been teaching for the last few months."

"Oh." She opens and closes her mouth, licks her bottom lip and bites it, like she's trying to figure out how to dig deeper without intruding too much. "Did you— I mean, what are you doing instead?"

"Mostly running," I confess. She looks embarrassed for both of us, like she's stumbled too far into the conversation and can't find her way out; like every possible door is a booby trap and she's trying to avoid them all.

"There was an incident," I offer, resigning myself to telling the story, trusting her with it. "My girlfriend, Chelsea, was one of the English teachers in my building."

"And you broke up?" She says it so hopefully, so sweetly, and I smile.

"Yes, eventually. After the incident."

She squints against the sun, and I see her trying to play it cool while she does the math in her head. "When did you get together? Because Nancy was trying to set me up with you last fall."

"Only in February." I laugh, remembering. "I was one of those chumps who asked out the girl right before Valentine's Day. And it was great. We got along really well, knew a lot about each other…" I feel the effects of the words before they ever leave my mouth, and my skin tingles at the idea of getting to know Gwen the way I knew Chelsea. "I was in the office one day, toward the end of the school year, making copies for our final exam reviews. I hear yelling from our principal's office, and then the door opens and Chelsea's booking it out of there. This guy—a parent of one of her students— follows her out, freaking out about a project she'd assigned. I guess he'd called a meeting to fight for his kid's right not to do this project. But anyway, this guy is just going off on both of them. Red face, screaming, swearing… all of it."

"That sounds scary."

"Yeah, well. It's the norm, now, having parents scream at you. But this was a book his daughter chose to read for an anthology assignment, and he didn't like it. Chelsea tried explaining it to him over and over, and he just wouldn't listen. He got right up in her face."

     MEGAN BECKER

Gwen leans in, hanging on every word. "What did you do?"

"I told him to back the fuck off. And when he didn't, I got in between him and Chelsea, and he kept coming at me, and I shoved him back."

"Oh. Good for you, protecting her like that."

"Well." I scratch the back of my neck and avoid meeting her eyes. "The district didn't think so. They suspended me, pending an investigation, for the year."

"Ohhh," she says, like everything's clicking into place in her brain. "So that's how you have the time—"

"Yeah."

"I'm sorry, Sawyer, I didn't know. *And* I'm sorry, because that sucks."

"Thanks. One of the conditions for me being able to go back then was to get some counseling for my 'anger management' issues, and my therapist recommended running."

"And Chelsea?"

"Ghosted me for two weeks before officially ending it."

Gwen swallows, and her voice comes out hoarse. "That's awful. I'm so, so sorry. I know how shitty breakups can be."

There's a story there, and she seems almost ready to tell it. But the sun is high, the temperature has risen, and my stomach growls.

She somehow hears it over the lapping water and plans the escape. "Maybe we should head back. Grab some lunch."

I nod, and we kick our feet out behind us and swim back to the cabana.

Gwendolyn

"YOU REALLY WENT all out for this trip," he says, wiping a spot of guacamole from his lips as we wrap up our lunch of shrimp tacos. Gram and Nancy finished a bit ago and wandered off in search of the pool, so Sawyer and I are alone again. He looks around the cabana and nods. "Seriously, let me know what I owe you for our share, and—"

"Absolutely not."

He looks up like he's been scolded. "Gwen…"

"Everything's covered. It's fine." It wasn't cheap, but Gram's been saving, and I've earned back the generous advance on my book, and we decided to splurge. Plus, there's no way I'm going to ask a semi-unemployed public school teacher to foot part of the bill for the things I'm enjoying on a luxury vacation.

I must have stalled our pre-lunch conversation as long as possible, because Sawyer (who has put his fancy shirt back on) stretches and dives back into the part of the conversation where we left off. "So. Bad breakups, huh?"

"Ha. Yeah." It all comes rushing back: the cold air in New York, what should have been one of the best nights of my life, everything crashing down. "I was dating this guy, Tristan, on and off for five years or so. He traveled a lot for work, and it was hard to find time together." I could stop there, and everything would be true. Nothing so far is a lie, but it's incomplete. And I think Gram would frown on incomplete. So I tell him the whole thing.

I tell him about the serendipity of being in the same city at the same time. I recall for him my disappointment that Tristan never showed up at the book signing and how I called him to just check in, to make sure he was okay. How he didn't answer. How his hotel was two blocks from mine, and when I asked for a key to surprise him they acquiesced, and how when I went into his suite, I saw him bent over the side of the couch.

Actually, I saw him bent over some random woman, over the side of the couch.

To Sawyer's credit, he doesn't interrupt. He just sits and listens, and he lets me spill it all out there, until I'm done and out of breath.

"And the worst part was," I say, feeling the burning of the tears that I try to hold back, "it wasn't even some assistant or coworker that he'd worked with for years and had some kind of friendship with, at least. It was some rando, a stranger, and fucking her was more important than being there for me."

"I'm so sorry that happened to you. You don't deserve that."

It's possible I obsess too much over language and word choice, but I hear the way he says 'don't' and not 'didn't', and I feel like I can breathe again.

"Are we disasters?"

"No." He shakes his head. "I just think we've both been screwed over."

"True. But enough whining, okay? I'll shut up, and I'll focus on getting to know other things about you."

He grins across the table at me. "Deal. On one condition."

"What's that?"

"We start with finding out who can make the bigger splash." He takes the steps upstairs two at a time, but I sneak under his arm and around his hip to beat him to the top. Then I send myself down the slide into the water and emerge, drenched again, laughing, refreshed.

There's a wide, square hammock built into the flooring just off the water. I hoist myself up with a boost from Sawyer after he launches himself down the slide after me. He runs a hand through his hair and rests his arms on the deck around the hammock. Droplets roll down the muscles in his shoulders and arms, and he nestles his chin onto his hands.

"There's plenty of room up here," I tell him, but he looks at the hammock and shakes his head. I scoot further to the side, freeing up two-thirds of the space. "Come on. I don't bite."

He evaluates again and gives in, climbing up and over the edge, until he's lying there next to me. "If you want me to get out, just tell me, okay?"

"Why would I want that?"

He shrugs, stretches one arm out to tuck a hand behind his head, and keeps the arm closest to me at his side with his hand resting on his stomach. "Just be honest with me. You won't hurt my feelings if you say 'Wow, Sawyer, you're so big and muscular, and you're taking up too much space on the hammock I paid for.'"

I pinch a tiny bit of skin on the underside of his arm, and the man flails. His arm shoots up over his head, exposing his obliques, and his whole body seems to leap three inches off the hammock.

"Geez, Gwen."

It's so hard not to laugh when those brown eyes go wide and look at me with such alarm. A cackle comes out and I say, "Sorry. I'm just shocked that someone so big and muscular would be hurt by a little pinch." For added effect, I drag my fingers over his abs and sides. It's such a reflex, joking like this, touching him like this, and I don't realize how inappropriate it is right away. But he lets me do it; his arm's still awkwardly overhead.

I should ask if this is okay. I should look for a sign in his eyes, or better yet, just back away. *Hands off the statue, Gwendolyn. Don't touch the art.* Instead I test the waters, creeping my fingers across his pecs, feeling his heart beating a steady rhythm, watching his chest rise and fall. He inhales deeply. Swallows hard. And then I'm curled up along his side, my head resting on his chest, our skin in contact along our

     MEGAN BECKER

torsos and the length of our legs. He tilts a foot in my direction and I answer, and then his arm is around me and he strokes my back with the backs of his curled fingers.

Neither of us says anything, because what would we say, anyway? 'Hey, sorry your last relationship sucked. This isn't a relationship but you can still touch me and I'll touch you and it'll be hot and magical and meaningless and then we'll go home and never see each other again'?

I could fall asleep like this if I wasn't so damn electrified by his presence. Everything about this feels so right and so wrong all at once, and I'm only mildly aware of the footsteps crossing the floorboards, pausing, retreating, and the hushed whispers that follow. Gram and Nancy must be back.

"Are you ready to kick me out yet?" Sawyer finally asks, his hoarse voice just above a whisper. I feel his breath across the top of my head, and his hand has lazily found its way to my lower back.

I pull in closer to answer his question, wrapping my arm around his waist and draping my foot over his shin.

"*Gwen,*" he exhales, pulling his arm back from my skin. He shifts at the waist, breaking the contact between our legs. Then he uses his free arm to readjust the waistband of his shorts and tug at the hem, leaving his arm to rest across his body when he's done. *Oh.*

"I'm an Aries," I blurt out.

"What?"

"You said you're a Pisces. I'm an Aries. I don't know if that matters."

"I don't think it does."

I sit up, giving him more space and freedom and less contact. And that's when I see it. On his hip, peering out from his shorts.

"Sawyer Dawson!" I poke at the line of ink and drop my voice to a giddy whisper so I don't alarm Nancy if she's not aware of what her grandson is rocking in his shorts. (Yes, that sounds weird. No,

I don't care. Because Sawyer is about to become even more interesting.) "Do you have a *welcome mat*?"

His eyes widen and he looks at the skin my fingers poke at. "A welcome mat? Really, Gwen?" He rolls his eyes and adjusts the waistband again, covering the ink. "Have you never seen a tattoo before?"

"Not there," I say, shaking my head. "Not on a guy. In person."

"It's really not that exciting."

"Agree to disagree. Can I see it?" I try to reach for it, to pull back the fabric of his shorts just enough to see what he decided to permanently decorate his body with, but he twists his hips away from me.

"It's, uh… It's a little low, I think." There's an unmistakable blush creeping across his cheeks.

"Okay," I shrug. "Let me know if you change your mind. You show me yours, I'll show you mine."

His eyes move over me. The swimsuit isn't crazy skimpy, but it's also a bikini, so I'm sure he's wondering if he somehow missed seeing it today or if it's just very well hidden. I like the way he looks at me, trying to see everything about me, inspecting my skin and dropping his gaze from my chest to my hips.

"Hey, Gwennie?"

I inhale, suddenly aware I've not been breathing since Sawyer began his perusal of my body. "Yeah, Gram?" I holler up onto the cabana platform. Sawyer swings his legs over the hammock's edge and submerges his lower half in the water.

"Did you two see the swim-up bar?"

SAWYER

IT'S EXACTLY THE interruption we need. The four of us wade out together, past the remaining cabanas and some floating beds, to do something Maggie added to her bucket list as soon as she and Nan started planning this cruise.

There are a few thatch-roof umbrellas in the water with little counters mounted to their posts so people can set their drinks down and relax close to the bar. Nan suggests they wait there while Gwen and I pick up the drinks, but Maggie is determined to sit at the bar and get her own drink. "That's the fun of it," she explains, winking.

I climb the ladder first, then offer a hand to the older women while Gwen helps them from below, and soon we're all at the floating bar, Maggie and Nan perched on stools (thanks to the guys that stood to make room for them) while Gwen and I hang back, standing along the railing that lines the bar's perimeter.

Once Maggie has her Sex on the Beach (this woman is shameless and lacks subtlety), she swivels toward us. "Having fun so far today?"

Gwen nods. "Yep. Just getting to know each other better."

The answer clearly pleases Maggie, and she and Nan recount their adventures, including a brief foray into snorkeling that ended when Nan saw a fin in the distance. "I keep trying to tell her, it was just a dolphin."

"And I keep trying to tell her, where there are dolphins, there are sharks. Except yesterday. Yesterday was just the dolphin."

Gwen dials up the drama in her voice and elbows me. "I don't know. I thought I felt something grab onto me at one point. Definitely not a dolphin."

Nan eyes her, confused, while Maggie snickers at the joke. It's confirmation that Nan missed the moment yesterday, luckily, because it was not my finest.

"Then we found mango daiquiris, and we played… what's that game again, Nancy?"

"Beer pong?"

"Right. Beer pong. But we made it daiquiri pong. Played with some nice boys, maybe a little younger than you."

"Gram! Tell me you didn't."

"She did," Nan answers. "And we ran out of daiquiri and had to order more, and I told her she should probably slow down a bit. She's not supposed to drink so much with—" Maggie glares at her, and Nan seems to pivot her statement. "Not with her age. Our age. Because we're old." She sighs and shakes her head, sipping her glass of wine. "Things to look forward to, kids."

We sink into a comfortable quiet, taking in the sounds of the sea, the water pulsing gently against the bar. Finally, Maggie checks her watch. "We should head back to the ship in just over an hour. Why don't you two go and start cleaning up the cabana? We'll catch up."

Gwen gathers her hair to keep it from blowing across her face. She twists it over one shoulder, but stray strands whip in front of her eyes. "Are you sure? We can wait and all go back together."

"We're much slower," Nan adds. "You two go on ahead. We'll be there in a bit."

"Actually," Maggie says, "would you mind just meeting us with our things at those loungers over there? Maybe in forty-five minutes or so? Then we can hop on the tram back to the pier."

Gwen studies her grandmother, then looks up at me. I shrug, and she nods. "Sure. Forty-five minutes." She and I return our empty cups to the bar and lower ourselves into the water, then paddle back to the cabana.

"I'll start gathering some things down here."

She nods and heads upstairs to the changing room, and I check all the storage areas for various belongings. I have Nan's tote ready and set aside, which was easy, because the only thing she removed from it was a book that she set down right next to it before we went for drinks.

My things and Gwen's are upstairs, so I make quick work of tidying Maggie's belongings, too. She's brought a clear bag for island toiletries, like sunscreen, bug spray, nail clippers, nail polish, floss picks… the usual. I grab her hand sanitizer from the coffee table and drop it in the clear bag. Something catches my eye as I reach for her tote—an orange bottle with a white cap and (upon further and totally intrusive inspection) a familiar-sounding name that I can't place. It takes a moment, and I don't mean to snoop, or to pry, but I realize I've seen the same drug name on pill bottles in our house, back when I was younger. They were things Nan couldn't throw away, no matter how much Mom begged her to.

"Hey, Sawyer?"

I drop the bag into Maggie's tote and zip everything closed. "Yeah?" I climb the stairs to answer Gwen's call. She's in the changing room with the curtain half closed, and she's clearly struggling.

"Can you help me?"

"Sure. What do you need?"

She peels back the curtain and turns her back to me, pulling her hair to the side again. Long blond waves, stained by the sea, cascade

over her shoulder. "Can you unhook me, please? This stupid suit…
I can't tell which way that little loop goes over the plastic hook
thing. I can't see it to figure it out."

"Um, yeah. Let me try." In barely three strides I've crossed the
entirety of the deck, and I clear my throat as I move in behind her.
Her skin holds the sun's heat, even now, when she's in the shade,
and my fingers trace the line where tan and white meet, just under
the edge of her swim top. I unfasten it easily, and she holds it in
place from the front as the back straps fall to the side. Her whole
naked back—from the waist up, of course— is exposed, and my
fingers float barely an inch off her spine, longing to follow that line
and the soft curves at her waist. Wondering if she'd let me.

"Sawyer." When I look up, she's watching me in the mirror in
front of us, and embarrassment floods my face.

"Sorry." I clear my throat and repeat it again. "I, um… I'll be
out here."

"*Sawyer*," she says, and she grabs my wrist before I can leave.

          MEGAN BECKER

Gwendolyn

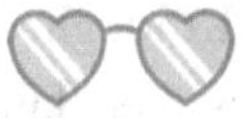

SHIT. SHIT, SHIT, shit. We're supposed to be on the ship in less than an hour, I'm a little more than half naked, and I'm holding onto him, bedroom eyes-ing him. Probably deer-in-the-headlights eyes-ing him, because *shit*, what am I doing?

What happens next makes no sense, even to me, unless you consider that when I feel nervous I turn to humor. And that is why I pull Sawyer's left hand onto my right breast, look him dead in the eye, and say, "This one felt unloved, after yesterday."

He looks horrified. Terrible idea. Abort mission, Gwen.

"I'm sorry… I don't know why I did that," I confess. I let go of his wrist and his hand falls, but we're both in this changing room and we're far too big for the space, especially with this new energy between us. "It's just that, I dunno, I really enjoyed today, and I thought we had a thing earlier, but I crossed a line and I'm sorry if I misread you."

Sawyer doesn't take his eyes off of mine. He licks his lips, and I watch his chest and his Adam's apple move with two breaths before he asks, "What do you want from me, Gwen?"

I want that hammock moment. That curl-up-against-him-and-feel-safe moment. That laugh-over-a-cocktail moment. And I want this next moment. The one that feels dangerous and adventurous and so unlike me, but so freeing.

I take a step backward, opening his view to more of me, and I let the swimsuit top fall to the floor.

To his credit, his eyes stay locked on mine, not shifting for a second. I'm slightly offended, but mostly impressed.

"I need you to say it, Gwen."

"I thought I just did."

"Gwen. Please."

Saying it is harder than I thought it would be. I've never been one to ask for help, and this feels kind of like that. "I want you, Sawyer." And I can't wait for him anymore, so I close the distance between us and pull his face down to mine. There's no easing into this—we're pressed for time, after all, and this need is too urgent, too intense, and my tongue is in his mouth before another second passes.

He pulls me tightly to him, against all the hard planes of his body. Then he moves forward, pins me against the wall, raises my arms over my head and holds them there, dropping his mouth to my neck. He palms one breast and plants desperate kisses on the other, and I feel like I could explode right this second.

"Touch me, Sawyer. Please. Touch me."

"I thought I was," he says, but now is not the time for smart-assery, because I fucking need him.

He lets his hand glide down my stomach, over my swimsuit bottom, and his fingers work to get between my still-wet swimsuit bottom and my skin. When Gram told me to let him in, I'm not sure this is what she meant. Actually, knowing Gram, it probably is.

"It's so tight, Gwen. The swimsuit, I mean."

It feels so good just to feel something *real* there, not just something battery-powered. And as Sawyer moves his hand and presses his body against me instead, I realize how good *he* feels— every long, solid inch of him.

He frees my hands so he can put both of his on my body: on my waist, in my hair.

I press my lips to his neck, his jawline, his shoulder, and back. "We could really have some fun, you and me," I say against him, my teeth grazing his skin.

"Gwen, I just need you to know—" his hands still, and he rolls his head back. "I don't do flings," he growls, his neck humming under my kiss.

"Neither do I." I draw part of his ear between my teeth, press my hand against his length, hear the sound each act draws from him, and crave more. As a rule, I don't do hookups, one-night stands, and flings. But Sawyer Dawson promises to be a very hot, much-needed exception to that rule.

DAY 7
Miami

MEGAN BECKER

SAWYER

12:42 a.m.:   Stare at the ceiling.

1:27 a.m.:   Sit on the balcony and hope the ocean lulls me to sleep.

World's largest white noise machine.

2:53 a.m.:   Watch the clock flip to 2:54 a.m.

3:02 a.m.:   Pick up a book. Realize it reminds me of her. Put down the book.

3:18 a.m.:   Go for a walk. Pass her room. Fight the urge to knock on the door.

4:11 a.m.:   See my relationship with Chelsea implode for the fortieth time as the scene plays on a loop through my mind. Mix in flashes from yesterday: Gwen cuddled next to me on the hammock; Gwen's laughter on the slide; Gwen's willingness to listen. Take note of how different it feels.

6:15 a.m.:   Get up. Lace up. Time to train.

Gwendolyn

"BIG DATE TODAY?" Gram jokes as I smooth a wrinkle on my white sundress and check my reflection in the full-length mirror.

I groan. "He's been avoiding me since yesterday."

"I think he's been avoiding *me*," she says, and she's probably right. Hell, I want to avoid her, too, but even if I could get away from her, the sound of her shriek will never stop tormenting me. "Hopefully he finds you, because that dress deserves to be seen by more than just the U.S. Government."

Since this is our first port back in the U.S., everyone needs to leave the ship and go through Customs. I was planning on lounging on a half-empty ship today, but I've heard horror stories about some people having to wait hours before getting back on the ship, and I don't feel like sitting in a crowded room for hours with people who are hangry and hungover.

"I'm sorry again, about…" She trails off; neither of us needs or wants her to finish that sentence, because even though she brought me on this cruise so I'd hook up with Sawyer, no one expected her to walk in on him grinding his hips against me—swimsuit bottoms on, thankfully—with his hands all over my naked upper half. He skipped dinner again and hasn't even tried to find me to talk, and I'm worried that this might have just as much to do with regret as it has to do with embarrassment.

"Let's not talk about it," I say, avoiding her gaze in the reflection, feeling the heat creeping up my cheeks.

"You're a grown woman, Gwen. You're allowed to have

desires. You're free to make your own choices."

"Gram, please. I'm begging you. I am very interested in ending this conversation."

"And that man is very interested in *you*," she taunts. "But fine. No more mention of it." She picks a piece of lint from the arm of the chair as I fix my makeup. "What's your plan for the day?"

Gram and Nancy are doing some celebrity mansion bus tour, not listening when I remind them that basketball season is in full swing so the chance they'll get a photo with LeBron James is highly unlikely. They're determined, especially after watching that Tom Brady movie, and they also won't listen when I tell them the whole movie is fiction.

I shrug my crossbody bag over my shoulder—it's straw and shaped like a pineapple and maybe a little juvenile, but oh well— and slide my sunglasses into my hair. "Not sure. I think I'm just going to check out Little Havana, get a nice, big Cuban—"

She whips her head to look at me, her brows nearly meeting her hairline.

"The sandwich, Gram," I clarify, and I don't want to know if she'd assumed I'd meant a man or a cigar. "Anyway. I probably won't stay out too long."

Then she says the same thing she said every time I'd drive back to school after coming home for the weekend: "Have fun, but be safe."

We meet up with Nancy to disembark, and Sawyer's hulking form lurks in the background. I see him in my periphery and avoid looking his way; if he wanted me to see him, he would've joined our little caravan off the ship.

Nancy follows my gaze and pats my hand. "Forgive him, dear. I don't think he slept more than an hour last night." She looks back at him and shakes her head. "Come to think of it, he's been weird ever since we left the island yesterday. Did something happen?"

My eyes dart to Gram, impressed that she hasn't spilled the beans in the last twelve hours. "Nothing at all," she says, putting an end to the conversation. Though I'm pretty sure there's an 'I'll tell you later' dying to come out of her.

We're caught up in the current of the crowd, swept off the ship and into the line for Customs, and then I wait with Gram and Nancy outside for their shuttle to their bus tour. Once they board, I hail a taxi. I'm sliding into my seat and trying to shut the door, but there's resistance in the form of a large hand that holds the door open.

"This one's taken," I say, peering into the sun at the person trying to commandeer my cab.

"Hey." Sawyer bends, propping his arm against the doorframe.

"Hey."

"Mind if I…" he nods toward the seat next to me, and I slide over, making room.

I shrug. "Sure."

He climbs in and shuts the door, and the driver takes off. I stare straight ahead, not sure what to say, and also convinced I don't want to say anything. If either of us owes the other something, I think the debt is his.

I feel his eyes on me: the length of my body, then my face.

I fold my hands in my lap and swallow.

"Where are we going?" he asks.

The driver glances in the rearview mirror, his eyes connecting with mine, like he's asking if it's okay that this random man has hopped in with us despite not knowing where we're headed. I offer him a smile and answer Sawyer. "Little Havana."

"Oh. Okay."

We ride in uncomfortable silence until we reach our destination. I tip the driver and take off with Sawyer trailing two steps behind me.

"Hey, Gwen." He reaches for my arm and finds my elbow, his fingers gentle as they wrap around my skin. There's nothing possessive about it, just tender, like he's missed this connection since yesterday. "You're avoiding me."

"Me?" I'm dumbfounded; my jaw drops. "That's rich, coming from the guy who felt me up and bolted, then ghosted me all night."

His ears turn pink and his jaw clenches, like he wants to say something and can't decide if he should. I'm acutely aware of the people around us, but right now I don't care. This was all a stupid idea, from the very beginning. I don't know why Gram thought this would help me move on past Tristan, when neither man seems to care about how his actions affect me.

"I didn't leave my room for hours."

I can't help but to roll my eyes. "Well, some of us can't hide from our problems." The problem, in this scenario, being my grandmother and her eyes that have seen too much.

"It was mortifying, when your grandma—"

"No shit." This is not a conversation I want to have, and especially not on the streets of Miami. "Look, just forget about it, okay? I don't want to talk about it." I stare at the place where his hand meets my skin, waiting for him to take the hint and peel his fingers off of me. Finally he backs away, and I spin on my espadrilles and continue on my way. Sawyer trails behind me, but he doesn't try to talk to me or interfere with my day. Generally, he sulks in storefronts while I browse, and he takes out a few crisp bills when I buy churros from a cash-only stand and realize I only brought my credit card. It was nice of him; I share the churros.

Above the traffic noise and the bass beats from the convertibles, Cadillacs, and open Jeeps that cruise the street, the melody of a guitar drifts toward me. I follow the sound, turning down a nearby alley. "Where do you think it's coming from?" I ask, though I don't really care if he answers or not. It's getting louder, so we have to be close.

Two blocks later, when the alley spills out onto another side street, we find the source.

Zamira's is scrawled in red script over the wide-open front door. Matching awnings shade black-trimmed windows along the crisp white exterior. It's no wonder the doors are hanging open—there's a palpable energy from within that can't be contained by tinted glass.

"Would you like a table?" asks a man with a heavily-gelled pompadour and the brightest smile I've ever seen.

"Oh, we just—we weren't really looking for lunch yet," I answer, very aware of the churro wrapper in my hands and the dusting of cinnamon sugar that lingers on my index finger.

"Maybe a spot at the bar, then," he replies, flashing his smile again.

"It's not even noon—" Sawyer protests, but it falls on deaf ears. The employee has already grabbed two menus and leads the way to a huge wooden bar inside, gesturing toward two empty seats on the side. Past a row of tables is a massive dance floor, and it's already filled with people.

As if reading my mind, he says, "We host salsa lessons a few days a week. In the evenings, especially on weekends, there are so many people out here you can't even see the floor." He slides two glasses of water toward us and leans in, resting his forearms on the bartop. "You should check us out tomorrow night if you're around. Half-price mojitos and a beginners' salsa competition. Couples love it."

Sawyer nearly chokes on his water. "We're not—" he begins, "—I mean—" He must feel the weight of about half a dozen gazes on him, and his ears redden. "We just met."

The employee quirks a brow at me, and I shake my head. "We're on a cruise. Not together, obviously. We just happen to keep bumping into each other." Okay, it's really hard to keep the word vomit down when this guy's smiling, amused by my flustered fumbling.

"Wait! I know you guys!" cries one of the patrons a few stools away. "You're *Knock-Knock* Joke Girl from the bar by the pool the other night. Remember? *Knock, knock. Banana.*" Cargo Shorts Guy has leveled up to Dan Marino Jersey Guy and I wonder if he has any grown-up clothing to his name. He shakes his head, laughing, and returns to his beer.

"That's me," I say with a shrug. "I'm Banana, I guess."

"Well, Banana, I'm Javier. My friends call me Javi."

I extend an arm. "Gwen. Gwendolyn."

"Gwendolyn." Javi says it like he's sampling it, seeing how it feels. "Beautiful name," he says at last, but it's the unsaid words that taint his voice that make my cheeks burn.

Sawyer shifts next to me, and I wonder if he's uncomfortable because of the stool or because of Javi.

"So, how long have you worked here?" I ask, taking a sip of water.

Javi busies himself with mixing ingredients, and a half-smirk crosses his lips. "We opened last summer," he says, scooping ice into a metal shaker. "It was my pop's dream to have a place like this, so when he passed we decided to make it happen."

"We?" Sawyer inserts himself into the conversation.

Javi nods and smiles. He gestures his head toward the band on stage and raises his voice to be heard over the rattling ice cubes as he shakes the drink. "My sister—she's the lead singer. We named the place after her. Well," he says, grabbing two glasses from a rack below the counter. "I named it after her. She thought it was too much, but she's the star of the show." He shrugs, then fills the glasses, setting each on a napkin in front of us.

Sawyer raises a brow. "We didn't order those."

"On the house, boss," Javi answers with a smile. His response is much more gracious than mine would've been. "Where are you visiting from?"

"Near Philly," Sawyer answers, examining his glass. I realize we haven't really talked about where we live. Not that it matters, since I have zero desire to see him again when all of this is over if he keeps going with this cold-shoulder-when-things-get-weird thing.

"What do you do?" Javi's trying to keep the conversation alive. He can't be more than twenty-five, but the way he tries to engage gives an air of years of experience. He seems to be made for a job like this, with his easy smile and knack for friendly conversation. But Sawyer doesn't give him much to work with, so he turns to me for help.

"I'm a writer," I volunteer.

This seems to interest him—though I'm not sure if he's more interested in my career or the fact that I'm actually responding to him.

"A writer? What do you write?"

This is the part of the intro when I always hesitate, because I never know whether I'll be met with intrigue, indifference, or laughter. (Luckily, I was only met with a creepy inquisition once.) I take a sip of the smooth mojito passed my way. "I, uh, I write romance novels." When I look up from the glass, he's smiling warmly.

"That's cool. I was afraid you were going to say you were a travel blogger."

"Would that be a bad thing?" Sawyer asks, finally taking part.

Javi shrugs. "They're alright. Not sure we ever see a bump in business from their write-ups, but they always expect everything for free, regardless."

Sawyer's gaze drops to his drink, and Javi clears his throat and quickly changes the subject. "How's the vacation so far? Or is this more of a work trip for you?"

"It's great, for the most part," I answer, and I catch Sawyer shifting in his seat again.

Javi's eyes dart toward the movement as well, and I'm not usually one to put too much thought into how people perceive me, but I'm beyond frustrated that Sawyer's grumpiness is making me look bad. Especially considering that he inserted himself into my free day.

"But—" I say, to draw the attention back, "I'm doing some work, too. I have a deadline in two months, so I've got to get some writing done."

"What's the book about?" He's cleaning the shaker and scanning the bar and restaurant, but when his eyes meet mine he gives a quick smile that says he really wants to hear more.

I lean in, giving a conspiratorial glance over my shoulder. "Between us?" Javi nods in reply. "I have no idea."

He laughs. "Well, Banana, Miami is a great place for inspiration. Great beaches, beautiful people, and salsa." I follow his nod toward the dance floor where multiple couples are swaying and moving to the music.

"So, you like knock-knock jokes?" he asks. "Here's one, if we're sticking with a fruit theme. Knock knock."

"Who's there?"

"Honeydew."

I try to guess the punchline and wrinkle my nose, unable to think of what it could be. "Honeydew, who?"

"Honeydew you want to dance with me?"

Of all the times to take a drink. Rum burns in my nose as the question lands.

"Oh, I—"

But Javi laughs. "Relax—it's just the joke. Besides, I'm not much of a dancer."

An older woman passes a stack of menus across the bar to Javi.

"Don't believe him. He may not have spent years in classes, but I taught him everything he knows. And I—"

"Placed third at the Southeast Regional SalsaFest of ninety-two," they finish together.

"Mamá, we know," Javi says, rolling his eyes.

She grins and pinches his cheek, and color spreads across his face. "It brings me such joy to see you dance. Your sister is up there, living her dream, and you're hiding back here working so hard all the time." She turns her attention to Sawyer and me. "Good for you two, having fun, taking a break. You honeymooners?"

"Mamá, *por favor.*" Javi drags a hand down his face. "I have fun."

I stifle a laugh at the contrast between his words and his pained expression.

"When? When's the last time you allowed yourself to just enjoy the moment?"

"How about right now?" Her words feel like a challenge, and mine feel like a mistake. But I said them. They're out there. Time to own it.

I look at Javi and repeat, with as much confidence as I can muster, "How about now? If you have time, I mean. For a dance."

A smile tugs at his lips. "Sure," he answers, setting down the menus he's been straightening and coming around to my side of the bar. "Have you danced salsa before?" he asks as he whisks me toward the crowd in the middle of the dance floor.

In college, one of my best friends insisted that we go to a few salsa lessons at a local bar where her crush just so happened to work. She said she wanted to pick up a new hobby, and I said 'hobby' was an interesting pronunciation of 'Hailey.'

"A few times," I tell him. "But it was a while ago."

"Same. I mean, in front of people."

"Wait—you mean to tell me that you own, like, the hottest new salsa club in Miami, and you don't even get out there to enjoy it?"

"I enjoy it very much," he replies, pulling me toward him and holding me in frame. "I just choose to enjoy it from behind the bar."

He leads me for a few moments, and once we settle into a rhythm he looks over my shoulder, back to where we left his mom and Sawyer.

"I watched my parents dance for years. Mom was technically brilliant from all her training, but my pop—he had this passion for it. A spark, you know? And I'd watch my parents salsa and laugh and whisper. Sometimes they'd just take a break in the middle of doing the most basic thing, like washing dishes. And it felt special, you know? Like dance was this intimate thing." His eyes meet mine for a fleeting moment before he clears his throat and looks away. "Anyway. I like to know I created a space for people to have that, you know? And someday, I'm sure I'll have someone to come out here with and have that same connection my parents did, before."

It's a lot to share with a total stranger, both the words and the intimacy of dance. "That sounds really beautiful. And I'm sure you will."

The music stops and we break our hold to applaud. Javi leans in so I can hear him and jerks his head toward the bar. "I'm sure you will, too," he says. Then he thanks me for the dance and kisses the back of my hand before taking off toward the growing line at the front door.

When my gaze shifts back to the bar, I catch Sawyer's eyes on me. They seem heavy with hope or dread as he throws back the last of his mojito and pushes off from his stool.

After yesterday—well, after *the way things ended* yesterday—the idea of being close to him, with structure and rules and an audience to keep us in line, sounds really nice. I try to soften my expression, as if to say *Come on over, I won't be a jerk.* I can feel it working, and the upturned corners of his mouth tell me that the hesitation in his step is about something other than me.

Unfortunately, Dolphins Jersey Guy doesn't hesitate at all, and he drunkenly throws an arm around my shoulders. "So you're a romance writer?" he asks, more a statement than a question.

"I am," I answer. Sawyer's only halfway to me and he stops, rooting himself to the floor.

"I have a joke for you," the guy says. "What do women and salsa have in common?" I'm afraid to guess, so I wait for him to deliver the punchline. He squeezes my shoulders as he drops his voice. "I like 'em both real spicy." He raises his eyebrows suggestively and drops his gaze to my cleavage.

"First of all, where I fall on the Scoville scale is none of your business," I say. "And second of all, and I mean this with all the respect you deserve, *ew*." I try to shrug him off of me, hoping he'll get the hint.

Spoiler alert: he doesn't.

His cackle is interrupted by a firm voice from a dozen feet away. *"Hey!"*

The music plays on, but there's a definite record-scratch moment in my head, when everything else stops and I'm hyper-focused on what's happening around me.

"Why don't you let her go, man."

Jersey Guy's arms tighten around me. "Why would I do that?" It's more possessive than playful.

Sawyer looks like he belongs here, with his fitted tan shorts and his gauzy white button-down. The top three buttons are undone, showing a tan, muscular chest I was stubbornly ignoring earlier today, and the fabric ripples as he unbuttons the cuff of one of his sleeves. He flips the cuff up and rolls it over itself until I can see his flexors twitch with restraint. "Because I'm telling you to," he growls, and he repeats the process with his other arm, staring down this stranger as he does and taking a restrained step toward us.

"Maybe she doesn't want me to let her go," he counters, but I very much do. Sawyer takes another step forward, clenching his fists, but he reads my warning expression perfectly and keeps a safe distance.

"Actually," I say, twisting, trying to put more space between myself and this guy. "I should probably get going."

"Why?" he asks. He pouts, playfully possessive. "Stay, pretty lady. Let's talk more about romance."

I shiver at his creepy tone and unfocused leer.

"She said *no*." Sawyer's next to me, his fingers wrapped around my wrist, and I've never been so grateful for his height as he towers over this man, clearly intimidating him.

I'm sure the standoff is drawing attention, and my thoughts are confirmed when Javi slides toward us. He speaks through gritted teeth and a forced smile. "Everything okay here?"

Apparently, when both a man eight inches taller than you *and* the bar's owner approach you, you have a change of heart. Jersey Guy removes his arm from my body; the world's worst game of tug-of-war has ended.

"We're heading out," I say, offering a smile to Javi. "Thank you so much for the drinks and the dance." He starts to respond, but I rush to grab my bag from my seat at the bar and head outside into the fresh air and sunlight.

Sawyer's right behind me. "You okay?" he asks, glancing both ways before following me to the opposite side of the street.

"I'm fine," I answer, though I'm not sure I fully believe it.

"That guy was a creep."

"Yeah, he was." I still smell his drunken breath, still feel gross from having had his hands on me.

"You have to be more careful. You were flirting with the owner, and I saw the way he looked at you. The way they *both* looked at you—"

"Are you trying to make this my fault? Because I *talked* to Javi?"

He says no, but he means yes. I can feel it. And I want to ask him how *he* looked at me, if he even bothered to look, why he didn't come take my hand instead if I shouldn't have been dancing with a stranger. I want to ask him how it's my fault that some men look at me a certain way, and scream that I can't control their gazes. All of it bubbles below the surface, like a bottle of Mountain Dew that's been kicked down the stairs, but the cap is super-glued on.

"He was all over you, Gwen."

I know he's talking about the creep from the ship that I hopefully will not bump into again for the remainder of our trip. I know, I really do, that he's not talking about Javi. But I wouldn't mind if he was jealous that another man asked me—and then I asked that other man—to dance. "What's your point? It's not like you care."

He takes my arm and pulls me to the side of the walkway, letting a family pass with a stroller. "Of course I care, Gwen. I—" He cuts himself off, and his Adam's apple bobs. "Forget it." He raises his hands in defeat before running a hand through his hair and checking his watch.

"You *what*, Sawyer? Don't think you're getting off that easily."

He looks up and closes his eyes, and his forearms flex as his hands open and close. I swear I hear him count to five. "It brought back some feelings. That's all. There was something about his face, and I didn't want him to... to hurt you."

It clicks: the way he approached us, the restraint, the counting... He's trying to control himself and not repeat the school office incident that landed him in hot water and led to the end of his relationship.

"It's like he was taunting me, daring me to do something. He's seen us together twice now, but he still felt like he could touch you like that, like he had a right to put his hands all over you. Like he wanted me to challenge him. And it just reminded me—"

"Hey." I press a palm against his chest, over his thudding heart. When he doesn't meet my eyes, I rest my other hand on his cheek and stroke the stubble that's been growing the past few days. "It's okay. I'm okay. We're okay."

He takes my hand in his, kisses the inside of my wrist, and takes a deep breath. I can feel his pulse return to normal as he releases my hand. After a few moments like this, he breaks the silence. "I didn't get to tell you earlier, but you look beautiful today."

"Oh." I'm so flustered, my own heart pounding in my chest after the whirlwind of the last five minutes, all my calming energy transferred to Sawyer, leaving me with none. So his comment lands differently than it might normally. I blush. "Thanks."

"I know I screwed up yesterday," he adds. His hands are deep in his pockets again, and he toes the ground with his boat shoe. "I was embarrassed. Like, want-to-tie-myself-to-the-anchor embarrassed. And then I couldn't sleep. And I thought about coming to talk to you, but I didn't want to wake you."

"How do you think I feel? I have to put up with her after this is all over. You at least get to go home and never have to look Gram in the eye again." I laugh, but he studies my face, and he opens his mouth like he wants to say something again. He closes it, deciding against it.

It's just as well; we've accidentally wandered again, and there's a crowd gathered down the street with more live music pulsing from the speakers set up in a small park.

"Come on." He takes my hand again and pulls me toward the scene. It's a week-long dance fest, and by the looks of the sign stapled to the telephone pole, we're about to get a tango lesson.

"We don't have to stay," I say, angling my head up so he can hear me better and so I can gauge his reaction. The salsa at Zamira's was like an appetizer—I'm hungry to dance more, but only if Sawyer's okay with being my partner.

He shakes his head. "No, it's fine. Just… don't let go, okay?"

WE'VE SPENT HALF an hour learning the basics of tango, which means we've stood mostly side by side to learn the separate men's and women's steps, which means she let go. But she keeps looking at me to reassure me we're still connected in some way, which grounds me.

The air has grown humid as clouds have rolled in, and she's swept her hair up into a messy bun, though loose tendrils stick to the sweat at the nape of her neck. When she makes a mistake, she laughs it off, shakes her head, and gets back to trying to perfect the steps.

Finally it's time to put our moves together, and our bodies come together naturally into the hold position. Her hand is warm and damp in mine, and I know I'm drenched in sweat, but other than feeling bad for her having to touch me I certainly don't care, and it seems like she's okay with it, too.

She moves easily, though she watches our feet and counts the steps the whole time. "They make this look so much easier on *Dancing with the Stars*."

"And in spy movies," I laugh. "Like everyone knows how to do those quick turns and dips and everything."

"Oh, you mean like this?" She spins herself away from me and turns back in, wrapping herself up in our arms. Her back is pressed against my chest and she bends at the waist to run a hand up her leg. It forces her ass into my hips and I bite my lip to distract my brain from sensations in other parts of my body.

A gentle rain falls, and if she feels it she doesn't care. When she's straightened back up, she raises an arm over her head. I drag my fingers down the silky skin from her elbow to her shoulder and over the now-damp fabric along the side of her torso. Her back arches away from me and she bends her arm, tangling her fingers in my hair as she bends lower, down through the tangled loop of our arms. When she's free, she spins out, stretches to the side, twirls in so my arm is wrapped around her back for support, and sinks into a dip. The rain slaps the pavement and people start scattering, but she holds the dip for a few seconds, reaching back with a free hand to let down her hair.

Finally she snaps back up, steadying herself against my shoulders as my arm tightens around her waist. Her chest heaves under the clinging white fabric of her now semi-sheer dress, and she pants, trying to catch her breath.

"Where did you learn that?" I ask, tucking a rain-soaked section of hair behind her ear. The rain has gone from sprinkle to torrential downpour in less than two minutes, and most others have sought shelter in their cars or nearby stores. But she seems unfazed by it; if anything, she delights in it.

"Mr. and Mrs. Smith," she says.

"The movie?"

"No, my neighbors. They own a dance studio." Her breathing calms and she beams this radiant smile right at me, but I can't bring myself to return it. "What's wrong?" she asks, her smile fading. Water drips from my hair and rolls down alongside her nose, and we probably look ridiculous out here.

Specifically, I look ridiculous, because I'm literally just standing here staring at her, afraid to break this attachment, evaluating my feelings in the rain.

"Hey. Sawyer, are you—"

I don't even let her ask the whole question before my mouth is on hers and my hands draw her closer. She's so firmly pressed against me I don't know how we could be any nearer than we are now, but I'm desperate for the connection and I try to pull her body even closer to mine.

She dives in, too, twisting her fingers into my hair, using her other hand to claw at my back, digging her fingernails into my skin through my shirt.

In need of oxygen and assurance, I pull back, and Gwen licks her now-swollen lips. She takes a step back without breaking eye contact. There's a hint of a shiver across her shoulders, which is fine, because we need to return to the ship and I am hoping to keep her warm once we get there.

"Do you want to head back?" She scrunches her face and closes an eye against the pounding rain.

I nod and clear my throat. "Gwen?"

"Yeah?"

"Thanks for not letting go out there."

"Never," she says, and she drapes my arm around her shoulder—her arm around my waist—as we walk toward cover to wait for a rideshare.

SAWYER

IT'S POSSIBLE, IF cruise ship showers were larger, that we may have stayed together once we reboarded. Instead we headed to our separate rooms with a promise to meet up at her suite. Her suite, which she's sharing with her grandmother, instead of my room, which I have to myself. I'm not sure whose choice that was, but it's probably for the better: we're dangerously close to 'fling' territory as it is.

She's in a tank top and jeans when she answers the door, scrunching her dripping hair into a towel. "Hey," she greets me. Her smile is soft and warm, and although the early afternoon's fire is missing from her eyes, she seems happy to see me.

"Hey, yourself." Smooth, Sawyer. Very smooth.

She rolls her eyes playfully and turns away to finish drying her hair. "Make yourself comfortable!" she calls over her shoulder as she disappears into the bathroom. She closes the door most of the way, dulling the hum of the hairdryer.

I let the front door latch shut and take in the suite again. It's a good size, definitely more comfortable than my room. Gwen's floppy hat hangs on the corner of the TV, and the desk chair is wearing her oversized cardigan. Her laptop has been pushed to the edge of the workstation, making room for a journal, a paperback, a newspaper, and a makeup bag, the last of which spills its contents over the laminate desktop.

After I straighten the laptop, I pick up a tube of lipstick with a cherry red sticker on the end, and I wonder if she'll be more likely to wear it if I stand it up front and center in her haphazard collection of cosmetics.

"I'm not sure that's your color," she says, emerging from the bathroom. Her hair's still damp, and she twists it into a messy knot on top of her head. My eyes flit to her lips, and I imagine them full and red and sipping wine across from me at dinner at some swanky New York restaurant that I probably can't afford. Finding a new job jumps to the top of my to-do list for the real world, because even if the school approves my return, I'm not sure I can stand to be in the same building, with the same administrators and parents and Chelsea.

"So," she continues, sliding into a pair of flip-flops. "What do you want to do?"

There's a list of what I *want* to do and another of what I *should* do, and I need to make sure to not let the first overtake the second. "Did you want to visit the casino?"

She shakes her head. "Can't. It's closed when we're docked."

"Oh. What about trivia?"

She scrunches her nose. "I think Taylor Swift trivia is coming up, and I lost track after the *Reputation* era."

"Then you're missing out, because *folklore* was great," I say, and she rewards me with her laughter. She might think I'm joking, but I always let my students request music when they're working on projects, and that particular album gets a lot of airplay in my classroom.

Got. *Got* a lot of airplay.

"Is it stupid," she begins, and her cheeks go pink, "to take a nap?"

"You tired out from all that dancing today?" I ask, and I immediately regret it. Her smile falters. "I mean, your tango skills are impressive."

She graciously moves past my accidental reference to the less pleasant part of our day. She chews the inside of her lip before admitting, "I didn't sleep much last night." She extracts the lipstick from my hand and sets it back on the desk. "You in? For this nap situation?"

I survey the room again, consider that Maggie could walk in at any moment, and contemplate if it would be better or far worse to suggest we go to my room.

"Relax, Dawson," she says, rolling her eyes. "I'm not going to try to seduce you. That would be weird."

"Why would it be weird?" I cringe as soon as the words come out. I'm okay with being straightforward in relationships and general communication, but that felt just plain *forward*, like *why would it be weird to seduce me?*, and I'm relieved when her smile reaches her eyes.

"Because. We're going to have an audience."

Lying so close, I can smell her fruity shampoo. Mango? Papaya? Something tropical. Mixed with the scent of her skin, an intoxicating combination of coconut sunscreen and sea salt, she's like a Caribbean cocktail, and damn, I could be drunk on her.

By some magic stroke of luck, there was a large daybed available in The Retreat. Rain still dances off the glass ceiling above us, and the constant thrum of the hot tub jets and pool equipment helps drown out the sound of people's voices. There's a fair amount of activity here, but Gwen tuned it out and drifted off to sleep a few minutes after we arrived.

My arm's asleep under the weight of her head on my shoulder, but I don't want to move; she's tucked into my side, her arm like a seatbelt across my chest and stomach. Every few minutes her fingers twitch, tickling the bare patch of skin she created for herself at my waist. I breathe her in and brush wayward hairs from her cheek.

She's not what I was expecting—not after that first meeting, just a few yards from where we lie now. It was fun to mess with her that day, because she seemed so miserable and I didn't care if I pissed her off. But things have changed since then, and now, frankly, I want to piss her off. And I want to make her laugh. I want all her passion, good and bad, because it would mean she cares the way I do.

Gwen stirs, and I can see that she's watching her own fingers trace the subtle v-cut on my side.

"Welcome back." Without thinking, I press my lips to the top of her head and freeze. This is how mornings are supposed to be, and lazy, rainy Saturdays, and hard days and good days and movie nights and making up. And despite the fact that we're surrounded by strangers, this feels like the most natural, most quietly intimate thing in the world.

She stretches her legs, pointing and flexing her toes over the edge of the day bed. "How long was I out?"

I shrug, or attempt to, considering the arm that's asleep. "Maybe thirty, forty minutes?"

"Oh." She glides her thumb across my skin. "Do we need to be getting ready for dinner?"

To check my watch I have to pull my arm tighter around her. She adjusts with the movement and presses closer to my side. Between her body heat and the room's humid air, I'm regretting the sweatshirt I pulled on after my shower. "We probably should soon, yeah."

"Okay." She lies there a moment longer, not tearing herself away like I expect her to. "This is nice, right?" She twists her head to look up at me, and I expect her to smile, but her eyes are tinged with sadness. It catches me off guard.

   MEGAN BECKER

"Yeah," I say, wondering what's behind the sudden shift from her gentle touches to this new emotion.

She closes her eyes and exhales, and when she sits up, she's herself again. "I'm going to change. Meet you at dinner?"

I nod. "Sure. I'll see you there." And before I can even slide into my flip-flops, Gwen is gone.

Gwendolyn

IT WON'T WORK.

He's too nice, and it's too easy, and that's not how these things work. So it won't work. It can't.

It's the refrain I repeat the whole way down to my deck and to my suite, and I gulp the fresh air when I throw open the balcony door.

"You alright, dear?"

I hadn't realized Gram was sitting there, but now I'm stuck. I'm hyperventilating, and it's not the first time she's seen it, and she's going to want to go into Fixer Mode. Except she doesn't. At least not right away.

I lower myself into a seat and tuck my knees to my chest. "I didn't think I'd actually like him, Gram."

Sometimes it's best just to rip off the Band-Aid. The admission is easy: clearly I like the guy, or why the kissing and the dancing and the snuggling? But the realization is hard: I don't trust it to work out, which sucks, because clearly I like the guy.

"I mean, obviously he's very attractive. And he's funny. And he's smart, and like, really thoughtful."

"He sounds terrible, Gwennie."

A long sigh passes through my lips. "I don't know how to make this work in the real world."

Gram resituates herself in her seat. "Who says you have to?"

When I look up, she's leaning toward me, her eyes bright. "Wasn't that the whole point? For you and Nancy to get us to date?"

"If you like each other, and you date, great! But if not, that's okay, too. We thought you'd be a great fit, but at minimum we just wanted you to meet so you'd know that there are good ones out there. For each of you. No one's expecting you to run off to the chapel on board or anything." A smile tugs at the corners of her lips. "We just wanted you to meet someone nice and to have a little fun, and based on what I saw yesterday…"

"Ewww, no," I object, shoving my fingers into my ears. Gram cackles, and I point an accusatory finger at her as I retreat into the room. "That's gross. Never speak of it again. Please."

"No promises!" she shouts after me.

Fun. I can do Fun. *I don't do Fun.* But I'm going to try to do Fun.

The Fun starts when I greet Sawyer before dinner and pull him into a hug. It continues when his hands run along my bare arms and he entwines his fingers with mine. It's really Fun to see the way his eyes dance at the sight of me in the strapless, tropical-print jumpsuit I put on. There's more Fun at dinner, where we share a bottle of wine—though I drink most of it—and we trade stories about college and our travels and ourselves.

We chase Fun to the sports deck where I beat him at a game of mini-golf, and Fun follows us to the bar where he beats me at a game of pool, but not before we have another round of drinks.

I'm sufficiently tipsy, and my cheeks hurt from laughing so much. Gram was right, we *can* have Fun. And what's more Fun than dragging Sawyer away from the velvet settee where I sit in his lap and play with his hair and throw my head back laughing at his jokes to go to the ship's theater so we can see The Couples' Game Show play out live?

Volunteering to be in the show. That's more Fun.

GWEN IS CLEARLY comfortable on stage, but I like to stay behind the scenes these days. Being the tallest person in the room most of the time draws enough attention; I never needed to seek it out elsewhere. Also, my track record with attention is not great.

I'd like to be able to say, 'Why I agreed to this, I'll never know,' but the startling reality is that I *do* know, and the answer is seated with her back to mine.

When Finn, our cruise director, asked the audience who thought they'd been married the longest, a few hands went up. The winners were a couple on board to celebrate their 65th anniversary; they'd been together since middle school. Together, they're Contestant Number One.

Then Finn wanted to know who'd been married the shortest period of time, and he already knew the answer because he'd officiated that couple's wedding three hours before the game started. Thus was born Contestant Number Two.

Finally, to select Contestant Number Three, Finn wanted a 'fun-loving couple' with a story to tell. Gwen's hand shot into the air. She jumped and waved, trying to catch his attention, while I tried to coax her back into her chair. But the damage was done: by trying to attract Finn's attention, she caught the eye of three book lovers in the audience who happen to be on a self-proclaimed "Smut-cation" (the name needs work), and they gestured wildly to Gwen and me while yelling to Finn that Gwen was a celebrity and he should totally pick her. Of course Finn was intrigued, and moments later Gwen and I were ushered to the stage wings to be given the full rules and sign the requisite waiver.

Somewhere around dotting the *i*'s she sobered and pulled my face to hers. "You're my boyfriend. It's been two months. We're very happy. And if there are multiple-choice answers, answer in the order of BAC. I don't care what the question is or what the choices are—let's at least make sure we match on something."

"That's cheating, Gwen."

"Eh, I've seen worse," she says, running her fingers through my hair and smoothing a wrinkle from the shoulder of my polo. Her face pinches, and I'm sorry I used the word cheating after what she shared with me on the island yesterday. It clearly still affects her.

We're tied for the lead after the first round, when I left the stage and Gwen answered three questions about me on her mini whiteboard. There was a multiple-choice question, and luckily 'B' was objectively the best answer.

The older couple pulls away in round two, when the opposite person leaves the stage. These people must tell each other everything, and they've had plenty of time to, because he knew which celebrity she'd use her hall pass on and which brand of underwear she wears. (The audience had a laugh at his original answer of 'sexy black ones that vibrate' before he changed it to 'Hanes.')

Unsurprisingly, he also knew the "shirt or dress color your partner wore on your first date." When Finn asked the question, my mouth went dry. Whatever answer I gave here could be telling: should I say 'navy' for that first night at dinner, 'silver' for formal night, 'what she's wearing right now,' because tonight has felt incredibly date-ish. I gambled and wrote down 'she wasn't wearing a shirt or dress.' The fans ate it up when Finn read it aloud over my shoulder, and heat rushed to my cheeks.

But Gwen answered the same way, and my whole body went warm, unrelated to the heavy stage lights. When I showed my matching whiteboard, the audience roared with laughter, and Finn turned the mic to Gwen for an explanation. Without an ounce of shame, Gwen flirted with the entire theater, flashing them a sideways smile and batting her eyelashes. "Wouldn't you like to know?" she asked Finn. The audience ate it up and she grinned, then stretched out her hands and motioned for them to quiet. "For our first date, I wore a black bikini." She turned her smile to me and it softened into something real.

Luckily, again, 'A' was the best answer to the second round's multiple-choice question, so I didn't feel too guilty when we both got that right.

Now in round three, we're trying to reclaim the lead, even though we know we really should let one of the real couples on stage win. We're back to back; I have her shoe in my left hand and mine in my right. We're in the middle of nine questions where we are the only answers, and I feel Gwen's soft curls against my neck when she throws her head back laughing at the question, "Who has more tattoos?"

I guess that Gwen has more surprises waiting for me, and when I hold up her shoe, we're a match. Finn banters with each couple, and when he asks Gwen about my tattoos she smirks and says, "If he wanted everyone to know about his tattoo, he would've put it in a place more people could see it." The laughter crescendos at the salacious innuendo, and at a blink-and-you'll-miss-it speed, her eyes dart to my waist.

At the end of round three, we're tied with the elderly couple. Finn apologizes to the newlyweds, and they're ushered backstage to a smattering of applause. We're heading into sudden death as a tie-breaker. We'll still sit back-to-back, but each person will be given a whiteboard. Finn will ask a question, we'll have five seconds to record our answer, and then we'll see if we match. The first couple to produce an incorrect answer will be eliminated.

Question one is easy enough. "We're looking for *her* eye color,"

Finn says, and I don't have time to write down 'gray with flecks of gold, except sometimes they turn blue and amber,' so I simply write 'blue.' Gwen's answer matches, and the older couple gets it right too, so we all move on.

"Where would *he* rather get a snack: Pizza Plaza on Deck Five, or Ice Creamery on Deck Fourteen?"

Again, Gwen and I match answers with 'Pizza Plaza,' while the other couple moves forward with dual 'Ice Creamery' responses.

"These guys are good," Finn says to the crowd. In my periphery I can see Gwen's hands flexing in anticipation of the next question, which happens to be multiple-choice. "This is about *her*, about Gwendolyn and Lizette. Where is she most herself? A: In a big city. B: At the beach. C: Wherever you are."

I'm supposed to say 'C,' but I can't. Gwen was so serene in Bermuda, so tranquil and comfortable yesterday on the private island, floating and turning her face toward the sun, basking in the warmth of the sky and sea. Plus, I can't lie about this, and I don't want to cheat.

Finn has Matthew and me flip our boards first, and Lizette giggles with excitement. It's clear she's selected the same answer as her husband.

When the women flip their boards, the audience cheers and Finn congratulates Lizette and Matthew on their win. My eyes are fixed on the giant letter 'C' on Gwen's board, with a tiny heart just to its right. Her mouth curls up at me while she enthusiastically applauds the winners. The loss doesn't seem to bother her, and she's all smiles while she poses with a few fans for photos as the theater clears out.

She wraps herself around my arm when she rejoins me and rests her head against my shoulder. "That was fun."

"It was."

"What do you have there?" she asks, pointing to my other hand. The effects of the earlier alcohol are mostly wearing off, but she's still a little tipsy.

I hold up the bottle of champagne. "This is just my prize for being part of the show. One of the staff guys gave it to me while you were being famous and fabulous."

"Oh," she says, turning, looking back toward the stage. "Where's mine?"

I feel the laughter in my chest. "I think this was meant for us to share, seeing as how it was The *Couples'* Game Show."

"Oh. Right." She rests her head against me again and smiles and waves toward the few people still lingering just outside the theater. "Where should we go to drink this?"

"There might be some seats down the hall here," I say, gesturing midship.

She shakes her head. "Too busy."

"The library?"

"We can't talk there."

"Upstairs by the pool?"

She wrinkles her nose. "It just seems too braggadocious, doesn't it? To drink our special champagne around other people? Like, 'look at us, paupers… look how swanky we are.' This might be a more private champagne experience."

"Okay," I say. "So, your suite then."

"What about your room?"

I wave off the idea. "What about it? It's small. You actually have room to move in yours."

"Yeah. But I also have Gram. And I don't want to have to share this with her." Her fingers slip between mine, and she looks up at my face with clear blue eyes, a smile, and hope.

A lump rises in my throat, but I swallow back against it. "Sure. Okay," I answer.

SAWYER

GWEN SINKS BACK against a pillow on the arm of the couch after passing me the bottle. I'm not usually a fan of the stuff, but this is surprisingly good. Her feet are in my lap, and she wiggles her hot pink painted toes. Her shoes—gold high-heeled sandals—are dropped just next to the couch. I need to be careful not to accidentally step on them if I get up then, because I am sure they're expensive and I don't want to damage them, but I'm also sure they could impale me easily.

The thought of getting up anytime soon is so far from my mind, so it shouldn't be a problem. I'm good right here.

"You came in clutch with that tattoo answer," she says. She tilts her head to see me better. "How'd you know I had more than one?"

"You implied, yesterday, that you had one hiding—" I motion toward her torso, "—there, somewhere. Then, I don't know, I just figured you had a pencil or something that I hadn't noticed. Maybe 'live, laugh, love' in Morse code or something trendy like that."

"I am appalled that you would think that about me!" She pulls the pillow from behind her head and chucks it at me. I save the champagne, but just barely. "I have two, sort of. One is still a work in progress."

"Are you going to tell me more, or am I supposed to keep guessing?"

"Please, I can't take any more of your awful guesses." She swings her feet off the couch and sits up, climbing onto her knees and twisting to roll down the back of her jumpsuit. "See this?" She

     MEGAN BECKER

moves her hair out of the way and aims to point out four thin rectangles, but she can't quite reach. "Those are supposed to be the spines of my books. And then every other book I write will be stacked on top of it."

"Much better than my idea," I admit. I'm about to ask questions about the three of her books I haven't read when she continues.

"And you saw the birds." She readjusts her outfit and sits back on her heels.

"Birds?"

"Yeah. Yesterday." She reaches her hand across her chest and pats at an area at her upper ribs. "The birds." Surely she can read the confusion on my face, and she grabs the champagne and takes another drink. "Sawyer. Are you that oblivious? They were out there on full display!"

My hands go clammy with the playful scolding. If she has a tattoo of birds, I certainly didn't see it. "I was a little distracted. My focus was not on the side of your body."

Color rushes to her cheeks, but she doesn't seem uncomfortable with the reference to yesterday's, shall we say, excursion. If anything, she seems emboldened by it. "So when do I get to see yours?" she asks.

"Only once you can prove you'll never make fun of me for the location of it."

"Well, shit. So, never, I guess?" She grabs the bottle, takes a sip, and extends the champagne to me again.

I take it and shrug. "Knowing you, probably not." When her laughter fades, I run a thumb over the label on the bottle. "I'm sorry I got that last one wrong. I just couldn't say 'C.' Not after seeing you these past couple days, the way you seem to come alive when you're near the water."

"It's okay," she says, and her voice is calmer, more reserved.

"It wouldn't have felt right to lie. I mean, I'm not judging you, for sticking with the plan. I just—"

"What do you mean by that?" she asks, shifting her body.

"Nothing. I just… I know you'd said, B-A-C was the order, and the first two were fair, but I didn't want to give a bogus answer just to win."

She whispers something, and I have to ask her to repeat it. "I just said, it wasn't a bogus answer."

My breath catches and my heart beats a little heavier than it did two minutes ago. "I—"

"Don't be weird, okay?"

"It's a little too late for that."

She slinks toward me like a prowling cat, her eyes trained on my lips. Her fingers tuck back a loose tuft of my hair and trace a path behind my ear while she rises up and straddles my waist. Her mouth finds mine, tentative at first, and she lowers herself onto me with a moan.

I'm already solid under her. If she keeps grinding her hips into me this way, kissing me this way, she'll undo me within minutes. "Gwen."

Her lips move to my neck, and I lean my head over the back of the couch, hungry for her affection. I grip her waist but let her control her movement. "I said don't be weird." She unbuttons the second button on my shirt and lets her hands in.

"Is it weird to have some questions about your answer?"

She pulls back, and her chest rises and falls as she narrows her eyes at me. "Normally I'd say no. But right now?" Her gaze shifts between my eyes and she rolls hers. She reaches for the champagne on the end table and takes a few gulps as she slides to my side. "Look. I wasn't expecting any of this. Quite literally, any of it. Not you being here, not you being some…" she gestures a hand up and down my torso, "…I don't know, some living statue of a Greek god or whatever all *this* is. I didn't expect you to be decent—"

I don't expect to be the one to resume the kiss, but I need her against me again. I want to taste her lips and her skin. I want

     MEGAN BECKER

everything.

She runs her hands up and down the length of my chest as her tongue tangos with mine. I reach to wrap my arms around her, but it's not enough. I'm desperate for her now; I pull her over me again. She kneels, still lighting me on fire under the touch of her hands on my skin, and my hands slip to her thighs. Nothing feels as important right now as having her legs wrapped around my body.

When I stand up she lurches against me, tightening her legs around my waist, weaving her fingers into my hair and pulling, running her tongue along my throat. She guides me by the grip she has on my hair and leans back, lowering my face to her chest. I want to devour her.

"We shouldn't do this," I say, pressing a kiss into her cleavage.

"The hell we shouldn't."

"You've been drinking."

"I'm not drunk, Sawyer." She kisses my mouth and resumes unbuttoning my shirt. "I, Gwendolyn Pierce—" another button, "—being of sound mind—" her teeth scrape my ear, "—hereby ask you, Sawyer Dawson—" her mouth is on mine, and I kiss her wide, wicked smile when she says, "to fucking *take* me."

She arches her back and guides my hand to her zipper, and the soft fabric falls around her waist after one smooth pull. I know her bra is lace without even looking as my hands memorize every swell of her, and I crave the sensation of unhooking the clasp in the back and picking up where we left off yesterday. After all, I do have a tattoo of birds to look for.

Gwen's hot against my chest as she finally undoes the last button. She bites her bottom lip as her fingers waltz across my Adam's apple, and the look in her eyes is equal parts pleasure and pleading. I want to pin her to the wall and taste her until she begs me to stop.

We're at an impasse: no more clothing can be removed like this, with her legs still wrapped around me and our bodies pressed together. Not fast enough, anyway. Her gaze shifts to the bed, and I swallow hard. I'm not like this, normally. I'm careful and logical, even with women, and maybe that makes me not the most exciting lover out there, but I'm thorough and detail-oriented, and I know that counts for something. These last few months, focusing on self-control… it all seems to disappear. But I feel grounded, if a little wild, being with Gwen. It's dangerous and safe, all at once.

I lower her onto the bed, kissing her neck, my fingers running the length of her sternum. I back away only long enough to pull the jumpsuit off her legs. She rises then, skimming her hands up my chest, and yanks the shirt from my arms. Then her hands are on my belt buckle, and I scoop her up and slide her toward the headboard. She works her way back, inches at a time, while she nips at my lips and works the buckle. Once she has my pants undone, she shimmies them to my ankles.

She props herself on her elbows and looks at me. The boxer briefs leave nothing to the imagination, and when her hand makes contact with me through the tight fabric, I drop my head to her stomach and groan. I kiss her there, then an inch lower, then the inside of her thigh. She writhes and reaches for me, pulling my face closer to hers.

"Do you have something?" she asks, her throat rumbling under my tongue.

I finish my kiss and repeat the question. "Do I have some—Oh." It takes a moment to decipher her meaning. "No. You?"

"No. Why would I?"

"Why would *I*? I thought I was just vacationing with my—"

"Don't even say it." She puts a hand against my chest and her eyes go wide. It's true: it would be a mood killer to mention Nan now. "You didn't like, I don't know, get one, somewhere?"

I feel my eyes narrow as I mull over her words. "Where would I even—?"

"The gift shop. They sell them, right?"

It must be comical, the closeness of our bodies, the way they're tangled together so intimately, frozen in a frenzy of limbs and needing to talk about the best place to buy a condom on a cruise ship.

"Probably? Maybe?"

"You didn't look?"

"*Why would I have looked, Gwen?*"

She stares at me, exasperated and sexy, her lips full and her cheeks flushed and her chest heaving. A smile teases up the corner of her lips, and I can't tell if she's annoyed or if she finds this whole thing hilarious. "Because obviously this was going to happen. Tell me you didn't see this coming."

Gwendolyn

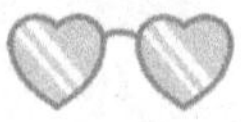

TONIGHT HAS DEFINITELY been Fun. Holy shit. So capital-effing Fun.

Sure, the game show and the mini-golf were great, and drinks and a game of pool were enjoyable. But sitting on the couch with him, chugging prize champagne, joking and learning about one another—I didn't expect anything to get better than that.

And all that was before I ended up in his lap. Then in his *bed*. Despite what I said to him, I did not see this coming. Even after yesterday, after The Incident That Shall Not Be Mentioned, I didn't think we'd end up here.

Though, *here* is an interesting idea. *Here* is right on the edge of something that is sure to be mind-blowing. *Here* is a leap into the unknown with a man who is still largely a stranger to me. *Here* is lying half-naked in Sawyer Dawson's bed, with his forehead on my shoulder, as he controls his breathing and groans into my breasts.

My voice comes out timid, with all the confident energy we both shared a few moments ago evaporated in an instant. "Do you want me to go look in the gift shop?"

"They close at eleven," he says, his words mumbled against my skin.

I glance at the clock: 11:42. *Shit.* "Do you want me to start knocking on doors? 'Cause I will."

"Not even a little." He shakes his head and kisses my neck. "With our luck you'd probably knock at all the rooms that have little kids sleeping inside."

"So. That leaves us with three options."

Sawyer shifts and sits back on his heels, letting his fingers draw invisible pictures on my thigh. "Do tell."

"Well," I say, bracing myself as I throw the idea out there. "I mean, we could just go for it anyway. But option two is just third-base stuff."

He stifles a snicker. "Who ever would have guessed that Gwen Pierce would be in my bed using sports analogies to talk about sex."

"The *third* option, Mr. Smartass, is that we just call it quits here for the night and probably put more clothes on."

"What do I do if I hate all of these choices?"

I shrug. "You hate all of them? Even option two?" I can only imagine how good it would feel to let him put his hands everywhere and to let his mouth follow.

"Gwen, let's be real: if I go for option two, I might as well choose option one. I don't think I could stop at third base when—"

"When there's a chance to score?"

He shakes his head and chuffs. "I was *going* to say, I don't think I could stop at third base when you're in the game."

My cheeks burn, because despite the terrible analogy, that was pretty sexy. After everything that happened with Tristan last year, this kind of honesty and he-can't-control-himself-around-me interest is refreshing.

Sawyer hangs his head. "So. Option three, then, I guess." He avoids my gaze as he slides himself backward, but I can tell from his body language and the way his eyes linger that he's as disappointed as I am. He disappears into the bathroom and the sink faucet starts to run.

"You okay in there?" I can see part of him reflected in the full-length mirror hanging on the closet door, and he's bent over the small vanity, splashing water on his face.

He calls back over the flowing water, "Yeah. Just trying to cool down."

Cooling down sounds great, actually. Sawyer's got a folded sweatshirt on the desk, so I swipe it for myself and head out to the balcony once I'm a little more covered. Standing out here feels like riding in a convertible on an autumn morning: the air is crisp; the breeze is constant. I gulp in the cool air and consider that maybe Sawyer's answer at the game show—that I am most myself at the beach—might have been the best choice. But then he emerges through the doorway and I stand by what I put on my whiteboard.

"Gwen," he says. His voice is maple syrup, smooth and rich, and I'm stuck on it. Stuck on him. He's wearing his zip-up hoodie open over his bare chest and a pair of gray sweatpants. He's a total trope, but so am I, leaning against his railing in a sweatshirt that's three sizes too big for me. He scans my body and licks his lips, and his mouth twists into a partial smile.

"This a good look for me?"

"*Everything* is a good look for you." He moves toward me with trepidation in his steps.

My hands retreat into the too-long sleeves and I hug myself for warmth against the midnight air. This man makes me so hot all over that it gives me the chills. He's like a fever, and I'm in no hurry to find a cure. "You cooled down enough?"

He shoves his hands into his sweatshirt pockets. "Yeah."

I turn my attention back to the nothingness in the distance and feel an old but familiar pang in my chest. I felt it growing up, I felt it a year ago, and the only name I can give it is *rejection*.

Sawyer slides closer to the railing, and I feel his eyes on me. "You're upset."

"I'm fine," I say, shaking my head. "I just—I thought this night was going to go a little differently."

"Yeah. Me too." He shifts again and tucks some wind-blown hair behind my ears. His fingers linger by my jaw, and I nuzzle my face into his hand. "Gwen, I—" he starts, his thumb stroking my cheek. "I just need you to know, choosing option three… that has nothing to do with *you* and what you do to me. I just… I can't fully control myself around you, and I didn't want things to go too far. I don't want there to be any regrets."

All the good heat I felt earlier morphs in an instant, and suddenly this fever makes me feel sick. I swallow hard against the sourness in my throat. "No regrets. Got it."

"Shit. No, Gwen. I don't mean I'd regret you—I could never— I just don't want you to regret things, either."

Either. What. the. actual. fuck.

"None of this is coming out right."

"I sure hope not."

"Gwen," he pleads, but I'm already past him and back in his room. He reaches for me and grabs my sleeve, swinging me around to face him. His breath is warm, his breathing urgent, his eyes desperate. "I want you. So much it's probably bad," he says. His eyes drop to my lips and he closes the distance to kiss me. His hands move to my hips, sliding the sweatshirt up over my underwear as he sinks down and kisses my stomach, then my thigh. "If you really want me to, I will show you right now. In great detail."

I want the warmth of his skin against me. I want his mouth on me and his hands on me and his body against mine, but I swallow hard and press back on his shoulders. He rises and searches my eyes, and I snake my fingers into his hair to pull him into my kiss. When it's over, he rests his forehead against mine. "I don't want you to regret me," I confess.

He shakes his head, and his Adam's apple bobs. "Never, Gwen. Never you. Just, maybe, going somewhere we aren't both intending to go."

"Then we won't go there. Not tonight," I say, and it takes everything in me to back out of his arms and kiss him on the cheek instead of ripping off all our clothes and diving back into bed. "I'll see you tomorrow." I grab my things and head back to my suite.

DAY 8

At Sea: Formal Night

Gwendolyn

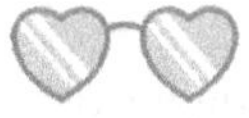

THERE'S A SPOT where the water churned up by the ship cascades over itself, where the most brilliant blue appears, rimmed in white, then greets the rich navy of the depths beyond us. Nowhere on the ship is this more beautiful than the view from the stern, where this electric blue trails us for what feels like miles, where it fans and widens and rolls over and over itself. I could watch it forever from my perch on Deck Fourteen, the wind flinging my hair into my face.

That's where Sawyer finds me. Rather, that's where he stumbles across me during what I assume—based on his sweat-drenched shirt, gym shorts, and sneakers—is another training run.

"Tired of the treadmill?" I ask as he jogs toward me. He wipes his face with the hem of his shirt, and his abs are so perfectly defined and glisteny that I consider that he might be a vampire from a YA novel. A vampire who showed incredible restraint when his mouth was on my neck yesterday.

"View's better here." His voice draws my eyes from his core. When I look up, he's half-smiling down at me.

Though last night didn't have the ending we wanted, everything leading up to it was great. I wonder if he's thinking about an encore, imagining how much better first and second bases could be now that we know what draws euphoric gasps and moans from each other, what causes the other to arch and writhe and tighten their grip. I wonder if he also thinks we'd hit it out of the park, and I wonder if he's stuck thinking in baseball analogies like I am. Mostly

I wonder if he's hungry for me the way I crave him.

"I like your sweatshirt," he says. I'm still wearing his from last night, though unlike my midnight sneaking from his deck to mine, I'm wearing pants with it this time. Well, turquoise biker shorts, but same thing.

"Thanks. I'm never taking it off."

He drops his gaze to my chest. "We'll see about that." Then a family walks by and he clears his throat, and red rushes up to his ears. He motions toward the railing, away from the passersby and out of range of possible eavesdroppers. "Listen, about last night…"

"We don't have to talk about it," I say, waving a hand between us.

"I want to." His eyes are fire, and my chest goes warm. "I told you the other day, I don't do flings."

"I know you did." Does it count, if we didn't actually sleep together?

"I meant it, Gwen."

"I know you did." So this is the part, where he tells me it's over before anything really begins.

"Which is why I want to take you out."

I squint up at him. "Out?"

"Out. Like, on a date. A real one, where we actually call it a date before it happens, and not just afterward in front of hundreds of people."

"Out," I repeat. I've been asked out a few times in the last year, usually by guys who want to give me their pitch so I'll put in a good word with my agent or my publisher. It was so annoying I gave up, which I'm sure is also why I ended up here, on vacation with my grandmother. "I could go out."

"Great." His eyes light up. "Do you have plans tonight?"

"Yes. Very *big* plans."

He doesn't register my meaning until I drop my gaze to his shorts. Then he takes my hands and pulls me to him, rolling his eyes and laughing. "And what about the rest of the day?"

"Probably writing," I shrug. The breeze picks up; the sky carries a distinct feeling of rain. After busy days in the sun, a lazy day indoors honestly sounds incredible. "What about you?"

"Maybe some reading. Maybe swinging by the gift shop at some point. Hard to say."

"Maybe a shower?"

There's a telling twinkle in his eyes as he meets my gaze again. "Gwendolyn Pierce, are you trying to seduce me before our date?"

I wrinkle my nose and smile, tugging on his still-sweaty shirt. "No. You legitimately smell awful."

"Fair point." He kisses my forehead and takes a step back. "So…"

I've written enough of these scenes—from the book that hit it big and a few rejected manuscripts before it—to know this tension. This will-they-or-won't-they, what-comes-next tension.

"You could come over then. We could hang out in the suite. Spend time with Nancy and Gram."

"Sure," he says. "That sounds nice." He cuts his training run short and I follow him back to his room, lingering while he showers.

He comes out, a towel wrapped low around his waist. We might need to find a place with a giant walk-in shower so we can have shower sex, because his body looks incredible wet. A sliver of his tattoo teases me from his towel, and I see a peak of black ink.

It's a good thing I'm across the room, because all I want to do is undo the towel and get an up-close view of this mystery art. "Have I proved myself worthy of seeing the tattoo yet?"

He grins and runs a hand through his hair. "You're getting there."

"Maybe later?"

"Definitely later. If you want, I mean." He pulls a T-shirt over his head and disappears into the bathroom with shorts, reemerging a few moments later fully dressed. "You ready?"

"Very."

He smiles again and reaches a hand toward me. When our skin connects he pulls me into him and kisses my mouth with restrained urgency. It's different: yearning and sobering and knowing and familiar. I wish we could change all the clocks and fast forward to tonight. But then he brushes a thumb against my cheek and looks at me with his melty chocolate eyes, and I'm glad we have all day to be together.

He grabs a few items and opens the door to leave, but we're greeted by a couple standing outside Nancy's door. Sawyer eyes them, confused.

"Can I help you?" he asks.

The woman in the hallway gapes at him, not even trying to hide her lust. I might be jealous if it weren't for the fact that Sawyer has demonstrated multiple times in the last few days that he's uninterested in the other women who've made their attraction known to him. I also get it. He's objectively hot, and I can't fault other people for recognizing it.

People, because this guy in the hallway swallows hard when he lets his gaze drop over Sawyer's frame. "We, uh. We're just trying to see if anyone's in here," he says.

"What for?" He rolls his eyes and sighs. "Did she con you in the pool hall? I swear, this lady's a shark." The couple steps back as Sawyer advances to knock on Nancy's carefully decorated door. "Gwen, never let my grandmother talk you into pool, spades, or drinking games. She's a little devil sometimes."

"Sorry, man. Did you say 'grandmother'?"

Sawyer looks from the man's face to the woman's, and then the man and woman look at each other, faces twisted in matching grimaces. "Yeah…" he drawls.

"Must be some confusion then," the woman says. She wraps her arms around the man's elbow and starts tugging him away, but not without one last long look at Sawyer.

"Sorry to have bothered you," the man adds, and they take off power-walking down the hall.

Sawyer looks more confused than ever as he turns toward me. "I'm going to need you to give them the people-watching treatment for me, Gwen. Help me understand what just happened here."

I bite my lip. I'm slightly horrified, but I'm also holding back laughter. I peel a few of Nancy's decorations from her door, including a pineapple that someone must have inverted as a prank. "No worries. I'll explain on the way."

"OH, GOOD. YOU'RE here." The suite door slams behind me, and Nan and Maggie look up from their seats on the couch at the sound.

"Hi, Sweetheart," Nan greets me. "Where else would I be on such a gloomy day?"

"Thankfully, not in your room." I drop the stack of magnets onto the coffee table.

"You had some visitors," Gwen offers, and if this was anyone else's grandma I'd laugh. But this is my grandmother, and *ew*.

"Why did you take down my decorations?" Nan asks, eyeing me suspiciously. "Didn't you like them? I thought they were nice. Pineapples are a sign of hospitality and welcoming."

"Oh, they were welcoming, alright," I snort. Gwen wraps her fingers gently around my bicep and nudges me aside.

"Nancy, on a cruise ship, certain… imagery… carries certain meaning."

Nan looks at Gwen, then at me, then back at Gwen, who now looks as uncomfortable as I feel. Maggie starts laughing, and Nan's eyes land on her.

"*Swingers*, Nancy. An upside-down pineapple means you're a swinger."

It takes a moment, but Nan's cheeks flush with understanding. "*Oh!*" she cries. She buries her face in her hands, her body shaking. When she looks up, she's got tears streaming from her eyes and one of the biggest smiles I've ever seen on her face. "Can you imagine what would have happened—" she gasps, in hysterics, and I can barely understand her, "—if I had been there and answered the door!"

Gwen has dissolved into laughter, and once I get over the shock of it all, I have no other option but to join in, too.

Gwen's perched on the arm of the chair opposite the couch, and I sink in, reaching for her instinctively. I consider that we haven't shared any of the physical details of last night with our grandmas (at least I haven't) so instead of pulling her into my lap like I want to do, I end up with an arm wrapped behind her, my hand grazing the outside of her thigh.

She doesn't seem shy about showing some affection, and she strokes my neck and plays with my hair. My fingers tighten on the armrest and Maggie hides a knowing smile behind her coffee cup as Nan's eyes flit between Gwen and me.

"Are you having a fun vacation, Gwendolyn?" she asks.

Without skipping a beat, Gwen answers, "More and more every day." Her long nails drag a line up the base of my skull. I shift in my seat and watch a smile flash across her mouth for an instant.

"Any fun plans today?" Maggie wonders aloud.

"I thought maybe we could all do lunch together," I say.

"Especially if we're not having dinner together tonight," Nan adds, mouthing 'sorry' in my direction when Gwen glances sideways at me.

I shake my head toward Gwen, a 'don't-worry-about-it' gesture, and turn my gaze back to the other women.

"Lunch sounds great," Gwen says. "Maybe after, we could—"

"So help me, if you even suggest we play another round of trivia," Maggie interjects.

Gwen rolls her eyes and smirks. "I was going to say, we could see if the spa can squeeze us in. My treat."

A massage sounds great. Normally I'd be opposed to someone wanting to treat me to something as pricey as a massage, but considering the rest of the night I planned for us, the only way I can afford it right now is if someone else pays.

It's on the earlier side for lunch, but since the rain still hasn't started we decide to enjoy a game of mini-golf before heading to the buffet. Gwen and I go up ahead to call the elevator, and I steal a kiss while we wait for them to catch up with us. She's still wearing my sweatshirt but has changed from shorts into leggings; paired with her neon sneakers and wavy hair, it looks incredible. Or maybe it's because I know what's underneath and because I'm anticipating the experience of learning even more tonight. Regardless, I want to be next to her and in her and around her... basically, if it's a preposition that indicates some sort of close proximity, I want it.

"So, what's this about dinner?" she asks with a wink.

"You'll see," I tell her.

Gwen's practically a pro at the mini-golf course, after beating me handily last night. A devilish grin forms on her face at every innocent reference to 'putters' and 'strokes,' until I'm sure she's going to double over laughing when a nearby golfer shouts about getting it 'in the hole.' It's refreshing to see this side of her, and it's such a difference from that first day's meeting, when I thought she was stuffy and patronizing. I want to keep being surprised by her, keep learning more about her until there are no surprises left.

I snake my arm around her waist and pull her close to me as Maggie and Nan finish the final hole. Maggie bends to get their balls from the cup but stops halfway down and stumbles backward. I rush to her side and offer support, helping to lower her onto a nearby bench. "You okay?"

She gives a delayed nod. "Thanks, Sawyer." Gwen appears at her side a moment later with a cup of water from the nearby beverage station. Maggie takes a sip and chuckles. "All of you making such a fuss about an old lady who just got a little dizzy from the heat."

It's not that hot, and Nan eyes me with concern. She and I

briefly discussed Maggie's diagnosis the other day, but the rule is that we're not mentioning it on this trip, so I don't push further.

Gwen doesn't seem to pick up on the disconnect between Maggie's words and the mild temperature and instead ushers her grandmother toward the air-conditioned buffet hall. She finds a table near the window and offers to fill a plate for her. I do the same for Nan and follow Gwen, holding three plates to her one, letting her dish each item. She sends a couple nervous glances toward the side of the room, but she doesn't say much as we weave our way through the food lines.

Lunch goes by uneventfully, and by the time everyone has finished eating, Maggie seems fine and Gwen seems content. It's a short walk to the spa, so we head there together. There are four massages available, but because all the regular rooms are booked, we'll have to divide into two couples massages.

"Great!" Maggie says, gripping my elbow. "So I'm with Sawyer, and you two…"

My heart stops for a second, until their laughter makes it obvious that she's joking (with Maggie, it's hard to be sure). She pats my hand and moves next to Gwen, but Nan wrinkles a nose at me, too.

"I haven't seen you naked since you were three, and I'd like to keep it that way," she says.

"I think if you're seeing the other person naked during the massage, you're doing it wrong, Nan."

"Or, you're doing it very right," Maggie snickers. Gwen's eyes light up at the joke; it's clear she loves her grandma, and it's obvious where she gets her sharp wit.

In the end, Gwen and I are partnered up and led to a large room overlooking the ocean. There's a sliver of sun in the distance, with two teak loungers angled toward the panoramic window.

"Feel free to take some time to relax," the hostess says. "Your massage therapists will be here in about twenty minutes to begin your treatment. When you hear this sound—" she pushes a button on the wall, and low chimes play over the spa music, "—we ask that you make your way to the tables and lie face down. Do you have any questions?"

I shake my head, and the hostess leaves.

"I have a question," Gwen says, once we're alone. She pulls the sweatshirt off over her head and twists her hair into a loose knot.

"What's that?" I focus on my own undressing, because if I watch her striptease I'm pretty sure I'll end up getting kicked out of the spa.

"Do I get to see the tattoo *now*?"

"What tattoo?"

"Sawyer. Come on. I just paid for these massages."

I'm down to my boxers, and I pull the provided robe over my arms. I leave it open when I turn to her; she saw the same display last night anyway. "I'm sorry if I gave you the wrong impression, Gwendolyn, but I am not going to let you objectify me just because you buy me fancy things."

She recoils until she sees my face, then a smile forms on her lips. She's in her robe, too, which she has tied loosely so it gaps across her chest when she moves. "Is that so?" she asks.

"It is," I answer, brushing my thumb over her lips. "I'm going to let you do it for free."

Gwendolyn

WHEN THE CHIMES sound, Sawyer's eyes go wide and he dives onto his massage table, covering up quickly with the warmed white sheets. I'm glad we're starting face down, because I felt the way he pressed against my thigh during that teasing kiss and he needs some time to get himself under control.

It feels good to laugh, even to hold back laughter, as the case may be. But within the first few minutes of our massages we've each busted up laughing numerous times, until the therapists ask if we're ready to continue or if we would perhaps prefer the salon.

I stifle the laughter and try to think of something other than Sawyer. It's hard to do, because so much of the last week has been spent with him at my side. Then his words from last night ring in my ear, and I begin to picture the gentle lapping of the Bermudian waters, the graceful gliding of the sea turtles swimming around us, the hammock, and the ocean breeze, and I'm calm. Sawyer must be calm, too, because from the massage table a few feet away I hear his gentle moaning.

I turn in the headrest to see him, and the therapist looks like she is about to die laughing. She mouths to my therapist, 'I think he's asleep,' and honestly, good. So many people want to make sure they stay awake the whole way through their massages to really experience relaxation, but the ultimate relaxation might just be found in nodding off during their appointment while their muscles are still soothed and loosened.

She finds a way to massage him while he's face down for the

whole hour, and she makes a little extra noise when she's wrapping up to wake him gently.

When we're alone in the room, a sheepish grin curls up his lips. "Thanks for that," he says. "I've actually never had a massage before."

"Are you serious? Don't you need them, with all your running and stuff?"

"I think we should have a serious conversation about the definition of the word 'need,' Gwen."

I roll my eyes as I pull on my sweatshirt (yes, I'm calling it mine now) and let down my hair. "You know what I mean. I'm going to have to get you a gift card or something."

"Or," he says, "we could go together sometime. This was nice."

"It was." It seems unlikely that we'd actually meet up for a spa day, but the idea is sweet. I check his watch, and it's already 2:30 p.m. "What time am I supposed to be ready for our date?"

"Five-thirty." He says it like it's obvious, and I guess it should be, because it's our normal dinner time. "And don't forget it's formal night," he offers.

"You're *kidding*." Finn has been reminding everyone via the PA system since six o'clock last night to 'dress our best' and that 'formal is better than normal.' But Sawyer doesn't laugh. He almost looks nervous. I cup a hand around one side of his face and kiss the other. "Any plans from now till then?"

He kisses me so firmly it moves my whole body backward, and I find myself trapped between the massage table and his hips. Then he smooths my hair, which always looks terrible after a massage, and twists his lips into an unconvincing smile. "I think we should spend some time with our grandmothers."

Gwendolyn

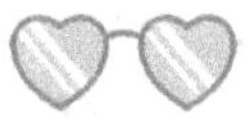

GRAM LOVED HER massage, and she's telling Sawyer all about it. When we gave her and Nancy the option to do whatever they each wanted to do, getting coffee was at the top of both lists, and now we're traversing the length of the ship to the café.

Nancy hangs a few paces back with me, and we laugh at the bits and pieces of the conversation we overhear in front of us. Then she looks up at me and straightens her smile. "He's a good boy, Gwendolyn."

I'm surprised she feels the need to tell me; it seems pretty obvious to the world that Sawyer Dawson is inherently good. "I can tell."

"He's been different this week." I don't know if this is a compliment or not, so I wait for her to reveal more. "You're good for him."

My mouth feels dry. I manage a "thanks."

"When I met you last year, I knew you'd be a good fit for him. I knew you would challenge him and respect him. He was single then, and very lonely, but when he started dating Chelsea he was a little better."

"Were they happy?" I don't have a right to ask the question, but I feel like I need to know.

"Mm," she sighs, tilting a hand back and forth. "Happy *adjacent*, I would say. He had someone to spend time with, and she was pleasant enough. There wasn't really a spark there, but growing up without a happy relationship to observe, I don't think he knew he should look for one."

Sawyer turns back, laughing at something Gram must have said. His wide smile fades to something sweet, if not slightly suspicious, when he sees us talking together. Nancy waves, and Sawyer resumes his conversation with Gram.

"I couldn't believe how things ended, considering the way he stood up for her. What he put on the line for her," Nancy continues.

"It's terrible to be ghosted by someone. To not even get closure."

"Yes, that was definitely hard for him. But I think two things hurt worse. First, knowing that he'd lost everything by standing up for the person who was named Teacher of the Year in their building a few weeks later."

I stop, feet glued to the floor. "Seriously?"

"Mhmm. Now, did she deserve it? Probably not. We think the school was trying to appease the teachers by recognizing her, since they had to follow up on the parent's complaint, too. Which was bogus, by the way."

I nod, and we resume walking. "You said there were two things?"

"Oh, yes," Nancy says. "Sawyer had left some things at her apartment. Not that he was spending a lot of his nights there, of course—" she adds, like she's afraid it'll bother me that he stayed over at his girlfriend's place. "Within days, she'd had it all dropped off on his porch. I don't even think she did it herself. It just showed up one day, like someone rang the doorbell and ran."

"At least he got it back. That's good, right?" I feel a tinge of guilt knowing that I immediately trashed everything of Tristan's that I'd had access to. Except the photos—those I shredded, then burned in my sink like I was in a fire-making challenge on *Survivor*.

"It is," Nancy agrees. "I think he almost hoped she'd keep something, though, like a souvenir of their relationship. To show that it meant anything to her. But even some of the gifts he gave her, like that very first Valentine's Day gift, were thrown in the box and sent back without a word. Then through the grapevine he hears that she said he was too toxic for her to be attached to anymore. That her reputation was in danger just by associating with him."

"That's awful."

"It broke my heart to watch him fall apart. He lost everything, Gwendolyn. But this week something's different. I think he's starting to find it again."

"Find what?" If she says 'love,' I'm going to have to jump overboard.

"Himself."

Gwendolyn

"JUST WAIT TILL he sees you," Gram says from the doorway between her bedroom and the living room.

I'm threading an earring into place—a dangling gold starfish to match the stack of rings on my index finger—and turn from the mirror to smile at her. "This old thing?" I wink, and she laughs.

"Are you still mad? That we tricked you both to get you on this trip?"

"No." I shake my head. "I was for a few days. Honestly, it felt a little manipulative. But I know I'm too stubborn to have agreed to come, had I known your plan."

"I know that, too," Gram says. She sidles up next to me at the mirror and adjusts the sparkling black jacket she's wearing over a silky turquoise shell. "I'm sorry we lied to you. But I'm also not sorry that you seem to be having a great time."

There's an odd sensation in my chest that radiates toward my fingertips. "I'm having a wonderful time. Sawyer's nice. He's different."

"I think you are, too." It's her turn to wink at me. "It's been a while since I've seen you so happy, Gwennie."

I don't want Gram to get her hopes up, so I say, "It's just one date." But in reality it's been a while since I've *felt* this happy. Here, I'm separated from the writer's block and the loneliness and the pressure to be everything people expect me to be.

There's a knock on our door, and Gram moves to answer it. I give myself a final glance in the full-length mirror and twist to make

 MEGAN BECKER

sure the back of the dress is tied evenly and that everything looks okay. When I packed this dress for formal night, I was not expecting to wear it for an actual date. But now it feels like overkill, from the near-backless design to the hint of side-boob, from the form-fitting fabric to the crimson color. I contemplate changing, but it's too late. The next knock is interrupted by a friendly greeting, and then Nancy is in our suite.

"Gwendolyn, you look absolutely gorgeous."

I thank her for the compliment, noticing the way her hands clasp together and the way her eyes take in my hair and the dress. It feels like senior prom all over again, and it's not lost on me that their phones are in their hands and not tucked away in their purses. I'm really hoping we can make it through tonight without having to pose for a hundred photos. "Thanks, Nancy. You look beautiful, too." Her black and white dress reaches just below her knees, and a row of beading trims the neckline and sleeves. She smiles.

"Sawyer sends his apologies—he wanted to pick you up himself but had an errand to run first. Want to walk down with us?"

"Sure," I answer, and that funny feeling fills my chest again. "I just need one more second." I rummage through my bag for my go-to nude lip gloss, but I can't find it. When I turn to my makeup scattered on the desk, I see one tube standing up, reach for it, and smile.

AT 5:15 EVERYTHING'S in place: red rose petals scattered on the bed, Gwen's favorite wine chilling on ice, and now, thanks to Frisma from the room service team, a tiny little snack smorgasbord with bite-size cookies and chocolate-covered strawberries and gummy bears and mini-cheesecakes will be waiting for us here in two hours.

It's too much and, somehow, not enough.

I open my wallet to tip Frisma and realize as he walks away that it is *not* enough, because there is one very important thing I've forgotten.

Which is why I send Nancy to pick up Gwen and Maggie for dinner instead of going myself, and which is why I find myself checking my watch (it's 5:24) while I stand in line at the ship's gift shop, red-faced because the two-year-old peeking over his mother's shoulder in front of me keeps pointing at the box in my hand, saying "Was-sat? Was-sat?", and because his dad has answered him back, "That's a sure sign of a good night now and a good night's sleep nine months from now, buddy."

Post-purchase, I pop into the restroom next door and fill my wallet with the foil pouches. This looks ridiculous. I should just keep two and throw the other half dozen away, but there's a finite number of these on board, and I don't want to be wasteful. A few get shoved into my jacket's inner pocket out of necessity before I throw the empty box away.

At 5:30 I'm in position, waiting near the entrance to the main dining room. I'm winded, which is only slightly attributable to the mad dash from stateroom to gift shop to bathroom to here. Mostly, it's because Gwen is descending the grand center staircase, and she's easily the most beautiful woman on this ship. It's one of those occasions where correlation *does* equal causation: she's breathtaking.

The fabric of her dress clings to each curve from her chest through her hips. Her skin peeks out on the side, and with her hair brushed in soft waves over one shoulder, all I can picture is brushing my fingertips over the skin of her neck and following the same path with my lips. I can't take my eyes off of her, and I swallow, trying to get my breathing under control. There have been a few times on this trip—last night being one of them—when we've been starved and hungry. Tonight, though, I want to savor every moment of her.

I make my way through the crowd that's gathered for photo ops along the main thoroughfare. When she spots me, her cherry-red lips part, then curl into a smile. She takes my hand for the last few stairs, and I take her in, head to toe.

"Gwen—" my voice catches in my throat.

"Hi!" She practically yells because it's so loud in here. I'd tuned out the crowd. As far as I'm concerned, it's just her and me.

I press a hand to her back and pull closer to her, leaning in to speak more privately. "You're stunning."

"Yes, we know, she's far prettier than we'll ever be," a familiar voice says. Gwen pulls back laughing, and Nan and Maggie appear at her side. Nan's waving her smartphone in my face. "So do we have time for a picture or not?"

We take a group photo, a photo of Gwen and Maggie, a photo of Nan and me, one of Maggie and Nan, and then they dictate a series of poses for Gwen and me.

"I hate to cut this short," I say, obviously lying, "but we need to be getting to dinner."

Nan and Maggie reluctantly agree, but their smiles are wide.

Gwen weaves her fingers into mine and starts following them to the main dining room, but I stay rooted in my spot. "Actually," I say, giving her arm a gentle tug. "We've got our own reservation."

"Sawyer."

The booth is small, tucked into a corner. The sunlight ricochets off the water and half blinds us, but it's something. It's private and special and has a distinctly 'date' feeling to it.

She slides into her seat and I take my place across from her. "This is beautiful," she whispers.

The words *"you're* beautiful" escape my lips before I can stop myself from sounding like a cheesy made-for-TV movie.

Gwen grins. "You look pretty good yourself." Then she folds her forearms on the table and leans toward me. "Can I tell you something?"

I gulp and nod, afraid to open my mouth in case any other proclamations are waiting just inside.

"I'm a little nervous," she says. Then, "Is that weird?"

"I am too," I answer. "So I'm inclined to say no."

"Why do you think that is? Especially after the last few days, when we've…" she pauses like she's unsure how to wrap the words in something that can be said in public, "spent time together."

I shrug, grateful for the carafe of water in front of me. I fill our glasses, thinking. "Because it's different, I guess. Hooking up is easy. This is harder."

Somehow her lipstick stays perfect even after she sips her water, and I push some off-topic thoughts from my head. "What is

    MEGAN BECKER

this, Sawyer?" she asks, using air-quotes.

A waiter arrives, buying me a few moments to plan my response. He pours us each a glass of champagne (the same good stuff we had last night), and we order the chef's recommendations from the prix fixe menu.

I raise my glass to toast hers, but she eyes me instead. "So?"

"Okay," I say. "I think *this* is… conversation. It's learning, and caring, and effort. Objectively more challenging than just ripping off your clothes."

"Then you've never tried taking off a sports bra after a hard workout." I'm relieved that she's made a joke, and she lifts her champagne. "What are we drinking to?"

There are so many things I want to say: *To us. To new beginnings. To the future.* But instead a chuckle rumbles through my chest, and I say, "To the wisdom of our elders."

Gwen's lips spread into a joyful smile. "I'll drink to that."

It's comfortable just to sit in silence with her. It's not why we're here, of course, but there's something familiar in the scene: Gwen, gazing out the window at the sun setting over the waves, the stillness, the quiet, being together. Being content. Being happy, just like this.

"Have you always been a beach person?"

She turns from the window and traces the stem of her champagne glass. "No, not really. I think I loved the idea of the beach, but we never really went as a family."

"It suits you. Like I said last night, it seems like you're just kind of… I don't know… made to be here. With the sea and the sun."

She gives another long glance toward the Atlantic and exhales. Her face is an outward expression of the same kind of at-peace feeling I had at the spa earlier today.

Our first course is delivered, and just as I'd anticipated, the servings are small but artful.

"Can I tell you something else?" She picks up her outermost

fork and lets it hover above her plate.

"Anything. Please."

"My parents always thought the beach was silly. Impractical. All of our vacations were to places with museums, if we took them at all."

"You haven't really mentioned your parents before."

She gives a half-smile, and there's so much sadness in it that I want to transport us back to that hammock with her curled up at my side, just to let her be content, and chase her down that slide again, just to let her laugh.

"We're not super close. We talk. We love each other, but they're not the most affectionate." She takes another sip of champagne. "Gram is my mom's mom. The apples fall far from the tree in our family. I'm nothing like Mom, and Mom's nothing like Gram. It's like Mom fell—the apple, of course—and rolled down a little hill, then grew into this giant tree that I fell from, but the tree was so big it towered over all the trees and so I just kind of landed back at the base of Gram. Gram's tree." She sucks in a breath and looks at me, her eyes wide. "Was that too much? Sorry."

"Don't apologize. That was a good way to describe it, I think. You're more like Maggie than your parents."

She nods, and the understanding helps her open up to share more. "My parents are brilliant. My dad's a professor of geopolitics, and my mom's an engineer. That's actually kind of the reason why Mom and I have Gram's last name. All her degrees were in the name Sophia Pierce, so when she and Dad got married she insisted on keeping her name."

"And they wanted to pass it down to you, too?"

"Yes, because Dad's last name is stupid."

"Do tell."

She shakes her head, laughter dancing in her eyes. "That's more of a fifth date conversation."

My heart leaps a little at the thought of a fifth date. "I look forward to it." She smiles and drops her gaze to her glass of champagne, and I resume the conversation before I think too much about the implication of a fifth date. "Your parents—they sound… a little intimidating. Like there are big shoes to fill."

"So you can imagine how very proud they were when their one and only offspring handed them a manuscript of a Y-A novel at the age of sixteen. Y-A means—"

"Young Adult. I know. But Gwen… sixteen? You'd written a book before you got a driver's license? That's incredible."

"I'd thought so, too. But apparently it was 'impractical' and a 'waste of a promising young mind.' They thought that if I was going to write, I should write about what they thought was meaningful: articles about capitalism or democracy. Things like that."

"Of course. The usual subject matter for a teenager."

"Exactly," she says, one side of her mouth quirking up.

"So what did you do?"

She shrugs. "I wrote another one. And then one more by the time I was twenty-five. Gram was retired at that point and kind of made it her special project to find me an agent and help me get published."

It's clear how much Maggie and Gwen love each other, and their bond was probably strengthened by Maggie's support for Gwen.

"I feel like I've been a disappointment to my parents for years. I wrote a bestseller, and that wasn't even good enough for them. Because if I was going to write, it should at least be something important."

"I'm sorry, Gwen. That sucks."

She fiddles with the ring on her finger. "It does." The hole she's chewing through her bottom lip indicates her desire to move the subject away from her parents.

"These books, though… the ones you wrote when you were younger. Would I have heard of them?"

"You might be a little old for them. But have you heard of Geri Wencep? The 'Griffin Academy' series?"

"Yeah. The books about the three friends who snuck into the all-boys school, right? With all the mythological creatures?" I take a sip of water to fight the dryness in my mouth; I want to shake the sudden flashback of the Book Brawl, as the local paper called it, out of my mind.

She sits back, nodding, and it's clear she's impressed from the way her eyes light up. "Well, that's my pen name. It's an anagram for Gwen Pierce. But those were my books." She's beaming. So much pride. "I got into romance more recently. But when I first started out I wanted to tell big, fantastic stories and create these bad-ass girls who could overcome any obstacle thrown at them. There's forever a spot in my heart for Daisy, Ashton, and—"

"Parker."

She looks at me, eyes dancing. "Parker. Yeah. Did you read them?"

"Gwen," I whisper, my voice hoarse. The room spins, and I grip the edge of the table to try to steady myself, despite my chair legs being rooted to the floor. "I lost everything because of those books."

It takes a moment, but realization crosses her face, draining the color from it. "*Shit*. Sawyer, I—I didn't—" She leans forward and places one of her hands on mine. "I'm so sorry," she says.

I'm not sure if it's because of the coincidence itself, or if it's the fact that this probably should be the worst date I've ever had *because* of that coincidence but still *isn't* the worst date I've ever had, but I start laughing. Hard. Which makes her start laughing after a healthy pause of stunned silence, and soon our main courses are in front of us and our waiter looks very concerned for our mental well-being.

"Did I tell you he broke my nose? He's trying to sue the district and make me basically unemployable because I separated him from another teacher, and he broke my nose and nothing happened to him." Suddenly this doesn't feel so funny anymore. It feels heavy and hard, and I press the heels of my palms to my eyes.

Just as suddenly, there are arms around my waist and a head against my shoulder, and a quiet voice telling me it's okay. And I know she doesn't mean 'it's going to be okay, so buck up, buddy.' She means 'it's okay to cry if you want to, so let it out; you deserve to have these emotions.'

Once I've got my breathing under control, I say, "Don't talk to Nan about this, okay? She doesn't know all the details."

"I think she knows more than you give her credit for."

I turn my head, and her big blue eyes are staring into mine. "How much did she tell you? And when?"

"A lot. When you were flirting with Gram after our massages." She loosens her grip. "Permission to speak freely?"

"Granted." I take a sip of champagne to give my mouth something to focus on other than frowning, and Gwen slides back into her seat.

"Chelsea sounds awful."

I nearly spit out my drink.

"With what she did to you after the incident, it doesn't seem like she ever really appreciated you. You deserve to be appreciated, Sawyer."

"And what about you?"

Her eyes move between mine. "What about me?"

"What do you deserve, Gwen?"

She bites her lip, and I can see so many thoughts flash across her expression. Which Gwen will win: witty Gwen? spicy Gwen? Neither: it's genu-Gwen, all warmth and kindness. "I'm still working on figuring that out," she says. "But I know one thing, Sawyer."

"What's that?"

"I appreciate you."

Gwendolyn

OF COURSE IT'S raining. Not a single part of this date is going the way Sawyer planned, and I'd feel bad for him if I wasn't having such a great time. I feel terrible knowing that he's in trouble with his school because of my books (even indirectly). I feel terrible knowing that the second part of our date was supposed to be mini-golf, and now it's closed. But I'd be lying if I said I didn't feel incredible every time he looks at me or touches me. Thus, I'm having a wonderful time.

I'm not opposed to the idea of a Netflix and chill kind of night, even if his intention is truly to sit there and watch a movie, start to finish. But before he settles on that he checks the list of on-board activities one more time.

"Are you finally going to serenade me?" I ask as we arrive at the bar. Karaoke will be over in about ten minutes, and then it'll be time for live music.

"Oooh, sadly, there's no time." Sawyer gives a theatrical shrug and searches the room for some open seats. It's packed, but there's a booth hidden around a corner and tucked away so far you can't even see the stage from it. He leans close to my ear so I can hear him. "I'll go get some drinks."

I nod and claim the table, sliding in with my back to the rest of the room. The pleather against my skin feels cold, and I feel myself shiver as goosebumps run down my arms. Sawyer arrives a few minutes later. I scoot closer to the wall to make it clear I want him next to me and not across from me, and he lowers himself onto the bench.

"You're cold," he says, already shrugging out of his jacket.

"I'm fine." I'm clearly freezing.

"Try this." He helps me into it, the backs of his fingers grazing my arms as I slip into the sleeves. "Better?"

"Mhmm. Much better. Thank you." It's the same jacket I saw folded over my desk chair a few nights ago, and my heart quickens at the thought of clothing draped over furniture.

He loosens his narrow tie and straightens it under his vest. The navy three-piece suit looks great on him, and without his jacket I can see how the vest tapers at his waist, mimicking the cut of his muscles as they descend to his hips. "I don't know how you're cold, Gwen," he says, unbuttoning the cuff of his sleeve. There's a hint of sweat at his temple as he rolls his sleeves up a few inches.

"I don't know if you noticed, but I'm wearing significantly less clothing than you."

"Trust me," he says, glancing sideways as he raises his drink to his lips. His forearm tenses, his muscles and veins on full display, and I'm afraid he's going to shatter the glass. "I noticed."

I feel my face warm under his gaze, not used to this particular brand of quietly intense attraction. I'm also giddy, because he looks hot as hell trying to keep himself from acting on anything right here, and because I know the reason he looks so strained and miserable is because he wants me. What a rush that knowledge is. I sip the drink he ordered for me and realize my mistake: I should have had him sit across from me. I want to be able to see him better, like the way his eyes keep lingering on my lips or the way his jaw clenches and unclenches every few moments.

Actually, this side view is good for watching his jaw, and for sliding my hand onto his thigh.

At this movement, every muscle tightens. I feel his thigh contract under my fingers as they skim the length of his muscle, see his arm twitch and flex and tighten again. His free hand opens and closes, then grips the table, and his pulse pounds at his temple.

"Gwen," he utters a moment later, when my lips meet the skin just behind his ear.

My eyes close and my lips are poised to kiss him again. The way he says my name is everything. I feel the fabric of his pants pull under my hand, and my muscles clench in response and anticipation. I shift my fingers just a few inches toward his lap, but his hand comes down firmly on mine. Then he throws his head back and a groan morphs to desperate laughter as he draws his free hand down his face.

"Are you trying to make me come right here?"

"Only if you can handle three times in one night."

"*Three?*" Even in the dim light of the bar, I can see the color rush to his face and his eyes go wide. "Have you—no, you know what? I don't even want to know."

When I pull my hand back and twist my fingers into his, he tenses again and downs the rest of his drink. "Did you want another?" I ask, but he shakes his head.

"The only thing I want to taste right now is you, Gwen."

Now it's my turn, for the color-rushing-to-the-cheeks thing and also for the warmth-rushing-to-other-places thing.

"Can we get out of here?" he asks. There's a new emotion in his eyes that I haven't seen before, and if the sound of his voice is any indication, I'm going to enjoy finding out what it means.

"Please." It comes out a whisper.

He stands, still holding my hand, and helps me out of the booth. I swipe my drink from the table and let him pull me through the crowded bar and to the first elevator we can find. Inside the empty car he pins me against the back wall, and the door is barely closed before he plants his lips on mine and works his tongue into my mouth. His fingers dig into the bare skin on my back.

He redirects his mouth to my throat, and my fingers grip the railing while I pant into the space above his head. I feel every inch of him against me, teasing me, making promises for the fun we're about to have, and it takes every ounce of self-control not to rip his clothes off and let him have me now.

"Sawyer. Maybe… maybe not right here?"

"Why not, baby?" he asks, and I gasp. I thought the 'baby' in Bermuda was just an act; I did *not* actually take him for a 'baby' kind of guy, but damn it, now I need him to call me nothing but 'baby' for the next two hours. And maybe again for another two after a quick power nap.

"*Sawyer.*" I sacrifice my grip on the railing behind me to snake a hand into his hair and pull back.

He breaks the connection, and his jaw drops. "Shit."

"Yeah."

He buries his head into my shoulder and hides his face. "*Shit.*"

"We've established that, *baby.*"

I feel his body shake with laughter, and he peels away to sink back against the wall next to me.

No, not the wall.

The window.

"I guess they all got quite a show," he says. He cranes his neck to view the five other glass cars. Luckily, most are stationed at much higher decks, away from us. It's quiet around here anyway, since most people are at shows or bars right about now.

"And you were worried about me and my dresses."

When the door opens on his deck, he moves at a much slower pace. Maybe it's because he's matching my much slower pace. "I should have asked, Gwen. Did you want anything from your room?"

It feels real. All the attraction and passion and desire from the evening turns into something palpable now, and it's a little intimidating.

"What would I need?" I ask, hoping he'll take the hint.

"I just thought, maybe, if there was anything you—"

"Just say it, Sawyer. Ask me the question."

His eyes scan mine and he swallows. My answer is already evident in the goosebumps on my skin, the way my fingers wind through his, the way my eyes dip to his lips. It's not a question anymore: it's a need, with all the yearning and longing I've ever wanted someone to feel for me in a moment like this. "Spend the night with me, Gwen."

My breath hitches. I'm rarely at a loss for words, but then again this man is helping me redefine myself. I nod and force out "Okay." It doesn't convey the excitement or want I feel, but I can tell from the way the corner of his mouth twitches he's more than happy with it.

He wraps a hand around mine, and I follow a step behind him to his room. He lets go just long enough to take out his cruise card and hold it against the door, but he pauses with the handle turned and the door unlatched. I let my fingers trace a line down the inside of his forearm until my hand is on his. A smile flashes in his eyes, and we push the door open together.

SAWYER

"SO WHERE DO we start?" she asks as she backs into my room. I ease the door shut and turn the deadbolt.

"I thought we could start with dessert."

Her lips part and her eyes rake over me, then she clears her throat. "Okay, yeah. Sure. Pick up where we left things downstairs." She seems nervous, and I kiss the top of her head.

"I mean actual dessert, Gwen." I nod toward the spread behind her, and she turns, taking in the platters of treats waiting for us.

I don't realize I'm holding my breath until Gwen's arms are around me and her head is pressed against me. I inhale her scent and feel her arms shift with the rise and fall of my chest.

"This is amazing." She turns and meets my eyes. "You did all this for me?" When I nod, she pulls my face to hers and plants the most urgent kiss I've ever felt on my lips. Not 'urgent' like 'take me now,' but 'urgent' like 'if I don't kiss you right now, my heart might explode.' Then she drags me over to the food and keeps one hand laced with mine as she inspects the spread. She grabs a massive chocolate-covered strawberry and moans as she takes a bite. "You have to try this," she says, holding it a few inches from my mouth.

I lean in and take a bite, steadying Gwen's hand with my own. My thumb swipes over the inside of her wrist, and I place a gentle kiss there before meeting her eyes. Gwen takes the lead by grazing her free fingertips through my hair, pushing strays off my forehead. "It's good, right?"

I'm convinced she's not talking about the strawberry anymore.

"It's incredible."

The further back her fingers crawl, the closer she draws to me. She glances at my lips, then presses hers against them. It's an eyes-open, rich-and-slow, I'm-safe-with-you kiss, made even more deep and wonderful by the fact that her free arm tucks up under mine and grips my shoulder from below as her eyes flutter shut.

If last night was raw, tonight is simmering desire. We both know where this is going. There's no need to rush it; it'll boil over eventually.

Her skin is warm when my hands find her back. She arches her shoulders back, making it easier for my fingers to slide beneath the strings that criss-cross her spine. I don't want anything between my skin and hers.

Without breaking the kiss, she's got my vest unbuttoned and is working on my shirt. "You look—so good—" she says. Her fingertips sink into my skin underneath, and when I kiss her neck she drags her nails down the length of my back. She arches again, this time pressing her hips tighter against mine. Her throat rumbles under the stroke of my thumb when she moans. "You *feel* so good, Sawyer."

"Gwen."

She doesn't say anything. It's like she can sense that I don't need her to; I just need her name in my mouth and my mouth on her skin. After she lets me press a kiss behind her ear, she pulls back, my tie wrapped around her hand. She tugs at the knot until it comes undone, then slides it off my neck and tosses it to the bed.

"This," she says, a smirk forming across her still-perfect lips, gesturing toward my now-exposed torso, "is pretty impressive. Think I should take up running?"

"This," I mimic, motioning in the same way she did, "came from strength training. You know what came from running?"

She shakes her head and bites her lip. "What's that?"

"Endurance."

Gwendolyn

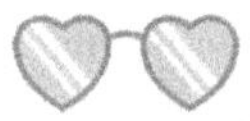

WHO KNEW? WHO knew that Sawyer Dawson could be so hot? And not just in the obvious, almost comically unfair physical sense, but, like, also in this smoldering, sexy, bedroom eyes, innuendo way.

My nerves are on fire with a singular realization: I want him.

His jacket shifts on my shoulders, and his eyes dart to the movement, then to the bare skin it's revealed. He inches closer, curls his fingers around the lapel, and slides it down my arms. As it drops to the floor, my skin prickles. It's slow and languid, the way he moves, but his eyes tell the real story: he's processing all of this as he goes, moving with intention. And I'm so tightly wound, just this look threatens to unravel me.

"Are you sure—" he starts, but I cut him off.

"Yes. One hundred percent."

"If you change your mind, Gwen, just say so."

"I won't. I've wanted this all day. But same, for you. You're allowed to say no."

He cups his hands around my face and presses his forehead to mine. His chest rises and falls with the warm breaths that play across my lips. "Baby, I've wanted this all week."

I can't wait another second for this, and I don't want him to have to wait, either. I meet his mouth and guide his hands down the sides of my upper half, from my neck to my chest to my waist and hips, then around to the tie at the base of my spine. When he fumbles with it, he turns me so I'm braced against the desk and he's behind me, trying to loosen the knot.

This man's desk is a shrine to me, from my favorite wine to my favorite snacks to a copy of my book in the corner. I catch his reflection in the mirror, see the way his brows knit, the way he bites his lip a moment before my dress loosens. Then he looks up and kisses the back of my neck while his eyes meet mine in the mirror and his hands grip my waist.

"How do you want this?" he asks.

Without a drop of irony, I bite my lip and say, "I'm an open book, Sawyer. Just read me."

There's a prologue, a gentle introduction in which he guides me back and lowers me onto the couch, whispering kisses into my neck, my shoulders, my ears. With this exposition, he reveals himself to me: first by shrugging out of his shirt and vest, then unbuckling his belt and sliding his pants down his toned legs as he stands in front of me.

Then the real story begins, because his eyes meet mine and I lean toward him. I trace the muscle of his naked thigh to the hem of his shorts, graze my fingers over the outline of his bulge. My hands are on his waistband, my eyes watching to see him spring free, and his fingers cover mine.

"Gwen," he says. I'm the protagonist, the heroine. The center of the story and the center of his attention. "You don't have to—" He cuts himself off with a gasp as I peel back the elastic and take him into my mouth, beginning a new chapter.

His knees buckle; he leans in to brace his hand against the wall behind me. "Fuck," he whispers, and my eyes meet his. "That's so good."

In our next chapter, I'm standing, facing him, re-introducing myself to him. I slide my arms out of the straps of my dress and let it fall to the floor, so it's just me and a V of black lace before him. His Adam's apple bobs and his eyes search mine, and as he drops to his knees he kisses my mouth, my breasts, the inside of each thigh, removing my underwear as he sinks to the floor.

"On the bed, Gwen. Please." His breath is warm on all the most sensitive parts of me, and I sit on the edge of the bed, lowering my back flat against the mattress. His tongue and fingers explore me, tease me, draw pleasure out of me. I'm coming undone, over and over and over again, and I need to feel the pressure of him inside me before I fall apart.

"Please—" I whimper, racked with the torment of another rush.

He stands, and his body is so visibly enjoying it that I don't understand the concern that clouds his eyes and voice. "Are you sure? We can't undo this, Gwen."

My brain does a quick recap of the week, from that first infuriating meeting to kayaking and sea turtles, from private islands and hammock snuggles to last night's laughter. I shake my head. "I don't want to undo any of it, Sawyer."

He's gripping a condom in his other hand and I take it, unwrap it, and slide it over every long inch of him. "Do you still want this?" I ask.

His answer is a kiss, and I taste myself on his lips and his tongue. Then he braces himself against the bed and eases himself into me. It's exactly the sensation I needed, and my muscles contract, coaxing him deeper.

In this story, there's plenty of character arc. Mostly, this main character's back arcs in writhing, why-didn't-we-do-this-a-week-ago pleasure as Sawyer increases the tempo and intensity of his thrusts. Maybe I'm not a book at all; maybe I'm a libretto or a score, because everything crescendos, rises and rises and never falls.

A new chapter: I roll on top of him, kissing his neck, his pecs, sinking my teeth lightly into his shoulder. He scoops my hair to one side, pulls back gently, finds my neck with his lips while he pushes up into me.

"Don't hold back, baby," he says when I bite back a scream. "I want to hear you like it."

"Mmm," I hum. "The walls—are too thin—" And I know who's in the room behind the headboard.

It's as if he sees it as a challenge, the way he lifts my hips and grinds into me. He runs a hand up my chest, caressing and kissing me, leaving my skin tingling from every point of contact with his electric touch. I gasp amorous whispers into his hair.

Each chapter of this adventure is expertly crafted. Every position brings new sensations; I'm partial to a throwback to last night, where he pins me against the wall and rocks me while my legs are wrapped around his waist and I can't control the way I beg him for more. It's from there that he carries me back to the bed, lays me down, and prepares for the most important part of the story.

The turning point is obvious—we're both ready to reach the climax.

My nerves are so incredibly sensitive that I can hardly take another minute. "No matter what, don't stop until you're there."

He brushes my hair from my face and his eyes meet mine. "Are you okay? Do you need to be finished?"

"No." I shake my head. Our chests heave against one another's and his length pulses against my thigh. "Don't stop."

They're the words I whisper as he guides himself back into me; as he dips in cautiously, watching my face with concern. They're the words I groan when he's plunging in faster, deeper; when I open myself to him and feel him fill me.

I muffle them with my arm when his hand sinks between us and he massages me with his thumb in quickening circles; when the pleasure reaches its peak and I contract around him.

"Please. Sawyer. Don't—stop—"

And we come completely undone together.

He kisses me while he finishes, and our hips rock slowly together until he peels himself away and falls to the bed beside me. I'm trying to get my heart rate down and regretting that I haven't taken up running when he snakes an arm under my neck, and we lie there for a few minutes in awkward *holy-shit-did-we-just-have-the-best-sex-of-our-lives-with-a-semi-stranger* silence until my stomach rumbles.

"You should eat something, Gwen," he says. He disappears into the bathroom and reemerges in a robe a moment later, then passes another robe to me, kisses my lips, and pours me a glass of wine.

We move his balcony chairs closer together and sit outside, snacking on sugar, stealing glances and kisses, finding ways to keep our bodies connected through our propped-up feet or our hands or mouths. The wind picks up so we head back in, tidying the discarded clothing from earlier. He's hanging my dress in his closet when I reach for his suit. I pick up the jacket and a string of condoms tumbles out onto the floor between us. Sawyer looks mortified, and I can't help but laugh.

"How many of these did you think you were going to need tonight?" I'm giddy from the wine and the high of one of the best nights in recent memory.

He tugs at the ties of my robe, drawing me closer to him. "At least one more," he says. His eyes are dark and clear; there's no joke here—he wants me again. Now.

I answer with my kiss when it meets his lips, my hands when they untie his robe, my words: "At least."

MEGAN BECKER

DAY 9

At Sea

Gwendolyn

"WHY BIRDS, GWEN?"

I'm curled up next to him, both of us still naked from last night's sex (which led to this morning's sex), our legs still tangled together. He rubs the backs of his fingers over the tattoo on my side. My fingers absently follow the grid of his abs. "Because they get to do what they want. They can build their nest anywhere. Fly away if they need to." I shrug. "They're free."

Gram wasn't necessarily the biggest fan of my tattoo (despite her encouragement for me to be sexually satisfied, she's still somewhat of a traditionalist), but with years of feeling caged by my parents' expectations, I knew I needed this symbol to remind me that I don't need to be held back by their wing-clipping words.

Sawyer shifts and wraps his arm around me, nestling me closer to him, and kisses the top of my head.

I know exactly what his tattoo looks like (being unclothed together for twelve hours tends to reveal things), and my fingers drift to that patch of skin. "Any hidden meaning here?" I ask, tracing the skin over the mountain, wave, and sun tattoo.

"Sort of. I designed it with Mom and Nan. Nan is the rock that's held us all together over the years. Mom is so gentle, so calming, so she's the water. And I'm the 'son.' So…"

"You light up their lives?" I ask, tilting my face toward his. He kisses my forehead and rests his cheek against it, smiling softly.

"That's what Nan said. It just felt weird to repeat it."

"Well. Nancy is the best. That woman deserves a medal after

having to overhear some things last night. God, I hope she had earplugs."

His face flushes. "I have it on good authority that she had a little slumber party in a friend's suite last night."

I press a hand on his chest, feeling a smile cross my face. "You really anticipated everything, huh?"

"No," he says. "I never could've anticipated how good this would feel."

"I'm sure you've had better sex than that before. Maybe. Actually, probably not. Last night… and this morning… it was—"

"I don't just mean the sex, Gwen. I mean all of it. This thing between us."

"Oh, it's a 'thing' now?" I chuckle, but he doesn't.

"Yeah." He pulls away and props himself on his elbows. "I told you, I'm not looking for a fling. You said you weren't, either."

"Well, I think I said I usually *don't* do flings. Which is true. But sometimes you find things you weren't looking for. And this was great. All three times. But realistically…"

"Fuck, Gwen." He swings his legs over the side of the bed, turning his back on me. "Fuck." Then he's pulling on his boxers, his sweatpants, his T-shirt.

I take the cue and slip into my underwear, then realize I don't have any clothes other than my formal dress with me.

"Top drawer," he says, his back still turned toward me. Inside, there's a sundress folded next to a pair of leggings and his sweatshirt, a pair of flip-flops underneath the clothing. He must have gotten all of this from Gram yesterday, somehow. I slip into the sundress.

"Thanks," I whisper. He really has anticipated everything. Except, of course, this argument I feel brewing, where he can't just let this trip be a perfect thing between us without ruining it by trying to force it into the real world.

When he turns to face me, his eyes sweep over the dress before darting to the dresser, and he seems disappointed. "I just thought we'd at least put in some effort. You owe me that much, Gwen." I recoil at the words and so does he, like they're a bomb he's thrown between us. "Look, I didn't mean—"

"I don't owe you *anything*, Sawyer. If you thought some nice dinner and wine and everything you did was some sort of deposit on a full-blown relationship with me, you're incredibly mistaken." I snatch my purse off the desk and rummage through, taking all the cash I have with me and shoving it into his hand as I push past him toward the door. "Consider my debt paid."

"You could at least *try*, you know. Regardless of what you think we should be, at least pretend to give a damn, for her sake, so she thinks you're on your way to something, before—"

"Before what?" I spin around to face him, and his face is flushed.

"Oh, come on. I'm not stupid. I saw the pills." "What pills? What the hell are you talking about?"

His eyes narrow, and his lips part. He lowers his voice. "You don't know, do you?" I cross my arms. "Shit. Forget I said anything, Gwen."

"No. Spill it, Sawyer."

He runs his hands through his hair and shakes his head, looking everywhere but my eyes.

"Never mind. I'll figure it out myself." I storm off and he follows me, objecting and apologizing the whole way to my suite. Gram's not here, so I start hunting: first her bathroom counter, then the shoe organizer hanging over the closet door, but I come up empty. I rummage through her purse; it's there that I find the pill bottles. I'm not a pharmaceutical savant, but I know these drug names.

"Gwen—"

I hold my hands up to stop him, and the pills rattle in the bottles.

"If you want to talk about it…"

I don't want to talk about it. But I'm not given a choice, because Gram and Nancy come bounding in after their breakfast.

"Oh. Sawyer, hi. What are you doing here?" Gram asks, her surprise at seeing Sawyer in her bedroom doorway evident. She leans in past him and catches me red-handed with her medication. She clears her throat and nods toward Sawyer and Nancy. "If you don't mind, I'd like to speak with my granddaughter in private."

     MEGAN BECKER

SAWYER

THE DOOR DOES little to conceal their voices. I hear the muffled arguing while I pace in the hallway just outside. Nan gnaws at her cuticles. "This isn't good," she says.

"No. None of this is good."

"I told Maggie, 'You need to tell her.' But she wouldn't listen."

I pinch the bridge of my nose. "They're stubborn. Both of them."

"And yet," Nan says, smoothing her wrinkled hand over my arm. "I imagine the two of you had a nice evening together?"

"We had a great night. Not that it matters, because she's made it abundantly clear that she's not interested in anything long-term. Not with me. And like I said, *stubborn.*"

"Oh, Sweetheart. Maybe she's right."

I halt my pacing and stare at her. "Are you serious?"

Nan shrugs and nods. "The logical thing is to end it here, have a clean break. It was fun while it lasted, but who really wants to do the long-distance thing when they get back?"

The complete one-eighty sends me reeling. "Wasn't your whole plan to help us meet and, I don't know, fall in love eventually? Isn't that why you tricked us into coming here?"

"That was the plan exactly."

"So why are you giving up, too, Nan?"

"Sawyer. Your whole life, you've wanted things to be practical. Logical. And this thing with Gwendolyn definitely isn't. Ending things now is logical. Letting this be some vacation fling is logical.

What Maggie and I did, well, it was a wild idea. We shouldn't have tried to meddle like that. It's not your thing, Sawyer, and it's not hers, either. But carrying on a long-distance relationship with someone you don't truly care about—" I open my mouth to object, but Nan holds up a finger to stop me and continues on. "Carrying on a relationship just so you can say you didn't have a fling is maybe the most illogical and impractical idea of all. Perhaps you should be content with the good times you had together and go back home tomorrow with some nice memories."

I truly don't know where all this is coming from. The words sting—an indictment on my character, a recipe for a boring and lonely future. Dating Chelsea was logical. And before her, being single was logical, too. I didn't have the time to pour into a relationship, not with getting my very practical master's degree, finding a practical job, setting up a practical future for myself.

It makes sense. My whole life, I've seen Mom and Nan—single women—making it work. Food on the table, bills paid on time, providing for me and each other. Practicality was the key to getting by. I think I was drawn to math because it was logical. The answer is always just a little bit of work away, and you can always check if you're right or not. Unlike the more subjective arts, there's no guessing, no interpretation needed. So I craved it. I wanted to have the right answers and build the stable life I'd known since I was a kid I was supposed to have one day.

And somehow, along the way, I didn't see what was underneath the surface of the way Nan's face would light up at a memory of Grandpa, or how she and Mom would laugh when telling stories about their family, or the pain in Nan's eyes when she missed him most: when I was learning how to ride a bike, when she drank her morning coffee, when Mom learned how to change the oil in her car, or when I went to prom or graduated Salutatorian. There, underneath it all, was deep, unrelenting love. The joy and pain of feeling something so strong it breaks you in all the best and worst

    MEGAN BECKER

ways, over and over again, even long after the person is gone.

I know I haven't known Gwen long, but that breaking feeling is happening already, and she's only on the other side of the door. "I don't want logic, Nan." I sink back against the wall and slide to the floor, ready to wait it out for as long as it takes. "I want *her.*"

She looks down at me and smiles with a wink. "It's about time you figured that out."

It's been an hour, and I can still hear their muffled arguments through the door. Nan went back to her room a while ago to rest her legs, leaving clear instructions that she is to be contacted as soon as the door opens to offer moral support, for whomever it's needed.

Then things quiet, with hushed bursts that no longer sound angry. One voice grows louder and clearer, and I make it to my feet as the door opens in front of me. Maggie stands in the doorway, her face shrouded in so much sadness I want to hug her.

"Hi, Sawyer," she says, emerging into the hallway and easing the door closed behind her.

"I feel awful, Maggie. I didn't realize—"

She cuts me off. "No. I should have told her months ago. You couldn't have known." Then there's pity in her eyes when she pats my hand and says, "I'm sorry, though. I think she just wants some time alone right now."

"Yeah," I sigh. It makes sense, but I don't want to leave her alone after having the conversation I know she just had. "Nan is down in her room, if you *don't* want some time alone."

"And what about you?" Her eyes are red and watery, but her

lips quirk up when I lower myself onto the floor again.

"I'm not going anywhere."

          MEGAN BECKER

Gwendolyn

EVERYTHING HURTS.

Everything's wrong.

Everything has imploded spectacularly.

Nothing is okay, and nothing is going to be okay.

This is my new mantra. The thoughts have repeated themselves for hours, jumping around every recess of my brain like they're the main feature in a game of Pong.

It's well past noon, and I haven't eaten anything. My head is reeling and I feel like I could be sick, but my rumbling stomach is not helping things feel any better. I swipe my cruise card from the desk, grab my phone, and open the door.

"What are you doing here?" It comes out harsher than I mean it to, but we'll blame that on the surprise of seeing Sawyer sitting on the floor just outside my room.

He scrambles to his feet, brushing off the back of his sweatpants. "I'm so sorry about earlier. I—"

"Stop. Please." I hold up a hand, and to his credit he listens. "I don't have the energy to do this right now, okay? I just need to get something to eat."

"I figured." He checks his phone before pocketing it. "Food should be here in less than five minutes." My mouth opens, but I can't find the words to say. But then he speaks, and I don't need to. "Listen. If you want someone to talk to, I'm here. If you want me to go away, I'll leave. If you aren't sure what you want, I'll sit back down right here until you figure it out."

I retreat a few steps, the proximity overwhelming. "I—I don't know. I don't know anything right now."

"No one expects you to. You've been through a lot today."

The tears are hot behind my eyes; I didn't even know I had any left in there. The past few hours I've cried angry tears, sad tears, exhausted tears, and I'm not even sure what kind these are that threaten to spill out of me.

Sawyer stands in front of me, shifting his weight, scanning my face before looking away, letting me have privacy with this torrent of emotions. Then there's a box of pizza in his hands, a five-dollar bill slipped to the person who placed it there. He sidesteps me into the room and sets the box on the desk, moving to leave, to be unobtrusive. His shoulders slump and his head hangs, and he seems so small again all of a sudden, like he did earlier in this trip. And I hate seeing him go back there.

"Hey."

He pivots toward me.

"You don't expect me to eat all of this by myself, do you?" I offer what I can, which is probably a hint of a wildly unconvincing smile.

"I do, actually," he says, and I wince at the words.

"Oh. Okay, I—" I messed it all up. I pushed him away. I ruined everything. The thoughts race through my head, but the words I could say to try to fix it get lost in my throat.

Sawyer reads me and his eyes go wide. "No! Sorry, I didn't mean…" He shakes his head and rolls his eyes. "It's just that, it's disgusting, this fruit-covered thing you call a pizza."

Then everything I've been holding back comes pouring out of me. All the heartache, all the unknowing, all the hurt. First it's laughing, then it's sobbing, and then Sawyer's arms are around me and his chin rests on my head. "I'm getting your shirt all snotty."

"I'll borrow one of yours. It's only fair."

I squeeze him tighter and burrow into his chest. "Why are you being nice to me right now?"

He tenses, then relaxes his grip on me and looks down. He smooths some flyaways behind my ears and turns up the corners of his mouth, though his eyes are all sadness. "I'm not being all that nice. I think you're delusional. You probably need to eat something to help you snap back to reality."

"Okay, fine." I shrug out of his embrace. "I'll go eat my incredible pizza all by myself." Sawyer takes a step backward toward the door, but I reach for his hand. "Not *by myself*. I mean, I want you to stay. If you want to."

"Of course," he says. I don't let go of his hand until we're on the couch, and even then I take the middle seat next to him. It feels better with him here. Not good by any stretch of the imagination. But not as shitty.

The pizza smells delicious, and I feel Sawyer's eyes on me while I devour the first slice. Not in a judgy way, just observing. I'm halfway through my second slice when his stomach growls, and I nudge the box toward him. "Please. Eat some of this."

He wrinkles his nose and leans in, picking up a slice and picking off the pineapple. "Thanks," he whispers, taking a bite.

"This was really sweet of you. Thank you."

He continues to chew, staring at his shoes. "No problem." At first I welcomed the quiet, but now it's awkward, like he's intentionally avoiding talking to me or even looking at me.

"I, uh… I'm not used to people going out of their way to do nice things for me, other than Gram." Even saying her name feels like a dagger to the heart, and I press the heels of my hands to my eyes. "I'm going to be completely alone."

He scoops me close to him before the tears fall; I look ridiculous, squished against him, sobbing, with an uneaten pizza crust in my hand. "You're not alone."

"I will be. She only has a few months left. A year, maybe. And then—" Gram's always been my biggest cheerleader. She's fought for me and given me my career. She's been my best friend for more than a decade, and I'm racked with grief at the thought of life without her.

"You still have your parents." He rubs my arm.

"Are you kidding? They're off doing their own things. I don't even know if they know the title of my last book."

"You have your friends." He pulls me closer.

"I don't have friends. I have acquaintances."

"Am I not your friend?"

I search his eyes. I don't know what we are, frankly, and I want a clue from him.

"You have me, Gwen. If you want me."

That's it: the magic words, like a hypnotist's phrase to put me in the same trance I was in last night, an outright admission. I twist, curling my arms around him, and find his lips with mine. He returns the kiss, hesitantly at first, then deeply and fully.

"We shouldn't do this," he says. Our lips part briefly, but then I'm back against him again.

"We should," I answer, as my hand reaches to cup him between his legs. "I need to feel close to you."

He winces when I make contact, finishing a long kiss, pulling my hand off of him. "Not like this, baby."

There's that 'baby' again, and it drives me completely wild for him. "Why not? I need you, Sawyer. Let's go back to your room, okay? We can be alone, and you can just make all this go away for a little." I lunge toward his lips again, but he flinches away and keeps me at arm's length.

"Gwen, stop." He raises his voice just enough to let me know he means it. "I am here to listen, or to talk, or to sit in silence if that's what you need. But I am not going to let you use me just to numb the pain. That's not good for either of us."

It's awkward. More than that—it's humiliating—sitting here with him stiff-arming me. He's supposed to want this, too. "Why

     MEGAN BECKER

did you even come here?"

"I told you, I wanted to be here in case you needed anything."

"What I need is a distraction, Sawyer."

"Okay. So let's go play mini-golf, or get coffee, or watch the belly-flop competition. Those are all distractions."

"You know what I mean. I need to be with you. You said I have you if I want you, and right now I really, really do."

He lowers the hand that holds mine and interlocks our fingers together, examining them as he rubs his knit brows. His expression softens with worry when he speaks. "I'm sorry that you're going through so much. I want to help, Gwen. I really do. But this casual, meaningless thing is the one thing I can't give to you." He deposits my hand on my own knee and rises, heading for the door.

"So that's it? You're leaving me, too?" The angry tears are back, a byproduct of the furor in my chest. "I need one thing from you, Sawyer. One. Little. Thing. And instead, you're bailing on me. Just like everyone else." I march after him, but he spins around, facing me.

"Let's be very clear about one thing, Gwendolyn." The sudden use of my full name startles me. It sounds cold and distant, not at all matching what comes next. "I'm not bailing on *you*. I'm bailing on this terrible idea. What you're asking for is not some insignificant thing. And if you weren't so damn stubborn, I would give you so much more." He looks down at me with brown, puddly eyes.

"Just—go." I gesture toward the door, and he dips his head before trudging to it and down the hall.

MAGGIE AND NAN find me on the pool deck, two drinks into an incomplete workout, and slide into the cushioned seats around me. Silently we watch the waves rise and fall, like we're parents watching a sleeping newborn's chest.

Finally, someone speaks. "I'm so sorry, Sawyer. This is all my fault." It's Maggie, her eyes sincere, her expression soft.

"It's not, Maggie."

"Why would you say such a thing?" Nan asks. Her eyes brim with tears.

"I should have told her. Months ago, I should have told her. And I shouldn't have lied to her about this trip, or about you, Sawyer." She shakes her head and purses her lips. "I really screwed up. And I'm sorry."

Nan's hand glides across Maggie's back, and her eyes flit from her friend to me and back.

"You don't have to apologize for anything, Maggie. You were just doing what felt right to you. There's no handbook for any of this."

She tilts her head my way. "If there was, dear, I'm pretty sure it would say in bold letters, 'Do not use a vacation to trick your granddaughter into meeting a man you want her to like.'" She offers a pitying smile and rests her hand on my knee. "This wasn't fair to her. Or to you. And I feel badly that she is refusing to spend time with you."

I set my hand on Maggie's. "Respectfully, I think there's just one person she wants to spend her time with right now."

Maggie inhales, slow and deep, and lets the breath *whoosh* out. "Would you mind terribly if I asked you both to come with me?"

"Not at all," Nan says.

Nothing is going to make Gwen want to see me, but I'm hoping a fresh latte will at least make my presence suck less. I get a head start and meet up with Nan and Maggie just outside the suite door.

"You ready?" Nan asks, and I can see the white ovals on her arm that halo Maggie's fingertips. Maggie holds her breath, nods, and opens the door.

Gwen pivots in her seat at her desk and turns away quickly. Her face is flushed, her hair is piled messily on her head, and she's wearing an oversized cardigan layered over the T-shirt and leggings she changed into since lunch. Most notably, her laptop is open, and her fingers are still curled over the home row, faint tapping audible as we file into the room.

"We should talk, Gwennie."

"*We* should," she says, her finger moving back and forth between herself and Maggie.

"Gwendolyn Pierce."

Nan stiffens, but Maggie's tone doesn't match the admonishing full-name usage. It's gentle, broken, pleading.

Gwen finishes her typing and closes the laptop, then turns fully toward us. "I'm not sure there's much left to say, Gram."

Maggie motions for us to sit on the couch, then lowers herself into the armchair and bends toward Gwen. "There's so much to say, darling. And I think that's the problem, isn't it?" Gwen's breath catches. Maggie's found Gwen's greatest concern: that their time of sharing, of going to her grandmother with her dreams and fears and mundane Tuesday stories is coming to an end. "I'm still here, Gwennie. We all are."

I set the latte on the coffee table. It's a peace offering, and she looks from it to me, then to Nan, then back to the latte. She bites her lip and crosses her legs, wiggling her dangling foot. "I hate that you didn't tell me, Gram."

"I know. It wasn't fair for me to keep it from you."

"No—" she presses the back of her hand just under her nose and shakes her head. "I hate that you didn't tell me, because I hate that you've been dealing with this on your own. I could have been there for you. I—"

"Gwen. Honey." Maggie's eyes meet Nan's, and they share a smile. "I haven't been dealing with this on my own. I'm lucky enough to have had the support of a very good friend over the past few months."

"My husband was given the same diagnosis. And although he passed before Sawyer was born, I remember it like it was yesterday."

Gwen's eyes move between the two women, then to me. I shake my head to convey that I haven't been keeping this from her. Her expression softens, and Maggie reaches to take her hand. "That's what I want for you, too. For you to have someone to lean on. To talk to. To yell at, if you need it. That's why we're all here right now. Nancy has been that person for me, and we all want to be that person for you."

"I know." Her voice is barely a whisper, and unborn tears cling to her eyes. "But right now, I just need you, Gram."

Gwendolyn

WE TALK THROUGH it all. Again. Calmly this time, over snacks and the coffee that Sawyer brought for me. And then we talk through a plan for tomorrow: Gram calls Nancy to make sure the plan will work within their schedule, and I cash in some points for two rooms at a hotel with views of the Hudson. An extra day to connect and relax together, since today was a bit of a bust, will be the right way to end this trip.

Once the plan is final and the rooms are booked, Gram raises her eyebrows at me. "Nancy's under strict orders not to tell him."

"Good." I want all of this to be a surprise. I want tomorrow to be like last night's dessert smorgasbord: unexpected and thoughtful. I want to see him smile and know that I'm the reason why.

She tries to play it cool, but her dancing eyebrows betray her. "We haven't even gotten to talk about the fact that you weren't here last night and this morning."

"I think that's all we need to say about that topic, actually."

"Gwen. It's okay to like him. It's okay to let him in." Her expression shifts, and a hint of laughter dances in her eyes. "Emotionally, I mean."

I squish my hands over my ears. "La, la, la! I can't hear you!" I sing, and Gram swats my arm playfully.

"Okay, okay," Gram chuckles. "Would you go see him, please? Put him out of his misery." She kisses my forehead, and I head down the hall and down the stairs toward Sawyer's room, ready to apologize for what happened this afternoon.

Oh God, this afternoon. It was definitely not my best moment, begging him to sleep with me, kicking him out when he said no. Because he should have said no. I'm honestly so glad he said no.

He answers before I finish knocking.

"Hey," he says, standing in the doorway with his arms folded across his torso. He looks so casually cool, like it's perfectly normal to be waiting by the door.

"Hi." My throat goes dry. "Can we talk?"

"Yeah, of course." He digs his toe into the carpet, looks down, then up. "What's up?"

"Can I—" I ask, gesturing into the room. He slides to the side to allow me in but stays close to the door once he's shut it. "Thanks. I promise, I will keep my hands to myself." It doesn't draw the grin I hope for, so I clear my throat and continue. "Look, Sawyer. About earlier—"

He waves off the comment. "We really don't need to talk about it."

"Yes, we do."

"Gwen." He takes a tentative step toward me, relaxing his arms, rubbing the back of his neck. "I cannot begin to imagine what you're going through. And I can't tell you the right way to grieve or process all of your emotions." Another step closer, and I can see the pain in the creases of his forehead. "All I *can* do is point out what's right in front of you, and that's me. To fight for you and alongside you and maybe with you, if that's what you need. In calm seas and stormy, to laugh and listen and cry. I can give you all of that. I just can't give you what you asked for earlier, for so many reasons."

"I know."

He stops, his jaw loosened, his brows furrowed. "You do?"

I nod. "I wanted to thank you, actually. For not letting things happen earlier." He's watching me now, waiting to see if that was his cue or if there's more. "It would have been a mistake. And you knew that, even when I didn't. Or at least, when I didn't care."

"To be clear, Gwen, I don't view last night as a mistake."

"Neither do I. But this afternoon… that would've been."

He nods, and his shoulders hunch forward.

"Don't do that. Please."

"Don't do what?" he asks, his brow knitted.

"Don't shrink away."

He looks at me like I'm crazy. "What?"

"You've done it a few times on this trip, where you kind of… I don't know, disappear into yourself, make yourself smaller. And I know there's a lot behind it, like being tall and the whole school incident, but you shouldn't do it. You deserve to be you and not feel like you have to hide."

I take a deep breath. For some reason it's so easy to compliment strangers, but so challenging to heap praise onto the people we care most about. I didn't get a lot of it growing up, so maybe I just never learned how. But regardless, he deserves to stand tall in the truth of how I view him.

"You're not a distraction, Sawyer." When his eyes meet mine, I see nervousness and yearning, and I want to wrap him in my arms. "You're one of the kindest people I've ever met. What you've done for me this week—what you've done for me *today*—I shouldn't have tried to reduce you to something so small, because the truth is, you're so much more than that. And I'm sorry for not saying all that earlier."

He straightens. "That might be the best apology I've ever heard." His mouth quirks up on one side, and he asks. "You some kind of writer or something?"

"I don't mean to brag, but I'm pretty good with words. I've even been called a dictionary before." I feel myself drift toward him, and the distance between us closes from both sides. It feels dangerous, the way his grin fades when he licks his lips and looks at mine.

SHIP MATES   245

He cups his hand around my jaw, his thumb grazing my cheek. I snake my arms around his waist, and he tilts his face down, pressing his forehead to mine, clenching his jaw. I try to read his eyes, but his face contorts with how hard he's trying to keep them closed. I've been there: on the precipice of something so monumental that if you keep your eyes open you have to own the truth, but if you squeeze your lids shut you can live in a daydream, like everything is okay and you get exactly what you need. I don't realize my own eyes have closed until I feel Sawyer's lips on my forehead, and it snaps me out of a vision of his mouth crashing into mine.

"So there's a second reason why I came down here." I snuggle my head into his chest, and his Adam's apple bobs.

"What's that?" he whispers, and I can't tell if it's hope or hesitation in his voice.

"I'm cordially inviting you back to our suite for the evening." He drops his arms and I drop mine, taking one step back to his two. "Nancy's coming over, too, and we're just going to play some games and have a slumber party, sort of. And I know it's not the most exciting way to spend your last night on the ship, but—"

"I'll be there," he says. "If that's truly what you want."

"It is. Yes."

"Alright then. I'm in."

A SLEEPOVER WITH my grandmother, the woman I'm falling for (and slept with last night), and her grandmother. This could be interesting.

Nan sits at the edge of my bed as I start packing my suitcase. I want to be as ready as possible for tomorrow morning's disembarkation, so I'm packing everything but what I'll need tonight and first thing tomorrow, which is basically just what I'm wearing now and a clean change of clothes, plus my toothbrush and toothpaste.

"Have you had a good trip, dear?" Nan asks.

"I've had a great trip. You?"

"It's been lovely, all things considered." She scoots sideways to make room for me to lay my garment bag next to her. "I'm so sorry about today."

I open the closet to grab my suit, and Gwen's dress from last night is still hanging there. My breath hitches, and Nan notices.

"Well." I can hear her smirk in her voice. "At least the day started out okay."

It did. And it went downhill quickly. And I don't know what to do about yet another thing in my life. "It's definitely been a bit of a roller coaster."

"So, what's next for you two?" She rises, begins tidying up the coffee table and the desktop, her hand hovering and recoiling when she gets to the pile of condoms that's still sitting there from this morning. Those can go to the bottom of the suitcase—there's definitely no need for those tonight.

"I don't think there is a 'next' for us, Nan." Sure, Gwen apologized for the incident earlier this afternoon, but she still hasn't expressed a desire to pursue anything beyond this week. "We're very different people who want very different things."

She laughs and waves me off when I ask what's so funny. "I think you want the same thing, dear. And you might do different things, but deep down, you have similar motivations. You're both funny, and smart, and you're both fighters, Sawyer. That's why I'm not sure why you're not fighting for a 'next' with Gwendolyn."

"Fighting is what got me here, Nan."

"And thank God you're here." Her tone changes, and she regards me sternly for the first time in a long time. "Sawyer Victor Dawson, enough with the whining. You did what you did, and it was the right thing to do. Everyone knows it. And that girl." She shakes her head. "That girl was an idiot, and she didn't make you happy. This past week I've seen things in you I haven't seen since you were setting up your first classroom. Passion. Joy. A real, honest-to-goodness smile."

"Nan—"

"No." She steps toward me, grips my elbows in her wrinkled hands, and locks her eyes on mine. "You told me this morning you want this woman. So why are you giving up already? Are you going to bail on your marathon as soon as it feels hard?"

"That's different. Gwen was very clear with what she wants, and it's not me. I want to respect that."

"Or maybe it *is* you, and you're not listening to what she needs you to be for her right now."

A *distraction*. A *mistake*. I can't get the words out of my head. And even though she apologized, even though she said so much more than that, all I hear is the rejection sandwiched between those words. It's what she needed me to be, and what I would have been, and I don't know how to be what she needs without her seeing me as some epic error—a chapter that needs to be cut from her story.

Nan picks up Gwen's book from my desk. It's got a sticker denoting that it's a part of the ship's library, and the bookmark is lodged at about the halfway point. "Were you planning to finish this?" she asks.

I'm actually on my third read-through since I discovered it in the library days ago. But the question feels loaded. "No." I take the book from her, turning it over in my hands. "I don't really want the story to end."

Gwendolyn

I SNIFFLE, WILLING myself not to cry. Not again. What started as laughter threatens to spill over into weeping, because I'm going to miss Gram's jokes. But tonight I don't have to miss them. Tonight she's here, her plate full of a sampling of the ridiculous number of desserts room service delivered half an hour ago, cracking up over her ridiculous puns. I finish a cookie that Sawyer had passed me, left over from last night, and catch him looking at me from across our little circle. He looks away quickly, but I keep staring until he turns back.

It should be awkward, the way we just examine each other like this. This unbroken eye contact and the soft shake of his head and his gentle half smile—it should all feel strange after this afternoon. But it's not awkward. In fact, it's almost lovely, the way we can be adults and deal with the weird thing that happened and communicate about it. Apologies accepted. We're moving on. I just don't know what that looks like for us.

"More Phase Ten?" Gram asks, and we answer with a chorus of groans.

"More wine?" Sawyer asks, and Nancy and I thrust our near-empty glasses toward him. He refills each, finishing off the bottle before he can top off his own, and raises his glass for a toast. "Here's to our last night of vacation."

Gram and Nancy exchange glances, then shift their eyes to me. Subtlety is not an area where they excel.

"What's with the eyes? What are you doing?" Sawyer's cheeks

     MEGAN BECKER

are pink, probably more from the heat in here and less from the wine, because Gram's been cold a lot recently and has the heat turned on in our suite.

"You didn't tell him yet?" Nancy whispers, completely audible to everyone in the room, and this I *will* attribute to the wine.

"Tell me what?"

Gram rests a hand on mine but looks at Nancy and yawns theatrically. "Oh my, I'm getting so tired. Nancy, don't you think we should get ready for bed?"

"Oh. Yes, I—" Nancy stretches, sloshing some wine over the side of her glass, and covers a fake yawn. "I do think we should begin getting ready. Why don't you kids go explore and let these old ladies get some sleep."

"I'll get this," I tell Gram as she stands to tidy up. I pull her in for a hug and hold her longer than normal. "Night, Gram. Night, Nancy." They retreat to the bedroom of the suite, where they've asked our room steward to separate the king bed into two twins tonight, and suddenly I'm alone with Sawyer. I feel his eyes on me while we clean up from dessert.

"So, are you going to tell me what that was all about?"

"Yes." I'm surprised by the fluttering in my stomach. I'm not normally a butterflies kind of person, but looking at Sawyer, knowing what I'm about to tell him… Flutter, flutter, flutter. "Can we go for a walk?"

"Yeah. Sure." He slips into his sneakers and waits while I look for an extra layer, but I've packed up a lot of my things already and can only find my heavy sherpa.

"Here," he says, pulling his old sweatshirt from his backpack and extending it to me. "It's yours, if you want it." It's this gesture that kicks the butterflies into overdrive, because it doesn't feel like he's just offering a sweatshirt. This is part of him. It smells like him, it's warm like him. His alma mater's logo is fading from the front. He's offering me himself, piece by piece, and I want to take it all.

He opens the door once I've pulled on the sweatshirt, and I slide my cruise card into the side pocket of my leggings. "Where to?" he asks, and we head upstairs so we can walk outside. It's a nice enough night, with a clear sky that makes it chilly but showcases thousands of stars.

We're nearly alone up here, and we're halfway through a lap around the deck when Sawyer breaks the silence. "So." He buries his hands in the pockets of his sweatpants and watches his feet. "You wanted to tell me something?"

I nod, though he's not looking over at me. It feels like the butterflies are climbing my throat, like speaking without nervous vomiting is about to be the greatest challenge of my life.

"Gwen? Are you okay?" He's stopped two steps ahead of me, and I realize that I stopped first. He steps to the side to allow another couple to pass us, nodding a greeting as they go around. *Another couple.* Is that what we are? A couple? Is that what we could be?

"I, um—" There's a tiny chip in my polish on my toenails. I didn't notice it until right now, and it's suddenly the only thing I can look at. It's safe to look down there.

"Gwen." His voice is like a blanket, all warm as it wraps around me. God, I love the way he says my name. I want his lips to breathe it like this forever, this gentle, *it's okay* tone, the care embedded in that one syllable.

I shake my head. "I have no right to ask you this." When I turn, ready to walk away and bail on everything tomorrow, he reaches for my hand and weaves his fingers into mine.

"Talk to me. Please."

I take a deep, shaky breath and find courage in the fact that he's still holding on, still here, asking me for more. "I wanted to take you on a date." There. The bandage is ripped off, and I lift my gaze to meet his.

Surprisingly, he's smiling. "You want to take me on a date?" he repeats.

"Mhmm." I nod. "Tomorrow. In New York."

Sawyer crinkles his nose. "I'm not sure that's a good idea."

This is not how I saw this going. This is not the reaction I had expected. "I'm sorry?" I pull my hand away and wrap my arms around my waist, holding myself together. I can handle rejection, but it's hard when it comes from a person I really don't want to reject me.

"You don't have to take me on some pity date, Gwen." He retreats to the glass half-wall that runs the perimeter of the deck and props his forearms on the railing. I follow him, annoyed.

"It's not a pity date."

"Then what would you call it?"

"I'd call it a date. Can't I just take you out because I want to?" I narrow my eyes at him, challenging him to push back again.

He traces lines along the metal rail. "I heard you this morning, loud and clear. We're looking for different things, and I'm fine with that."

"What if we're not, though?"

His fingers stop and he raises his gaze to meet mine. "What?"

"What if… what if I don't know what I'm looking for, but I still see you? And what if I know I really like you and want to see more of you?"

Earlier, his words were the key to unlocking my need for him. Now, my words seem to be that key for Sawyer. He steps toward me, draws my face to his, knots his fingers in wind-blown strands of hair, and kisses me. Ferociously, feverishly, he kisses me. Again and again, deeply, with sunburnt lips and dessert-stained breath and his soft tongue that tangles with mine.

"I can't promise you anything, Sawyer," I say, coming up for air.

"Just promise me you'll try." There's hope there, in the gravel in his voice, the rise and fall of his chest, the way he brushes wild strands of hair back from my face.

When I nod and whisper "yes," a grin spreads across his face, reaching all the way to his eyes. My back's against the railing, with his arm drawing us together as our lips collide again. And everything about this feels right: the way my heart and head feel so much lighter than they did this afternoon; the way he holds me like I'm his favorite thing and he can't bear to let me go; the way my body melts into his.

He's growing hard against me, his sweatpants offering little in the way of disguising the feel of him, or— yeah, no, they're not disguising the look of him, either.

I nibble at his lip, giggling. "This is a family-friendly vessel, sir."

"Aye, aye, Captain." He pulls his hips back, bending forward, and rests his head on my shoulders. "I am at the ready." His body shakes with answering laughter, and I collapse into one of the chaises beside us. He sinks into the neighboring chair and tugs his sweatshirt down over his groin.

"That was really excellent wordplay, Sawyer."

"You should hear what I was going to say about seamen," he deadpans, and suddenly we're howling. Tears stream down my face, and I even snort once, which causes him to crack up even more. When it finally dies down, he reaches across the space between our chairs and holds my hand again. His fingers are warm between mine, and his thumb draws gentle circles on my skin.

For a while, he doesn't say anything. He just looks at the stars, but my eyes are set on him. Finally he swallows and says into the perfect night air, "There are so many fish in the sea, but I think you're the most fin-tastic."

"That was an ex-squid-sit joke. Whaley, whaley good."

He flashes me a half-smile, stars reflected in the dark pools of his eyes. "What you said last night at dinner… that your parents feel that if you're going to write, it should be something important."

The complete change in subject catches me off guard. "Yeah?"

     MEGAN BECKER

is all I can manage to say, unsure where he's going with this.

"They're wrong. Romance *is* important. Giving people that outlet to feel happy matters. Being able to make people experience joy from words on a page is a gift. You're incredibly talented, Gwen."

If I had a pen in my hand, I could string together flowing prose and flowery language, fragrant with meaning and appreciation, a bouquet of gratitude too large to hold. But it's just me, out of my element, out here with someone who matters to me, who's praising my work, and I barely manage a "thanks."

"Should we head back?"

I could ask for a detour to his room. Could ask for another encore of last night and this morning. I'm trying, he knows it, and I'm sure we both want to. Instead, I bob my head once and walk back to the suite with his arm wrapped around me, and it feels equally intimate.

We brush our teeth side by side, and by the time I'm finished getting ready for bed he's got the sofa bed opened for me and is trying to make himself comfortable in one of the chairs, his hoodie and T-shirt folded neatly on the other.

"You can share with me," I whisper.

"I definitely should not," he growls, his voice low so our grandmas don't hear, and I feel myself blush.

"Can you sit with me at least, for a little?"

He looks at the bed, then at me, then back at the crisp white sheets. He lowers himself into the corner of the bed on top of the blanket, and I don't know which one of us he doesn't trust enough to allow himself to slip under the covers. It's probably me, biting my lip, staring at his tanned chest as I crawl toward him. He drapes an arm over the back of the couch: an invitation to curl up next to him, and I RSVP a very obvious *yes*.

His heart beats a steady rhythm under my ear, its pace quickening slightly before slowing again once I'm snuggled next to him.

"If you're too hot like this—"

"No," he says. "It's perfect."

And we stay like this for a while, wordless and wonderful, my fingers gliding across the hard plane of his torso, his fingers sliding in smooth strokes up and down my arm.

Earlier, I was fine. But earlier, I had distractions. I had dinner and games and a romantic stroll under the stars and a chorus of crashing waves to distract me. But I haven't figured out how to handle the stillness, and now it all washes over me again. It comes in waves, flooding my senses. Grief is a bitch. Sawyer wraps both arms around me and rests his chin on my head, and for the second time today I'm crying into him.

"It's okay. Let it out."

I do. I let it all come pouring out of me. Even the part that's the hardest to say. "I'm so scared of being alone."

His arms tighten around me, and I feel his Adam's apple bob. "You're not alone. You don't need to be." He pulls back and tucks my hair behind my ear, then guides my face to look up into his. "I know it's not the same, Gwen, and no one could ever replace her, but you've got me, and I'm not going anywhere."

Maybe my fears about being alone aren't the hardest part to admit. Maybe it's what lurks beneath, the reason why I feel so alone outside of my relationship with Gram. "What if I disappoint you, too? What if I'm not enough for you?"

"That could never happen," he whispers.

"You say that now, but—"

"Baby, trust me on this." He cuts me off, his voice gently firm. "I really like you, Gwen. Exactly how you are. And as long as you're you, that's enough for me."

It's all he says, and it's everything I've ever wanted to hear.

DAY 10
Disembarkation

MEGAN BECKER

Gwendolyn

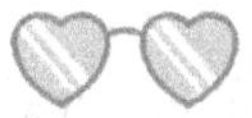

"RISE AND SHINE, Sleepyheads."

Sunlight streams through the open curtains, and outside there's a bustle of activity that confirms we're docked and the crew is working diligently to prepare for the next sailing in just a few hours.

I stretch, expecting to feel Sawyer behind me, but I see him shifting on the floor next to the sofa bed instead, squinting up beneath a messy mop of hair, reaching up to the seat of the chair on his other side for his sweatshirt as he swipes the back of his hand across his mouth.

Gram and Nancy stand just inside the doorway, each one holding a to-go coffee cup, a muffin in Gram's spare hand and a banana and foil-wrapped breakfast sandwich in Nancy's.

"Sleep well?" Nancy asks, setting Sawyer's breakfast on the desk.

He sits up and zips his sweatshirt. "Sure," he answers through a yawn.

Gram hands my breakfast to me. "Well, we disembark in forty-five minutes, so time to get up, eat up, and pack up." Then she and Nancy disappear again, heading off to who knows where.

"You didn't have to sleep down there," I tell Sawyer, standing to fold the sofa bed back into couch form like it's a soft Transformer. Actually, it's about as hard as I'd expect Optimus Prime to be.

"It's fine," he says, replacing the cushions.

"You looked super comfy."

He arches a brow and smirks. "It would have been more uncomfortable to stay in bed with you and have them hear or see something we didn't want them to see or hear."

"Touché." I take a sip of coffee and plop onto the couch. "It's date day today."

"So I've been told." He unwraps his breakfast sandwich and takes a bite. "Any big plans?"

I shrug. "A few plans. I don't know that any are 'big,' necessarily. Just normal-sized plans." In reality, I have big ideas, but very few actual plans, because it took half an hour on the ship's WiFi to book the hotel rooms for tonight, and I didn't want to press my luck with anything else. But now that we're docked, I need to get to work on solidifying details.

"You know I don't need anything, right? Just spending the day together is enough." *As long as you're you, that's enough for me.*

"I know," I answer. I know.

     MEGAN BECKER

WHAT A WHIRLWIND. For not having any big plans, Gwen has definitely planned a lot. First we navigated to our hotel, a little boutique not too far from Times Square with views of the Hudson. We helped Maggie and Nan to their room, then wheeled the luggage cart to our room four doors down.

"You're sure you don't want to share with Maggie?"

She set her overnight bag on the ottoman. "I'm sure. Tonight I'm sharing with you." It felt pointed and suggestive and very, very sexy.

Sexy like the familiar silver dress she slipped into after we'd spent the day with our grandmothers. First there were mimosas in the hotel lobby, then there was lunch at a place a friend of a friend of Gwen's owns down on Leonard Street in Tribeca, after which we played another three rounds of cards.

Sexy like her kiss on the elevator ride down to the lobby, ready to begin our evening together.

Sexy like a wink and red lips curling around a champagne flute at dinner, like a hand on my thigh and a head on my shoulder at a show. Like a hand slipped into mine while she talks to another fan who's recognized her on our way out of the theater.

She pulls me into a late-night bakery, just a few doors down. "This place has the best apple fritters in all of New York." She inhales the scent of vanilla and cinnamon and shimmies her shoulders. "Doesn't it smell incredible in here?"

"It does." She tells me a few of her favorites while we wait in line, and when it's our turn we put in a comically large order.

"Gram will murder me if she finds out I came here without bringing her back a scone," she says. She takes my hand and leads me to a table in the corner, just inside the front window. Between bites of late-night snacks and a cup of coffee that we're apparently sharing, we play the people-watching game again. It takes me back to one of those first days with Gwen. Really, to the day that everything changed for me.

"So that couple there—the lady in the purple coat." I spot who she's talking about on the sidewalk outside, walking toward us on the opposite side of the street. "She just wants to soak it all in. See how she keeps looking back toward the marquee? This is big for her, being here, and he is not having it."

"He looks like he's freezing."

"Look—she's checking out her playbill; I bet they just stood outside by the stage door for the last forty-five minutes for some autographs, and he's just over it and miserable." She shakes her head. "Your turn."

I discreetly nod toward the kid behind the counter, who doesn't even look old enough to drink. The bags beneath his eyes contrast with his energetic greeting. "Moved to the city. Trying to make it in the biz. Up early every day for a shift at the diner, then dance classes, then voice lessons, then working as a bike messenger?" I shrug. "Then here. Literally on the go, twenty hours a day."

She seems to think about it, then nods her head. "See how he's mouthing the words to this song? No one knows this song. This is old-school Broadway, a song only a true theater geek would know. I think you're right." She fumbles through her purse and takes out a twenty-dollar bill. I wince, wondering if it's one that she'd shoved at me yesterday morning. She drops it in the tip jar on the counter, and he smiles, grateful. "Okay," she says, linking her arm into mine as we take our box of pastries and hit the street again. "Find one for me."

     MEGAN BECKER

There are a lot of couples around us that look startlingly like the one she already analyzed, so no fun there. There's a stretch limo stopped at the red light a few car lengths ahead of us, two women in light-up necklaces emerging through the sunroof, drinking out of long tubes. "Are those penis-shaped cups?"

Gwen follows my gaze and doubles over in a fit of contagious laughter. "They definitely are."

I compose myself first, and the limo is gone. But it's fine, because coming toward us is a man walking solo, urgency in his stride, his eyes desperate, frantic. "Him," I say, and Gwen cranes her neck.

"Who?"

"This guy. Tan coat. Expensive haircut."

She scans the sidewalk again, and her lightheartedness evaporates. "Shit." She turns, grabbing my hand again, tugging me close to her like she wants to take off in the opposite direction, but between the crowd still gathered at the theater to one side of us and the traffic that congests the street, there's nowhere to go. Cool, sexy Gwen has transformed into panicked, hyperventilating Gwen.

"Hey, what's wrong?"

She locks eyes with me and taps the pastry box. "Two hands on this. Your job is to protect this box. Promise me you'll hold on, both hands, no matter what."

"Okay…"

"Sawyer. Promise me. Both hands on the box until I tell you it's okay."

"I promise, Gwen." Her eyes dart between mine and she bites that perfect cherry-red lip, and then the guy I'd picked out of the crowd stops three feet away.

"Gwendolyn."

She takes a sharp breath and brushes a hand over mine, then turns and faces the well-dressed guy in front of us.

"Tristan."

Shit is right.

"You look incredible," he says, and my hands tighten around the box when his eyes scan her body.

"You look the same as the last time I saw you, though there is something different…" She taps a finger to her chin, and this idiot beams like a compliment is coming his way.

"New suit? Custom made a few weeks ago."

"No, that's not it," she says. She looks him over once and fakes the lightbulb moment. "Ah, I know what it is. You don't have a stranger attached to your dick tonight."

His smirk vanishes. "Gwendolyn, that was all a misunderstanding."

"A misunderstanding? I'm sorry… did I imagine you standing there with your pants down with someone else, when you should have been with me?"

It hurts to hear the crack in her voice. It's been a year, but that crack sounds like fury and like pain. I don't want her to hurt anymore, partially because I don't want her to hurt ever, but also partially because if she's still hurt, she's likely not over the guy. And this guy is exactly the kind of guy I would have imagined for her that very first day: good-looking, put-together, successful. *Shit.*

"Would you hear me out?"

"No."

"Gwendolyn, please. Let's just talk." He pouts at her like he's not interrupting her date. Like I'm not even here.

I silently beg her to say no, but she searches my face and it's written plainly on hers that she needs this.

"I can wait on the red steps," I offer, but she shakes her head. "It's frigid out here. Why don't you head back to the hotel? I'll be back soon." She steps to the edge of the sidewalk to hail a cab for me.

"I'll walk," I say. "If you're sure you want to stay."

She bites the inside of her cheek. "I need to." Then she brushes her thumb over my knuckles. "I'm trying. I promise." She reaches up into my hair and pulls my face toward her, pressing her lips to my temple.

Tristan stands behind her, his arms crossed, his expression shifting from surprise to smug as my box and I head west, and I let the late fall air do its best to counteract the angry heat that surges through my veins.

Gwendolyn

"WOULD YOU HEAR me out?"

I waited for this question for so long. I prayed he would call me, apologize, offer some sort of explanation, and though I really believe I've moved on, the closure would be nice.

Poor Sawyer. This is not how this date was supposed to go. He offers to wait just up the block in Times Square, but I have no idea how long I'll be out here, so I send him back to the hotel with nothing but a promise that 'I'm trying.'

"Thank you. For giving me an opportunity to—"

"Let's hear it, Tristan. You're interrupting my date, so say what you need to say."

He reaches for my hand, but I roll my shoulder back and avoid making contact. Instead, I rub my arms against the biting air.

He gestures back toward the bakery and pushes back when I balk. "Your feet must be killing you, and you're clearly cold. Come on. Let's sit and talk over coffee."

One of the things that makes Tristan so good at sales is that he can read people incredibly well, and he's just demonstrated that for me. The dress was great for the Caribbean but paper-thin and not ideal for a New York City sidewalk on a November midnight, and the shoes are as painful as they are hot.

"Fine. One coffee."

He ushers me in, orders our coffees, and finds a private table at the back of the bakery near the restroom. "I'm so glad that girl tagged you in her post from the theater tonight, and that you were still here when I arrived." So this is no chance encounter. This is him seeking me out, forcing this conversation. Noted. "How have you been?"

"Better," I answer. "I've been better."

His mouth twists like he's holding back how pleased he is to hear this, and I'm torn between keeping Gram's health a secret and letting him know that 'better' has nothing to do with him.

"You look phenomenal. Really. It's different. Very sexy." His gaze drops down to my chest, but I won't give him the satisfaction of watching me squirm.

"So I wasn't sexy before? Is that why you didn't stick around?" Gram always said that when I was angry I got right to the point. That's why she sometimes likes when I get mad: much less talking.

Tristan flinches. "You're the one who left, as I recall."

Is he even serious? "I was supposed to stay? After…" I wave away the vision, which is still burned in my memory. "I just need to know one thing."

"Okay." He shifts in his seat. "Anything." His folded arms and jittery leg don't jibe with his cool-as-ice persona.

"That night. We were both here, in the city. And it was a huge night for me. Why didn't you show up?"

"I had work to do. It was important."

"I had work to do, too. And it was one of the most important events of the year for me, and you were supposed to be there."

He rolls his eyes, blinks, and tents his fingers in front of his pursed lips. "There's a difference."

"Oh? What's that?"

"I had real work—a real project to finish. I couldn't just leave for your little—"

"Little? My little *what*? My little *biggest event* of the tour? My little this-means-everything-to-me night?" And then it hits me: the real reason why he didn't prioritize it. "You don't support me. You don't think my writing's important."

"That's not what I said."

"But it's exactly what you meant." He raises a finger to interject, but I'm not done. I've been holding this in for a year; now it's erupting out of me, and someone's going to get burned. "What kind of project requires you to fuck some random person, anyway? That sounds like an in-demand position."

Another one of the things that makes Tristan so good at sales is that he truly believes everyone wants to buy everything that he's selling. Great for sales, terrible when he's peddling excuses to his ex.

"She was nothing."

"Which is the problem, right? That a 'nothing' was more important to you in that moment than your supposed something."

"It was just a fling!" He protests, and a few heads turn our way. He drops his volume and adds, "I screwed up. I don't even think about her anymore. I don't even remember her name."

The word hits me like a punch to the gut. Breathlessly, I repeat, "A fling?"

"Yes. Unremarkable. A mistake." He huffs, like he's the one who has the right to be upset. "I'm here now, aren't I? I came looking for you, in the cold, just hoping to find you. Can't you see I've changed? Can't you see how badly I want you back, Gwendolyn?"

And there it is, all wrapped up in a neat little package, my name the ribbon knotted on top, holding it all together. After a week of *Gwen*, a week of *I don't do flings* and being *enough* and someone putting in effort, I know exactly what I need right now. And it sure as hell isn't this.

"It doesn't matter, Tristan. I deserve to be with someone who isn't okay with letting me go in the first place."

I drop a few more dollars in the tip jar on my way out and hail a cab. "The Audrey Kay hotel, please," I tell the driver. "As fast as you can."

SAWYER

"OH, THANK GOD," she pants, standing in the now-open bathroom doorway. Steam swirls around her as it makes its escape.

"Gwen?" I contemplate covering myself, but it's nothing she hasn't seen before. She's not looking anywhere but my face now anyway, and I can tell she's been crying. "Are you okay?"

She doesn't answer. Her heels clatter to the tile floor, and she shrugs out of her coat.

"Did you run all the way up here?"

"Just from the elevator to the room." She steps toward me, careful not to slip. "I needed to make sure you were still here."

"Of course I'm still here. I told you, I'm not going anywhere." She steps over the ledge of the tile shower. "Your dress—"

She shakes her head. "The dress doesn't matter." Another step toward me, and now she's in the flow of the water with me, fingers feeling their way up my biceps, interlocking behind my neck, drawing my face to hers.

I was afraid I was imagining her. Maybe the water was too hot, messing with my head and making me see things that weren't there. But my hands can't grasp mirages; visions don't taste like hunger and desire and longing.

She clings to me while I shut off the water, and now she's drenched and still shivering from the lingering bite of the outside air. I wrap her shoulders in a towel, but it's no match for the waterlogged dress. She lets the white Egyptian cotton fall to the floor by the time I've got my own towel tucked around my waist, and she presses her body against mine, closer and closer until my back's against the wall, then raises her arms above her head. I lift the hem of her dress over her hips, then her chest, my fingers grazing every inch of her soaking wet skin along the way, until the dress has joined the towel and shoes and coat on the floor.

"Do you want to talk about it?"

Running mascara streaks her cheeks. "Yes. Later. Right now—" she places my hands on the small of her back, "I want you to kiss me like you'll never let me go."

That means something to her, and I don't know what kind of kiss that is. But I know that I don't want to let her go, that the thought of her leaving kills me, and had she been gone much longer I would've been curled up in the corner of the shower crying. So I bring all that into my kiss when my lips part to meet hers, and I trust she can feel it all. Her tension seems to dissipate and her body softens, molding into mine. "I won't, you know." I whisper it into her hair. "I won't let you go unless you ask me to."

She backs away, her eyes all earnest, still wrapped in my arms, leading me out of the bathroom and toward the bed. "Never."

My pulse quickens, and I feel it equally in my chest and my erection, this longing for her in every possible way, this euphoria that she's somehow already mine. She catches my glance to the bed and simpers, dipping her fingers between the towel and my torso. "Do you want this?" she asks.

"I want—" I turn wet strands of her hair over in my fingers, then I tuck them behind her ear and tilt her neck so her face is turned up toward mine. I kiss her jaw, her lips, her neck; I sink my face into the curves of her chest and plant a kiss there that I'll come back to nurture later. I breathe into her skin my secret, hoping it's enough. Hoping I'm enough. "I want you, Gwen. As much as you'll let me have."

She leans back, opening her neck to my mouth, and fumbles with my towel. "Good," she says, letting it fall.

     MEGAN BECKER

We move together onto the bed while we kiss, lying down next to each other, and I pull the covers up to keep her warm. We kiss and touch like this for a while, naked and nearly so, and I feel like I could come just from the way she exhales when I move my mouth to her shoulders, the way she digs her fingernails into my back when I nibble her ear, the way her body feels against mine when she wraps her leg around me.

I touch her, and her nails dig deeper, now tangled under my arms and coiling up to my shoulders. She shudders, and I'm filled with need. "Baby, I want all of you." She stretches an arm to the side, swatting at the nightstand drawer until she connects with the handle, and pulls out one of the condoms she tucked in there earlier while we were getting ready for our date.

She grips me and rolls it on while I massage her with my thumb in slow, intentional circles, responding to the way she responds to me with her hands, her writhing hips, her uninhibited whispers of pleading for more, her arching back. When she slams a hand against the bed and twists the sheets in her grip, biting her lip, I pull her on top of me.

Gwendolyn

"GOD, THAT'S GOOD," he whispers as I keep coming undone around him. He props himself up on his elbow, using his free hand to bring my mouth to his, then expertly unhooking my bra and letting it fall away. "You're perfect, Gwen." He rocks into me, bending his knees to move me forward, until the lines of our bodies are so entwined you can't see where mine ends and his begins.

It's a steady, slow rhythm: *soft, soft, deep,* anapestic, repeated while I'm on top, after he rolls me over, buries his face in my chest and draws me into his mouth. It's perfect—enough to tip him over the edge. I contract my muscles and he bites his lip and groans as he pulls out and hovers over me, his forehead pressed against mine, our huffing and panting mingling, mutually and deeply satisfied.

He excuses himself, disposes of the condom, and comes back in a pair of tight boxer briefs. Meanwhile, I've slipped into his button-down from our date. "That looks infinitely better on you than it ever did or will on me," he says before he deposits one more kiss on my lips, his eyes open, smiling into mine.

"Personally, I think you should just give up on clothes. This—" I gesture to his abs, his toned arms, "this works for you."

"And this is probably more comfortable for you." He hands me one of his T-shirts, tortured and tattered into sleevelessness. I make a show of unbuttoning the shirt seductively, and he hoists me up so I'm standing on the bed. He flings back the fabric like curtains and nuzzles into my stomach, a trail of heat from his breath running from my navel down. I gasp when his lips greet my skin, and I push

 MEGAN BECKER

off against his shoulders.

"We have all night, Sawyer."

"Hopefully more than one, though, right?" He lifts me down off the bed and watches while I trade one of his shirts for the other.

"I told you, I want to try." I sit, taking his hand, tugging him toward the spot next to me. "About earlier..."

He swallows and shakes his head. "You don't have to tell me anything. You're here. That's enough for me."

I appreciate that he doesn't need all the details about my conversation with Tristan, but I need him to know my realization. "I was wrong the other morning." Confusion tugs at his eyebrows. "I don't want to be a fling that means nothing, that maybe you talk to your buddies about over beers. I don't want to be this fleeting thing. I want to be enough. I want to be memorable... part of your story." I twist back a lock of his hair and cup his face in my hand. "I don't want to *try*, Sawyer. I want—I *need* us to be together."

"You need it?" His brows pinch, and I have a flashback to yesterday when I propositioned him.

"Not *it*. You. Not as a distraction. Not some quick fix for my issues. I need you because you're you. Because I'm better with you, and I don't think I completely ruin you."

"I want you, Gwen. So much," he says through a snicker. *Want.* "I need you, too, if you're curious," he adds, reading my mind. He pecks my shoulder, running over the skin with his finger. "Your shoulder's already peeling."

"Hm. Shame. Maybe I need to find someone who's better at applying sunscreen." I rise and he yanks me back into his lap, smothering me in kisses.

"Or, you need to not be so stubborn and take your shirt off next time so I can actually get it where it needs to go."

In one swift movement I strip out of his tank top and dangle it over his head. "This better?"

"Perfect." He twitches against the inside of my thigh, and a mischievous smile tells me it's time for more.

"I lied to you."

Not exactly what you want to hear when you're tangled in a mess of linens and limbs, sweaty and wet, coming down off the high of mind-numbing sex. I try not to startle at the admission, but with my chest pressed against his side and his fingers stroking the length of my spine, any little jerk is noticeable to him.

"When I said Nan didn't tell me anything about you, that wasn't true. She told me about you that first night, after your event, though she never told me it was *your* event. She said she'd met the nicest girl for me, a total firecracker, and I should have gone in with her instead of waiting in the bar down the street." He shifts, letting his nose rub against mine. "Then when Maggie told her you were single, she started planting seeds, saying how smart, funny, and beautiful you were…"

"She said all those things? Sounds like I'm dating the wrong Dawson."

He pulls back, beaming ear to ear. "Dating, huh?"

"Of course. I don't do flings."

There's one part on my side that is extra sensitive, where the slightest touch tickles, and he goes after it. I squirm, squeal, roll over so my back's to him, and pull his arms around me. He is a very, very big spoon, and being nestled into him is my new happy place.

Across from us, framed in an ornate stand in the corner of the room, bathed in the ambient light streaming through the window, is a full-length mirror. Sawyer already joked that we could have fun with it later, but now our eyes meet in the reflection.

     MEGAN BECKER

"When you finish this next one, I want to come along. I'll carry your suitcases across the whole damn country for the next tour."

"Okay, calm down back there. It won't be for a little while, at least."

"Regardless, I'm there. I don't want to miss a second of watching you shine."

It's 3:00 a.m. and I'm wide awake, energized by this affection from him. "What do you think people say when they people-watch us?"

He swallows, then shrugs against my back. "I don't know. You're the expert with this."

"I like to think I rubbed off on you a little bit this week."

"Just a little." He shakes his head, smirking. "I think they would say, this guy is one lucky bastard."

I poke his hand. "Be serious. I want to hear what you think." I could really get used to the way he presses his lips to my neck and shoulders and back, or the way he grazes my skin with gentle caresses when we lay like this: almost absently, but always with intention.

"I *am* being serious. I think they'd say you're way out of my league." He swallows a yawn. "They'd say, look at that happy couple over there. They're having a great time, so in love."

My eyes grow at the word. "We've known each other less than two weeks."

"Do you think other people think that? When they look at us together, do you think they see strangers? Or do you think they see two people who need each other, who are each better because the other is in their life?" He stifles another yawn and drapes an arm around my waist, pulling my hips more tightly to him. He closes his eyes and eventually drifts to sleep.

I settle deeper into his embrace, wondering what it's like to love and be loved by Sawyer Dawson.

Wondering if, somehow, I already know.

Post-Cruise Extension
A February Sunday
Coastal California

MEGAN BECKER

Gwendolyn

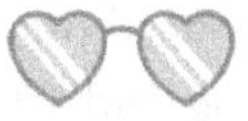

"IS THAT HIM?" Nancy peers around me. Her assignment: look for red shorts. She's pointing toward a man in red basketball shorts and a black T-shirt with a white visor strapped around his head.

"No," I answer. "He's wearing a light blue shirt, remember?"

"Right." She scans the crowd again, clapping instinctively as the runners stride past us. We saw him at mile six, then again at twenty, and now we're waiting for him at the finish.

The tracker app projects that he'll be here within the next four minutes, if he maintains the solid pace he's held for most of the race. Not that any of us cares about his time; we're all just so proud of him for being out here. And we all love him.

Nancy flew out with him last week so he could get in a few runs at the right climate. The winter back home has been rough, with biting winds and icy air, and he wanted his lungs to remember what it's like to run outside without getting freezer-burnt before having to do it for 26.2 miles. I think he also just needed a week away to really focus on himself and his running, instead of focusing on others twenty-four seven.

He and Nancy moved into my place temporarily while I've mostly stayed with Gram. They just showed up, about a week after the cruise ended, ready to help however they could. We cycle through shifts at Gram's place, I miraculously meet my deadlines, and Sawyer dives into the world of online tutoring and freelance work creating educational materials in addition to being Gram's favorite nurse, my therapist, and an athlete in training. Additional roles include: my boyfriend; possibly the love of my life.

Sawyer's mom and I flew out two days ago with Gram, who's just as feisty as ever, even on wheels. Mel was a huge help with navigating through the airport and ensuring we had all our luggage and our sanity when we traversed the country. I'd met her before; we'd celebrated Thanksgiving and Christmas together, and she's just as comfortable and kind as her son.

"What about him?" Gram asks, and I follow her gaze down the far side of the finisher corral to another man in red shorts. This one's wearing a light blue shirt and black sunglasses with bright blue mirrored lenses, and we all recognize him at the same time, erupting into cheers and screams as he approaches the finish line.

I gallop along the long chute, shouting his name and any encouraging words I can think of, but he doesn't look like he needs it. He looks incredible, and he finishes with a smile spread wide across his face. I wait off to the side, the rest of the group weaving through the spectators toward me.

Sawyer emerges from the finisher area with a bottle of water and a banana in his hand, and I crash into the medal around his neck when I throw my arms around him.

"You did it! I'm so proud of you!"

"I couldn't have done it without you. You really kept me going that last point-two," he says with a wink.

Mel slides in to hug him, not caring that he's drenched in sweat, as moms are wont to do. "Congrats, Honey. You did great." She holds him at arm's length and takes in his face, then musses his hair and steps back to make room for anyone else who wants a chance to congratulate him. Wisely, Nancy and Gram keep a safe distance when they offer their accolades. I don't care about the sweat, and he knows it. He pulls me against his side and munches on his banana.

"So, who had the idea for the matching shirts?" he asks.

Nancy and Gram exchange conspiratorial looks, and Gram

   MEGAN BECKER

answers. "Your grandmother felt I needed something to do to keep me busy."

He glances around the little circle, taking in the neon pink and fluorescent lime green tie-dye creations that Nancy insisted we wear. "I love them. It was so easy to find my cheering section."

"What was louder?" Gram asks him. "Your grandmother's chosen color palette or our yelling?" Like I said, feisty as ever.

He chugs some water and makes eye contact with each of us. "Thank you. All of you. For being here. This means a lot to me." There's a round of chatter, and Mel suggests we head back to the hotel.

"We've got a big day today, and you need a shower. Badly," she tells her son. When she looks away, he shifts his gaze to me and winks.

I pinch his side, squint against the sunlight, and return the smile he's giving me.

We wait for a bus that can accommodate Gram's scooter and head downtown, and everyone agrees that regardless of how hungry we all are, we're waiting until Sawyer has a chance to shower and change before we grab lunch. It's possible that's for our benefit more than his.

"Sure you don't want to join me, baby?" he asks, leaning through the bathroom door as I scroll through a string of emails from my agent and editor.

I swear he uses the pet name to lure me in, the same way he uses his slow striptease or the attention he draws to the boxers slung low on his hips, showcasing his tattoo. I don't give in, don't take the bait. Eyes on the phone, nowhere else. "Love to, but can't."

"Don't you love me anymore?" he asks, and he laughs when I roll my eyes. Because of course I love him, which is crazy. We met barely three months ago, but when you spend so much time with someone and see how they care for you and help you in the hardest times of your life, you know. Gram calls it *trial by fire*, us being thrown into domesticity while helping her, trying to work, and still learning so much about each other. I say we're forged: beaten and burned, a beautiful creation.

He told me in late December, during a weekend getaway when my parents were in town and staying with Gram.

We decorated gingerbread cookies at a bakery, surrounded by children who had more icing on their hands than on their cookies.

Then we went to dinner, Christmas sangria for me and a lager for him, soft candlelight and piano music waltzing in the air around us.

After, and the whole reason we chose the destination for our night away, a visit to Green Fable Gardens to see more than five million lights on display. It was there, after I nearly choked on my hot chocolate at one of his jokes, standing under a twinkling arborvitae archway, that his smile faded and he swallowed hard.

"Gwen," he said. "I'm in love with you."

I remember my heart plummeting and rising, diving to the pit of my stomach and then catapulting to my throat, before settling warmly where it belongs. It was the way he said it: 'I'm *in love* with you,' not just 'I love you,' the latter of which is actually the more important of the two, long-term, but can be platonic or familial. *In love* implies a fire, excitement, this feeling of falling into some abyss, deep and unknown, but diving in anyway. Dumbstruck, relieved, I didn't answer right away.

"It's too soon. I know that."

I shook my head, tears threatening to freeze in my eyelashes. "It's not—"

 MEGAN BECKER

"You don't have to say it back. I just… I couldn't keep that in anymore."

"Anymore?"

He nodded, dropped his gaze, met mine with a smile tugging on the corners of his mouth. "I've known for a while, I guess."

"Me too. I mean…That I love you. That I'm in love with you." My mittens—knit by Nancy—felt too hot, and heat rushed to my ears, toes, and cheeks, too. When he kissed me, there was something new there: some hope or promise we hadn't explored yet.

And there we were, a snowglobe scene, frozen while other visitors meandered past, taking photos and videos of the decorations, unaware of this momentous thing right in front of them.

We made love as soon as we got back to our hotel, tender and soft and tangled together, limbs entwined, *love* lingering on our lips.

Driving back the next day, he asked, "When did you know?" His thumb brushing over my knuckles as our hands lay interlocked on the armrest.

"The day you showed up at my apartment," I answered. His lips curled upward like he was pleased with the response. "I was so grateful that you showed up, that you wanted to stay." He deposited a kiss where his thumb had just been. "What about you? When did you know?"

He glanced in the rearview, flicked on the blinker, and changed lanes. "Bermuda. When you kissed me."

My jaw dropped. "No way. You didn't know way back then."

"It's only two weeks before you knew." He shifted into the exit lane, despite our exit to get back to my place being twenty miles away.

"It was the third day. And let's be honest, I did not make a great impression on day one."

His guffaw filled the car. Then he turned toward me when we reached the base of the ramp, waiting for the light to turn green.

"You definitely made *an* impression." He leaned over and kissed my head. "My sweet, obnoxious, cranky little dictionary."

I swatted at his arm and feigned anger, and he hung a left.

"Where are we going?"

"Detour," he said. He drove in silence for a few minutes, away from the highway and toward a quaint downtown with wreaths decorating the streetlights and a raised grassy median dividing the main road, with a sign welcoming us to Songbird Springs. We stopped at a coffee shop nestled between a bookstore and a stately bed & breakfast. "They have the best breakfast sandwiches here," he said, barely a bite into his ham and egg croissant. His neck flushed, and he changed the subject to my latte and gift ideas for my parents for the holidays.

"How do you even know about this place?" I asked as we waited to check out at the bookstore. I'd just signed their in-stock copies of my books, titles by both Gwen Dolan-Pierce and Geri Wencep, and Sawyer had selected a few tomes for my dad, a *Marvels of Engineering* coffee table book for my mom. I scanned the flyers on the bulletin board by the register: the book club schedule for the next two months, town activities for the holiday season, and a community Q&A session with the developers of the new neighborhood on the edge of town.

"There's this thing called the internet," he chuckled. He took my hand, held it all the way home. We hid ourselves away for the rest of the day at my place while everyone else was with Gram, then made dinner, made love again, and continued with the new rhythm of life we'd found ourselves dancing to. Work, Gram, us. Work, Gram, us. Cha-cha-cha.

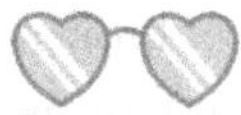

Now he's singing in the shower, and it takes me back to those first days again, when Nancy said he was shy, when he made himself smaller. To juxtapose that image with who he is today: marathon-finishing, tantalizing strip-teasing, *take-a-shower-with-me*, songbird Sawyer… it's night and day. Wide-open ocean and land. Cold and melt-your-face-off hot.

I'm contemplating shimmying out of my shirt to join him when there's a knock on the door, and I pull the bathroom door closed before letting Mel into the room. "He just got in about five minutes ago," I tell her. "I can tell him to hurry."

She waves off the update. "I actually came to talk to you, Gwendolyn."

"You did?" I'm not sure what she could want to say, except maybe *leave my son alone* or *let him get back to his life*, or something along those lines. He's spent so much time taking care of Gram and me that I can imagine Mel misses him.

But she nods and smiles, her eyes warm chocolate like her son's. "I just wanted to say thank you." She lowers herself into the desk chair and picks at a piece of lint on her sweater. "Sawyer has been my best friend for more than thirty years. I know that sounds a little weird to say, but it's true. We were the graham cracker, the marshmallow, the chocolate. The three amigos—"

"The mountain, the sea, the sun."

She flinches at the mention of his tattoo and I blush, because one does not see that tattoo casually. "Yes, the mountain, the sea, the sun." Her smile returns, and she clears her throat. "What I mean to say is, when my mother duped him into going on that trip, I was furious. I was excited for what he could find, and bitter because I knew it wouldn't last. How could it? You two were miles apart. I didn't want to see his heart get broken again."

Mel stands and paces the floor by the window. "When he met Chelsea, he was so ready to settle down. I think he believed that having someone he could coexist with was romantic love. I never got to model that for him. I failed at giving him that example when he was growing up, and I own that. I didn't do much to discourage their relationship, though, because I thought he was happy, and it meant he was staying close to home. He was making plans, and then his world imploded around him."

Making plans. What plans? Moving in together? More?

"He was a shell of himself when he left for that trip, Gwendolyn, and he came back full. Of life, of joy, of love." She snorts. "Hell, he came back full of *hope.* And when he said he was leaving to stay with you for as long as you needed him…" The shower stops and the curtain hooks screech across the rod. "I was resentful at first, Gwendolyn, I'm sorry to say it. But I get it now, why he's so willing to leave."

"Mel, I'm sorry, but I don't understand what you're saying."

She squeezes my hand. "I'm saying, be good to him. He loves you more than you know."

Then the bathroom door opens, and Sawyer emerges in a towel (thankfully). "Hey, Mom," he says, tucking a second towel around his waist for good measure.

"Hi, Sweetheart," she says. Her eyes go misty and her words catch. "Just seeing if you're ready yet."

"Yeah, soon," he answers.

"Great. Come find us when you are." Sawyer nods and Mel heads for the door, squeezing my hand as she passes.

"What was that all about?" Sawyer asks when she's gone.

"I have no idea."

IT'S CLEAR I'VE interrupted something, but what, I have no idea. Gwen looks equally confused. Regardless, my body is going to become one giant cramp if I don't keep moving, so I kiss Gwen, throw on some clothes, and towel as much moisture out of my hair as I can.

For lunch, we've found a little family-owned Italian restaurant with flatbreads that come as highly recommended as their extensive wine list. It's casual and quick, and I spend most of the meal answering questions about the race this morning over a bowl of gnocchi and stretching my legs under the table. At one point I accidentally kick Gwen, who is inexplicably across the table from me instead of at my side, and who keeps avoiding Mom's gaze.

"Everything okay?" I whisper to Mom when Gwen's deep in conversation with Maggie.

"It's fine," she answers. "It's just… it's actually happening, isn't it?"

It's a difficult question: across from me is heartache and hope; Maggie's health is fading, slowly but undeniably. When she's gone, Gwen will be devastated. We all will be, actually. Maggie is one woman who comes into your life and lets you know she's been there, leaving your pride wounded and your heart healed. She's a force to be reckoned with, and I remember Gwen telling me about her family, about how she's so much more like Maggie than like her own mother. Heaven help me if that similarity continues.

"Hey." Mom nudges me with her elbow. "Are *you* okay?" she

asks, always able to read me.

I use her own fitting words in reply. "I'm fine. It's just *actually* happening."

She rubs my back and drops her head to my shoulder, a discreet hug. She understands perfectly.

We leave the restaurant and head back the two blocks toward our hotel. Along the way, I spot a sign, and whisper my plans to Mom. She nods and continues onward with Nan and Maggie for some time at the hotel pool.

I pull Gwen into an indoor glow-golf course. "I believe I owe you a round," I say, bending to kiss her smile.

"Sure you want to get humiliated on your big day?"

For a second I can't breathe; I'm choking on her words. Does she know? But then I realize she's talking about the marathon, and the knot in my gut loosens. "Speaking of getting humiliated…when I walked out of the bathroom in a towel and saw that my mother was there talking to you—what did she say?"

She shrugs and takes a fluorescent pink golf ball. "A bunch of stuff. It was a little weird, if I'm being honest. Something about you guys being a s'more?"

It takes me back to the days of "camping" at home, building a blanket fort in the living room and sleeping on a pile of pillows, trying to roast marshmallows over votive candles, projecting shadow puppets onto the ceiling with a decade-old flashlight. The days when we all lived together, before we lived within a five-minute drive of one another, before—

"You're up," she chirps. Her ball teeters on the edge of the hole already, and when mine taps hers in she still writes down a two for herself. "Not to worry, I'll come by one honestly eventually."

"Your humility is one of the many things I love about you." It comes naturally, throwing that word around like confetti (and meaning it, every time), once I allowed myself to say it. Once it was too soon, but not *too* soon. Once I was sure my options were *say it* or *explode*. And here I stand, not exploded.

Back at the hotel, two holes-in-one from Gwen but a narrow victory for me later, Gwen has to meet quickly with her editor, so I grab a drink at the indoor pool where Nan, Maggie, and Mom are relaxing in the warm air.

After an hour I find Gwen back in our room, lying on her stomach on the bed, her bare feet kicked up behind her as she scribbles into a fresh notebook. "Don't judge me," she says, "but I'm working on the next one."

"I'm too happy to judge," I reply. "But we should get ready for dinner."

It's a perfect bookend. Not that this is an ending, by any means. But we're all together, so a dinner cruise seemed like the most fitting way to wrap up this trip.

"You don't think the dress is too much? Can I just go like this?"

"No and no." I pull her sparkling black dress and my gray suit from the closet, hanging them over the door. "Just think of it as another formal night."

I plug in the curling iron I know she'll want to use to touch up her hair, then brush my teeth. I'm dressed and waiting while she finishes her makeup.

"This okay?" she asks, emerging from the bathroom, putting the backing on a dangling silver earring. She's pinned up her curls, save for a few that frame her face, and her eyes have that smokey gray-black look to them, complemented by a softer red-pink lip gloss, nearly the same shade as the shoes Maggie bought her to wear tonight.

Only one word can fit past the lump that forms in my throat: "Perfect."

She finishes with her earring and tosses the robe on the bed, takes the dress from its garment bag, slides it gingerly over her head, and steps in front of me for help with the zipper. "The shoes are too much, though, right?"

"I think they're great."

"They're so… bright. And super matchy." She eyes my pink tie, then the shoes again.

"And they're also from Maggie. Are you willing to risk her wrath if you show up without them?"

She screws up her lips before sitting on the bed and sliding her feet into the shoes. "Good point."

The boat's not huge, but the waves seem to be, as if my stomach wasn't uneasy enough. Maggie, Nan, and Mom are all here. Maggie approves of Gwen's footwear selection, Mom straightens my tie, and Nan looks happier than I've ever seen her. Tables are set up inside, white cloths draped over each one, each carefully set under the weight of centerpieces of pink peonies and poppies. Most people have yet to board or are milling about upstairs, catching the last few minutes of sunset. It's perfect, because I don't need a huge audience for what comes next. I pray I don't need the smelling salts, either.

Gwendolyn

"THERE'S KARAOKE?" I ask Nancy as the DJ introduces Sawyer, cutting off a BBMak song that got me through college.

"Apparently there is." She resumes conversation with Gram, shooting sideways glances toward her grandson as he takes the mic.

He breathes, a little shaky, and waits for the song to start. It's an awkward pause, mostly because we're basically the only people in the room, other than a few people who've wandered to the bar at the opposite end.

Really? I mouth to him, certain my eyes are about to pop out of my head, just as the intro kicks in.

He gives a half grin, shrugs, and raises the mic. And then I'm impressed by what he brings to a fun Bruno Mars song: he's a showman, not at all shy, with a great voice. And the lyrics are a little absurd, sure, but he's drawing a crowd into the room. I hear them, feel the energy swell, but I can't take my eyes off this ridiculous man in front of me, owning the mic. I lose myself in the memories from that first week together: Sawyer propped against the doorframe while I sang at karaoke, unwilling to sing himself; Sawyer on stage during The Couples' Game Show, coming out of his shell; Sawyer splashing me with water in a kayak; Sawyer racing me to a sliding board over the ocean; Sawyer trusting me with his secrets. But never Sawyer the showman.

"Where did this come from?" I wonder aloud, and Nancy looks up at me through wet eyes.

"From you, dear."

Mel dabs at her own eyes with a tissue from the pack in Gram's outstretched hand, and I catch a glimpse of a familiar face in my periphery. It's not that Mom and Dad don't like Sawyer, it's just that they wouldn't fly halfway across the country to watch him finish a marathon. And if they did, why am I just now seeing them for the first time today?

And why is my agent here?

And who are all these other people, cocktail dress- and suit-clad, watching him, watching me?

The last verse starts and the music shifts, the sound of bells replacing the steady drum beat, and he sings, turns serious, the room's atmosphere altogether different as he approaches me, takes my hand, and draws me to him.

"What are you doing?" I whisper, tightening my grip around his hand as he lowers himself to his knee, crooning the end of the song, making it very obvious what he's doing. The showmanship fades and it's just the two of us, eyes locked, alone in front of so many people. He smooths his thumb over the back of my hand and the crowd erupts with quiet excitement. His skin flushes and he swallows against the knot of his tie.

The devilish grin I love on him flashes on his lips, and he holds up a finger to the waiting masses—a surprising number of friends and family, I've determined—before rising and pulling me outside onto the deserted deck, away from the ears of everyone inside.

"Feeling better out here?" I ask, as he gulps in the salty air.

"So much," he says. He cups my cheek in his hand and plants a kiss on the other. He takes a step back and holds my hand again, picking up right where he left off inside. "I never thought I'd get to a place where I could do that."

"What, kick ass at karaoke?" I grin up at him, but he doesn't laugh.

"Tell a room full of people how madly in love I am," he says. Then he shakes his head and his brows furrow. "Hell, Gwen, I

   MEGAN BECKER

never thought I'd get to a place where I could love anyone the way I love you."

Maybe I should stop him. Maybe I should tell him that it's too soon—*far* too soon—to take this step. This is the stuff of romance novels and fairy tales, not of real life. But I feel it, too. It *is* real: all of it, good and bad, from that first awful meeting to the tears we've shared and the ones we know we still have yet to cry together; from finding ourselves sharing a kayak to finding ourselves sharing a bed, and now, as he proposes, sharing a life.

"I know what you're thinking. You're thinking I'm crazy for asking you to marry me when we've known each other less than four months."

"I don't think you're crazy for asking." The words come out a whisper. "Do you think I'm crazy for saying yes?"

He swallows hard. "You might want to hear the whole question first."

I'm shaking, but he's visibly trembling as he lowers himself onto one knee again. "Gwendolyn Grace Pierce, will you continue to fill my life with joy? With love? Will you put up with me forever, whether I'm dripping on your laptop, or freaking out about snakes, or trying to rip your clothes off in elevators?" He turns the black box over in his hand and exhales. "Gwendolyn Grace Pierce," he repeats, his eyes moving to mine from the box, "will you marry me?"

"Yes, of—" I start, but he shakes his head again, opening the box, looking up at me with hope dancing in his eyes.

"Tonight?" he adds.

It feels like the wind was just knocked out of me. "Tonight?" I squeak. I clear my throat, and now my voice is a normal octave. "Tonight?"

"Tonight," he echoes. "I hear you were looking for something unexpected. Does this not fit the bill, Gwen?"

"Unexpected? Where did you—" He flicks his gaze through the

window and I follow. Inside, Nancy and Gram are huddled together, watching like the rest of the attendees at whatever this event ends up being. "Oh. Right. And the black glitter and hot pink."

"All Maggie's doing."

"Of course it is."

"I'm cramping up down here, Gwen," he deadpans, and it launches me into laughter, which is the last of the convincing I need.

"Yes." I answer. I want to say so much more, but I'm already dangerously close to ugly crying in front of everybody watching through the windows. I clear away the tears that have already landed on my cheeks and steady my breathing. "Yes, Sawyer Victor Dawson. I will marry you. Tonight."

He rises and slips the ring on my finger, kissing me firmly before turning to the window and throwing his arms in the air. "She said yes!" he cries, and the sound of the cheering from inside fills the air around us.

Obviously, all of this is unofficial. There will be papers to fill out when we get back home, an "official" anniversary based on whatever date we can get an appointment at the courthouse, but it doesn't matter. I want to be officially unofficially his, starting right now.

There's a quick shuffling as Mel takes the lead, shooing everyone out the back of the room and up the stairs to the outdoor upper deck. Nancy ushers Sawyer up shortly thereafter, and I'm left downstairs with my parents and Gram.

"I'm so happy for you, Gwendolyn," Mom says. She opens her arms and wraps me inside; it's the first hug I remember getting from her in a decade. Dad smiles, every feature of his face filled with emotion.

"Walk me down the aisle?" I ask them. "Halfway?" Then I turn to Gram, and she knows the question before I free it into the space between us.

   MEGAN BECKER

"Nuh-uh," she says. "Not dressed like that, kiddo." She mutters something about how no granddaughter of hers will be a bride dressed in black. I look to Mom and Dad for support, but their smirks show they'll be no help. Instead, Gram pulls open a closet door, and an ivory dress hangs inside. "Try this."

Of course it's a perfect fit. "How did you do this?" I ask, and she and Mom exchange a look.

"It started in December," Mom answers. "After you got back from your weekend away, he had a conversation with your grandmother. Which turned into many conversations with Nancy and Melanie and us, too. And we have access to your closet, so ordering a dress in your size was pretty easy." She circles me, ensuring the lightweight embroidered tulle of the simple dress is laying as it's supposed to. "It's all happening a little sooner than we'd expected, but he received a ringing endorsement." She chuckles. "Pun not intended."

"You're welcome for that five-star rating," Gram says, eyeing the dress. She plucks a peony from one of the vases and tears the stem, tucking the flower into my hair. "Much better, Gwennie."

I always thought I'd want something structured and satin for a wedding dress, but what they've selected for me is a dream. It feels light and romantic, like it was made for a beachy wedding, which is perfect for our love story.

"So you've known about this for months?" I ask Gram.

She snorts in reply. "Sweetheart, ever since Nancy told me about him—more than a year ago—I knew that this would happen." She fixes my hair and smooths my cheek.

Dad chimes in next to me. "How do you feel? Nervous?"

Truth be told, the butterflies are back, but I shake my head. "Not nervous. Excited." Calm washes over me, and I add the most important feeling of all. "Ready."

Upstairs, Sawyer mouths *wow*, then sinks his teeth into his lip, trying so hard to bite back tears. There are about twenty chairs on either side of the aisle and a pre-recorded piano melody playing through the sound system as Mom and Dad walk me halfway. Then I take Gram's arm for the rest of the trip, a bridge from the past to the future.

MEGAN BECKER

SAWYER

GWEN OWNS THE dance floor. She knows the lyrics to every song, dances choreographed routines from decades-old music videos, serenades me during the ballads when I hold her close to my chest.

This is free Gwen, like kayak Gwen and game show Gwen and *this one felt unloved* Gwen. The world is light, if only for tonight. If only for a song, and, if we're lucky, the one after that. She's across the room, nursing the same glass of champagne for the last hour. At this point I'm pretty convinced she's holding it just to give her left hand a reason to be on display as it curls delicately around the crystal. She winks, and I shake my head.

"Mind if I steal my wife for a moment?" I ask the couple she's talking to. If I remember correctly from the introductions earlier, it's her writer friend Hillary and her fiancé Dalton, but I was so focused on booking the venue and planning surprises that I put the guest list in our matriarchs' capable hands. Luckily, I'll have a lifetime to get to know her friends.

"Excuse me. My hubba-hubba-hubby is here to whisk me away." She nods, smiling at our guests, and takes my hand.

"Want to get out of here?" I ask, winking.

We go as far 'out of here' as we can, which is the top deck again, and the few friends up here wave in greeting but then ignore our presence completely as they laugh into the crisp night air and down their drinks.

"You're incredible, you know that?" she asks, leaning backward against the railing, propping her elbows on the smooth wood. "I can't believe you planned all this."

"I had help," I remind her. "The dress was a nice surprise, though. I had no idea—"

"Gram has this theory that brides shouldn't wear black at their wedding," she says, shrugging. Then she drops her face into her hands. "What a day this has been. Especially for you." She rolls to the side and rubs a hand along my back. "How are you feeling?"

"Legs? On fire. Back? Hurts like hell. Heart? Best it's ever been."

She shivers as she smiles, and I slide out of my suit jacket to drape it over her shoulders. The breeze blows loose wisps of hair across her face, but I smooth them back and draw her to me. Her fingers interlock behind my back and she rests her head on my shoulder, and we sway in the fog of the music playing below us.

"This feels right," she says. "The two of us."

A laugh rumbles in my throat, pressed to the top of her head. "I'm glad to hear you say that, Wife." There's no retort, just a shift in her shoulders as she winds tighter around me and exhales. "Gwen, if you want a real wedding when we get home, with more people or your choice of dress and color scheme and food—"

She turns her head upward, sticking her chin into my sternum. "Why would I want a wedding do-over when this one was absolutely perfect?"

"I'm glad you said that, because I didn't plan for that in my budget."

"Oh my gosh—Sawyer—what *is* the plan for when we get home? Where are we going to live, long-term? I can't expect you to just move everything to my apartment forever." Worry floods her eyes.

"I've done a lot of thinking about that, actually. Obviously, we stay put for now, for Gram."

The deep crease between her brows softens. "You called her

     MEGAN BECKER

Gram."

I shrug. "She's family now." A smile plays at her lips, lightening the concern in her expression more. "And once we're ready, I was thinking of a small town with a lot of character and charm, not too far from home. A little closer to Mom and Nan, maybe, but a place that's *ours*." I peel back the side of the suit jacket and reach into the pocket inside, pulling out a folded piece of paper, weathered at the creases and corners from the hundreds of times I've opened it, reviewed it, and tucked it away again in the past few months.

I found Songbird Springs by accident on the trip from Mom's place back to Gwen's one weekend, and it felt like home. It felt like a place to hold hands and walk to the coffee shop, or trudge through the snow to the bookstore on a wintry day. When I saw they were building a new neighborhood, it felt like a place where we could start fresh, someday. And when I took her there in December and she loved it too, it felt like it could be *ours*.

Gwen steps back while I open the paper and turn it toward her. She scans it, her eyes returning to the top after reaching the bottom, taking it all in again, then meeting mine. "It's perfect."

"I thought maybe we could take a little honeymoon up there. Stay at the B-and-B, meet with the builders."

"You just want their breakfast sandwiches."

I shake my head. "No, Gwen. I just want *you*."

"You have me. As long as we both shall live." She pulls my face down to meet hers. The taste of champagne lingers on her tongue as she parts my lips and kisses me like we're back in my room with our Couples' Game consolation prize.

Gwendolyn

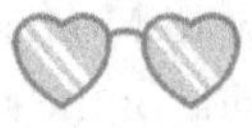

"DID YOU EVEN notice?" he asks, dangling the champagne bottle in front of me. We've docked again, said our goodbyes to our guests. Mel and my parents are tidying up downstairs while Gram and Nancy prop up their feet after a busy day, but someone had the bright idea to send us up here without supervision to "clean up," and there is no cleaning happening. Sawyer's hand is on my hips as we sway along with the boat's generic music, since the DJ has also packed up. He refills my glass as I try to read the label.

"Is that—"

"Mhmm." He nods. "Same as what we had on the ship."

"You really thought of everything, didn't you, Husband?" The whole night has been perfect, with touches of us sprinkled throughout in unexpected ways, from the music to the spread of desserts, from the champagne to the piña colada cocktails. From the vows he'd prepared months ago, using two lines from my first romance novel—lines he said he committed to memory the first time he read them because they moved him so much, to the fish pun I made in my own vows that I'd written in the thirty minutes between knowing I'd need them and actually saying them. Then there's the ring, which pulls in stones from both of our families: an oval diamond from Nancy's engagement ring, and a pair of pearls from a necklace Gram had bought for Mom when she was still a baby, combined beautifully in a modern but classic setting.

"Can you handle one more big announcement?" He grins, and I'm tipsy enough to fear for a second that there's a surprise baby

 MEGAN BECKER

involved, but I shake that off pretty quickly once I realize it would be pretty hard for him to know something that I don't when it comes to that subject.

"Sure," I lie, overwhelmed in the best way. I don't think I can handle anything else right now, and definitely not any more alcohol after that last thought.

"I got a job. A real one. A good one."

"You did? When?"

"The offer came through a week ago. And before you get mad at me for not telling you—" he says, holding up a finger to shush me before I even have a chance to scold him in the way he predicted I would, "I don't start for another two weeks, and I wanted to wait until I'd met the team until I officially accepted. That's part of the reason I came out early—they're based about two hours from here. I'll be working remotely, though."

"So, what is it? Data analytics for some tech firm? Are you a Silicon Valley snob now?" I gasp, mocking. "When do we get our self-driving spaceship?"

"Ha, ha. Funny," he says, and he kisses the tip of my nose. "Actually, it's working in education. There's a software company out here that's developing an app to create cross-curricular content, like incorporating math into other subject areas. I'll be in charge of making sure different states' standards are met in the process." The way he beams when he says it is everything. He still gets to help students, but without reopening the old wounds from his teaching days.

"How did I not know about any of this?"

He raises his shoulders, drops them, forms his mouth into a perfect grin. "Because I wanted to surprise you."

When I met Sawyer, everything was falling apart—even things I didn't know about yet. But now—with his hand in mine and his ring on my finger—everything feels like it's coming together.

"Can I make a request?" I peer up into his eyes, through the tousled hair that hangs over his forehead. The stars bear witness to the water gently lapping the side of the boat and the sparkle in his eye.

"Anything."

"For our honeymoon… can we take a real one? Maybe, I dunno…" I bite my lip, drop my gaze to his tie, straighten the loosened knot. "Maybe a cruise?" Somehow, I manage to hold in my laughter until I hear his. He pulls back and sets the champagne down, then takes my face in his hands. He shakes as he presses his mouth to mine, firm and hot and sweet.

"Gwendolyn Pierce-Dawson, I think that is o-*fish*-ally the best idea I've heard today." His lips meet my cheeks, my nose, my forehead.

"No, Sawyer Dawson-Pierce." I wink at him. "The best idea of the day was us getting married."

"Def-*fin*-itely."

     MEGAN BECKER

Acknowledgements

This is weird.

Normally I show appreciation with a little gift: a cup of coffee, some flowers, a Reese's Outrageous bar… So sitting here, trying to find actual words (the irony is not lost on me) to thank you for reading this book, is a challenge. While I would love to buy each of you sugar or something pretty, the logistics are a nightmare. Please accept my gratitude instead. You are making my dream come true, reader, and I am eternally grateful.

I need to thank the women who at least partially inspired Gram and Nan. I'm blessed to have some amazing grandmas and grandma-types in my life—women who are independent and beautiful and funny and loving and honest. I am so grateful for their influence and their love, and nearly as grateful that they never needed to meddle in my love life (aside from the infamous *fruit salad* conversation, but that was between an aunt and my husband and therefore not quite the same). Though none of you will cruise with me, I hope you know that our journeys to the mountains, the beach, WDW, and so many other places stick with me as some of my favorite memories.

I was recently reminded of the importance of showing up for people, and there are so many people who have shown up for me that I need to thank: Pocket Books Shop and Aaron's Books for stocking my work on their shelves. Everyone who read and reviewed *Coffee Dates* or *Ship Mates* or helped spread the word on social media. The Elegant Literature and Write Now communities for quite literally *showing up*, physically and digitally, to offer support and guidance. Also, Mickayla, for being just as excited as I was to bring this book alive via candle.

I'm beyond grateful to the people who first read *Ship Mates*. Laura, thank you for the many messages as you read Sawyer and Gwen's story. Your comments have kept me going. Emma, Kathleen, and Steve, I appreciate your thoughtful insights that made this book better! And to my Street Team: thank you for reading and reviewing and hyping this book. This voyage with you has been so much fun.

My gratitude goes to the people who worked on the guts of *Ship Mates*: RJ for your formatting expertise and your patience when I couldn't decide on graphics, structure, and fonts; Alexandra Aiken for making a cover that truly captured Gwen, Sawyer, *and* me; and Deb for your proofreading skills and incredible generosity. (Any grammatical errors are 100% my fault and sometimes a stylistic choice.)

To my family and friends who have been cheering me on: *THANK YOU*. Your pep talks and excitement have gotten me through all my overthinking and stressing, and I am so excited to share this with you—and to celebrate with a cocktail, hopefully!

Jeffrey, obviously none of this would be possible without YOU. No one makes me laugh like you do, and there is no one I'd rather cruise through life with: through storms and smooth sailing. You're simply the best. Your support means the world to me, though you could also let me win Ticket To Ride, like, *once*. I love you!

My tiny travelers, who are not so tiny anymore: may you always see the world with wonder. Sometimes it sucks, but it's glorious, too. Learn, love, laugh, and LIVE, and please don't think I'm copying those cheesy signs when I say that. I want all those things for you, from the bottom of my heart. Above all, be good people. Te amo // Wuv iz tiz.

A Note from the Author

When my friend Cara and I set out for a jog a few years ago, I had no idea that we'd brainstorm a list of *Mates* and *Dates* titles in thirty minutes. *Coffee Dates* was already a work in progress at that point, and I knew I wanted it to be part of something larger. Cara's creativity does not disappoint, and we made a pretty extensive list for a collection.

Ship Mates had to be my second book. What I love most about this title (and why I refused to change it even after someone told me it should be more "romance-y") is that it ties back to my years at Shippensburg University. It's the term for your *people*, and many of my own Shipmates had a hand in bringing this book to life. Also, I married one of them, and ours is still my favorite love story. I knew *Ship Mates* was going to be my sophomore romance; it just needed an idea.

I enjoy traveling, so I decided to write a romance novel set on a cruise ship. Forced proximity, only one kayak… it doesn't get much better than that! I'm not sure exactly when or how I landed on the idea of grandmothers arranging the world's longest blind date, but I'm sure glad I did. I also know that reading about a grandparent whose health is failing can be difficult, but I hope that you also find comfort in how Gwen, Sawyer, and Nancy all show up to support each other in the ways both Gram and Gwen need to be supported.

As individuals, and as a couple, Gwen and Sawyer are incredibly different from Hillary and Dalton, so adding a bit more spice into this book felt like a recipe for success. My goal is never to make people feel uncomfortable with the spice, but to tell a story that is true to the characters within it. I hope I found the right balance here.

Just as Gwen shows her appreciation to teachers, I also want to show mine. The work you do is so important and undervalued by far too many. To my former teachers, to my friends who are teachers, and to all the teachers out there: *thank you*. Sincerely.

Gram, Nancy, Gwen, and Sawyer were a joy to spend time with—and trust me, we spent a *lot* of time together. I hope that you also enjoyed their banter and wit, their connection and love. I hope you laughed and felt something and are happy you spent your time with them, too.

Book Club/Discussion Questions

- Were you rooting for Gwen and Sawyer to get together? Why or why not?
- Who was your favorite character, and why?
- If *Ship Mates* were made into a movie, who would play each of the main characters?
- Which moment prompted the strongest emotional response from you?
- Which location in *Ship Mates* would you most like to visit and why?
- In your opinion, did the dual perspectives help the book or hurt it?
- Did you like the "heat" level of this book? Or did it need more or less spice?
- Did the author balance romance with other elements, like humor and drama?
- If you could change something about the book, what would it be?
- On a scale of 1-10, how would you rate *Ship Mates*?

Also Available in the Mates & Dates Collection:

COFFEE DATES

Chapter One

The rain slows and a hint of sunlight peeks through the clouds visible between distant high-rises. A steady stream of commuters and tourists flows past the window next to me.

"I'm fine, mom," I say into the phone pressed against my left ear. To block out the noise of the milk frothers and other patrons, I squish my right tragus into the ear canal. I only know the word 'tragus' because my sister is one of those cool people who pierced hers to fight off migraines, and now she looks like a badass. Or at least a badass as far as her fellow accountants are concerned.

Mom's chirping something about being safe on the subway, but I can only make out every other word. I nod like she can see me and begin to pack up my things, hoping I can make it out in time before the fresh batch of dark clouds rolls in with more storms.

"Mom, it's fine. I've been here before. I know how to get around, and I know how to be careful." In hindsight, and thanks to the sideways glances of the nuns at the table next to me, I realize that hearing only *my* side of the conversation might make it sound like I'm looking for something I am definitely *not* in town to find.

My cheeks flush and I mouth *sorry* to the nuns as I gather my papers into a neat-ish pile and slide them into my backpack. Its water-proof material and the short line are all the convincing I need to get one more latte on my way out. If I get stuck in the next storm, at least my papers will stay dry and I'll have coffee to warm me up.

"Gotta go, mom. I promise I'll call you when I get back to Lindsey's apartment." If she argues, I don't hear it.

The barista raises an eyebrow as I approach the counter for the third time this morning. "Napkins are that way," she says, pointing to the end of the counter.

I plaster a smile on my face. "Thanks. I'm good, got them earlier," I say, hoping I look friendly and not idiotic. "Can I get another caramel-vanilla latte please?" and confirm that, yes, once again I would like the largest possible size while hiding my already jittery hands. My heart leaps inside my chest from caffeine and excitement and nerves. I pay for my coffee and wait in the pickup area, tightening and loosening my backpack straps like I did every middle school morning at the school bus stop. The sky beyond the windows is darkening again and I'll probably get drenched on my way to the subway station, but it's worth it for espresso and sugar.

I'm lucky to be here. Lucky that Lindsey is willing to lend me her spare room for two months while her boyfriend spends time back home with his ailing father. It feels weird to say I'm lucky that my life is in shambles, but if that's led to me spending time in New York, seeking inspiration and sharing time with my best friend since middle school, then sure, I'm lucky that I was fired from my job and dumped for a cat.

"Caramel-vanilla latte for… *Hellary*?"

I swear the nuns cross themselves. Maybe they hear me curse at the mixup under my breath, or maybe they feel the name really fits the person they think I am from that phone call earlier. I swear some people become baristas just to mess with the rest of us because sure enough, when I look at the cup, the "i" sure as *hellary* looks like an "e."

I plaster on that smile again and yell, "Thanks Candy!" to that initial, eyebrow-raising barista, whose nametag totally says Mandy.

There—karma for Mandy, I laugh to myself. I take a sip and look behind me as I walk to the door just in time to catch Mandy's annoyed eye-roll.

I'm two feet from the door when karma comes back for me.

A man—inexplicably not watching where he's walking in a coffee shop in the most crowded city in America—collides with me and sends my latte spilling down my jeans and onto the floor. *Karma.*

He kneels at the same time I do to try to clean up the mess. And he is the hottest man I have ever laid eyes on. *Luck.* Or maybe this is karma, too.

"I am so, so sorry," he says in a voice that's kind and genuine. "Let me find some napkins."

"I'll grab some," I say, rising. "I know exactly where they are."